Catherine Webb was just fourteen when she wrote her extraordinary debut, *Mirror Dreams*. With several novels already in print at nineteen, Catherine has quickly established herself as one of the most talented and exciting young writers in the UK.

By Catherine Webb

Mirror Dreams
Mirror Wakes
Waywalkers
Timekeepers

The
EXTRAORDINARY
and
UNUSUAL ADVENTURES
of
HORATIO LYLE

Catherine Webb

ATOM

First published in Great Britain in February 2006 by Atom

A CIP catalogue record for this book
is available from the British Library.

HARDBACK ISBN 1 904233 60 0
C FORMAT ISBN 1 904233 78 3

Typeset in Fournier by M Rules
Printed and bound in Great Britain
by Clays Ltd, St Ives plc

Atom
An imprint of
Time Warner Book Group UK
Brettenham House
Lancaster Place
London WC2E 7EN

INTRODUCTION

Murder

1864, London

In the west, the sun is setting.

It is orange and yellow fire, the sky sooty grey and brown smudge. The sky is full of chimneys and asthmatic birds. The fog is rising off the river, all the way from Greenwich to Chiswick, crawling up past Westminster and hiding the ravens sitting on the walls of the Tower, who blink beadily, waiting for something interesting and edible to happen in their lives. The fog is grey-green – grey from the water suspended in it, green from the things floating in the water.

In the west, the sun has set.

A man is running through dark and silent streets. He knows he's going to die, but still feels that if he's got to die, he might as well die running. In the world in which he moves, this is all a man can wish for, and tonight he has already seen his death mirrored in the death of another. The streets he runs through are silent and empty, their inhabitants either behind dark shutters hunched over their work by candlelight, or out, or asleep, or trying to sleep. He keeps running. A black bag bounces against his shoulder as he moves. He wonders how he ended up this way, and tries not to think of emerald eyes burning in his skull, the heavy weight of the body as it fell into his arms, or the blood now seeping through his fingers.

The rigging on the ships creaks as they rock slowly back and forth in the docks. The water that slaps around their long wooden hulls is brownish and just a little too thick for comfort.

And though he's running, he can't hear anyone following him. For a second he wonders if he's made it, if he's escaped, and knows that it's not that far to the Bethnal Green rookery from here, to the maze of shadows and cellars where anything and everything could disappear without a trace, knows that he could get there, knows that he won't. He half-turns to see if he's still being followed, bent almost double over the gaping knife wound across his belly, and stares straight into a pair of bright green eyes, burning emerald eyes, and a thin, slightly satisfied smile. He chokes on blood and steel and slips down into the shadows, clawing at the fine black sleeves of his attacker, of his killer, blackness that smells of dead leaves in a dying forest and burning wood and salty iron and black leaves falling on to a black floor like a black rain from a black sky and . . . and . . . and *don't look at the eyes* . . . He looks. The man holding the knife starts to grin, razor-sharp teeth, like those of a fish, bright green eyes, almost glowing, almost dancing with satisfaction and anticipation. The body slips to the ground. The bag falls off its shoulder and lands on the cobbles with a faint clank of heavy metal shifting inside.

The theatre halls of Shadwell are draining out in crowds of girls and boys cackling and clinging on to each other's arms. The fat man has reached the end of his song about the glory of Empire, Britain's majesty and amorous flirtations in barnyards. This latter aspect is what appeals most to his yelling, swaying audience. Down at Haymarket, the fat woman is dying to the mild applause of the bourgeoisie, top hats on their laps for the men; opera glasses held daintily in white gloves, and huge dresses spread like a map of the known world for the women.

A carriage rattles down a street, then stops. A door opens. A couple of horses stamp their hooves against the old cobbles, the sound muffled by centuries of rubbish and dirt, softening into a brown, thick sludge, through which the grey stones are rarely perceived. A voice says, very quietly, 'Mr Dew?' It sounds like black leather would, if it could speak. A man with bright green eyes stirs in the shadows and carefully wipes blood off the tip of a very long, slightly curved and highly ornate hunting knife.

'Yes, my lord?'

'He is dead?'

'Yes, my lord. He has joined his brother.'

'Very well. Give me the bag.'

The clang of heavy metal moving inside the bag, as it is passed into a hand gloved in white silk and attached to a body

3

clad in black velvet. The rattle of hands digging through metal. The faint glow of a lamp catches against gold. The rattling stops.

'It's not here?'

'My lord?'

'I said, it's not here!' And now, if the voice sounded like black leather, then that leather had just found itself driven through with nails, and wasn't pleased.

'He . . .' A little breath, steadying against fear of those burning green eyes, above a tight smile that makes sharks seem sympathetic, staring with the hardness of granite on a dark night. 'He said he had it, my lord . . .'

'And you killed him before he'd given it to us, killed them *both*?'

'I wanted to save . . . inconvenience?'

'If we cannot find it, you will pay. They will not tolerate further delay; her ladyship has already been sent here once asking questions!'

'Yes, my lord.'

'Hide the body! *Find it!*'

The thieves are hiding in the shadows under the bridges, waiting for their prey, fingers drumming on their knives. The policemen are trudging through the streets, rattles duly sounding as they whirl them around and announce the hour, long blue coats slapping against their white-clad knees. The horses are bedding down in the mews of Mayfair. The street-walkers are plying their trade in the gutters of St Giles, all false white faces and falser red smiles.

A dark carriage clatters away down a dark street, fading into the thick, choking green-grey fog that rises off the river and from the factories into an itchy soup in the air. It leaves behind nothing, except a dying gas lamp and a small red stain of blood, seeping gently through the cobbles and into the mud below.

The gas man is putting his ladder against the side of another black pillar along Green Park, and wondering whether his career prospects really do his talent justice. The girl has sold her last little bag of nuts and is going home with her few pennies of profit for the night. The master of the cress market below Shoreditch is laying out his trestle tables for the night's trade. The mechanics are wiping dirt from their faces as they walk away from the seething railway yards of King's Cross, with dirty hands rubbed on dirtier hankies.

And in the darkness of the carriage, a still man with a black leather voice carefully inspects his white gloves by the light of a bouncing lantern, observes a tiny speck of red blood on the tip of a finger, pulls the glove off a long, white, elegant hand, and sighs. He drops it on to the floor of the carriage for someone else to worry about. He sits back, and thinks very quietly to himself, *Soon, we will rise.*

As the driver pushes the carriage on into the night, he puts a hand inside his coat and feels for something to eat. He finds nothing but an immaculately intact knobbly peel from a small fruit, and a single round stone. He curses internally. He tells himself that he shouldn't have eaten the lychee, and throws both peel and stone away into the gutter. After murder, littering isn't really a priority. At least, it isn't tonight.

Almost five miles away, something went *click* in a darkened house. A window opened a few inches, sliding up from the sill.

A hand slithered inside, checked carefully on either side of the window, found nothing of interest except a pair of faded curtains, and pushed up the window a little more. The hand wormed further inside. It was followed by a scantily clad arm, a head, a pair of shoulders and, in due course, the remainder of its owner's body. The shadow dropped on to the floor, and very slowly started to walk. Halfway across the room it hesitated. It squatted down and gently ran its hand across the floor, until it touched a tile which sank, ever so slightly, under its pressure. It moved forward stealthily on hands and knees, avoiding the tile, and the five others its gentle probes detected. When it reached the door, it stood again. It ran a slim blade carefully down the side of the door, felt nothing, and opened it.

In the corridor beyond, a single candle burnt on a table. Nothing else here to give any sign of ownership. The curtains at the far end were drawn, one side slightly singed. The figure moved forward cautiously, and for a moment could be seen by the dim candlelight, before darting back into shadow.

It was short, had no shoes, wore a shirt and trousers that might once have been white, but which now would shame even the most scruffy of scarecrows. It had a tangle of dark brown curls sticking out in every direction from its head, and a pair of intently squinting and blinking grey eyes. It was, in fact, a girl, still young enough to get away with pretending to be innocent, but old enough to be very, very guilty indeed.

Halfway down the corridor, she hesitated, head slightly on one side. She looked up at the ceiling. She looked down at the floor. Then she went back the way she had come, past the door, to the end of the corridor and tried a different door in the opposite direction. It was locked. This didn't cause as much consternation as an innocent observer might have expected. The girl pulled out a small bottle from the deep recesses of a padded jacket favoured by shepherds the world over. There was the sound of something liquid. A smell rose up in the corridor, and a gentle hissing. A little click from the door, which was pushed gently open. In the room beyond sat a huge table, sagging under the weight of apparatus: bottles, strange flasks, tubes, candles, prisms, wires, tools.

The figure moved forward quickly, then stopped. Under the table a dog lay sleeping. It lay on its back, feet in the air, paws folded over, enormous nose twitching slightly, long brown and white ears sticking out either side of its head along the floor. It had the belly of a spoiled animal and the wagging tail, even in sleep, of a very happy one. It had the nose of a creature designed for hunting down prey at great distances, and the girl guessed that somewhere below the huge nose, there were teeth to match.

She watched it for a long while, cautious. Then, very slowly, when it was clear that this animal would wake for nothing (except, perhaps, food and affection), she shuffled forward, half-turning to keep it in her sight, moving a toe at a time. She went past the table to a row of cupboards hanging above a desk, in a corner. She opened them, started digging through, but found only notes, reams and reams of paper covered in an almost unintelligible hand and even less intelligible drawings. She frowned in exasperation.

Not having found what she was looking for, she headed to a side door in the room. This too was locked. She drew out her tools again, inserted the first one, and instantly something inside the lock flashed bright blue, a big fat spark leaping from the door to the ground. Somewhere above the door, something embedded in the ceiling went *thunk*. Something slow and ponderous began to turn. There was a sound like a marble running downhill on uneven ground. The girl tugged at her tool wedged in the lock, and heard a snapping sound. Pulled away, the end had boiled down to nothing. Not hesitating, not even bothering to waste time on thought, the girl turned and ran towards the other door, bursting out into the corridor, running along it for the window at the far end. At the point where before she had turned back, she ran on, and under her the floor shrieked, making her head shake sickeningly. Somewhere there was a hissing sound and hot steam exploded in a white cloud from the room she had only just left. She reached the window; a dog started howling, barking; she dragged the curtains back, heaved the window open, looked up, looked down.

There was the street twenty feet below, a gas lamp burning steadily outside, cobbles glistening in the rain. The girl leant out, saw a lead drainpipe, reached for it, grabbed hold and dragged herself out of the window until she dangled, feet scrambling against the wet metal. Clutching with hands and feet, she started to ease herself down. There was a long, screeching sound, like a banshee with indigestion.

The section of pipe she clung to lurched, started to bend away from the wall. Where it joined the section below, an unseen tube of linked metal plates started to bend, so that as the pipe fell back, it leant away from the wall like an arm. There was a snap and a long coil of rope, wound into a tiny cubby-hole in the red brickwork itself, started to unwind. One end was tied to the pipe.

It fell back slowly, the girl still clinging on desperately. It bent forty-five degrees away from the wall before the length of rope snapped tense. It stopped moving, and dangled there, the girl holding on to it with every fibre of strength in her thin, unprepared arms, as she wondered what the hell to do.

Around the street, she could hear people stirring, distant dogs barking, carriages being pulled to a stop, breaking their rhythm towards the corner at the end of the road. The window she had dropped from lit up a dull orange. Silhouetted against it was a dark shadow that might just have resembled a man. There was a long silence. Finally the shadow said mildly, 'Are you all right up there?'

'Yes, thank you, sir.'

'You sure? It looks like quite a long drop . . .'

'Really, sir, it ain't nothin' to be botherin' about.'

'Oh.' He looked slightly surprised, and frowned. 'It *was* you trying to break in, wasn't it? Only if there's been some kind of misunderstanding . . .'

She gulped. She could feel her hands slowly slipping on the smooth metal pipe. Falls seemed further when you were short, she reasoned. 'Oh no, no, no, sir! Can't think what you'll be meanin'. But since you happen to be mentionin' this pipe, sir . . .'

A front door opened on the other side of the street. A woman exploded out like a runaway train. She was carrying a meat cleaver, had blonde hair which trailed down her back, and wore a determined expression of bloodthirsty vengeance. The girl on the post shrieked and tried to climb higher. The man in the window blanched. The woman in the street screamed, 'Police, police!', saw the man in the window and gasped, 'Horatio?'

Horatio Lyle, who knew that manners were an essential social glue and that society was a fascinating phenomenon that deserved study and thus, preservation, smiled uncomfortably. 'Yes, Miss Chaste?'

'Horatio, are you all right?' In that split second, her voice had dropped an octave and become as soft as springtime rain, which was clearly disconcerting to Horatio Lyle, who began to reconsider the benefits of society after all. The girl clinging on to the drainpipe tried not to boggle at her.

'What in heaven's name is happening here?'

'Just a little . . .'

On the dangling pipe, the girl, who had been watching all this with keen attention began, ''Bout this pipe . . .'

'Horatio, is this another experiment? Only I do know that the last one went so terribly . . .'

'No, no, I was just ascertaining whether this young lady was or was not . . .'

'Oh, the young lady!' Miss Chaste's voice rocketed an octave, and two hands flew to two cheeks, as if they might burst with appalled indignation. 'She looks in such terrible danger, so distraught! Oh, good Horatio, you must . . .'

'Well, actually, she was in the process of . . .'

To everyone's surprise, including possibly the girl herself, she exploded. 'Please, miss,' the girl started yelling, 'please, I'm just an innocent child tor . . . torme . . . havin' a really hard time seein' as how I've been on the street tryin' to make an honest livin' in a harsh world . . .'

'I beg your pardon?!' squeaked Lyle.

The girl was unstoppable. 'Please don't let this horrid man

hurt me, I never done nothin' but he just don't listen to me and he chased me an' I said how I was lovely really and, please, miss . . .'

In the gloom of the window, Lyle's mouth dropped open. In the street the woman with the meat cleaver hesitated. She looked far too slim and pale to be holding such a large weapon, and indeed now that the excitement was cooling a little, its presence in her hand made her uncomfortable, and she tried to hide it behind her voluminous white nightrobe. Ladies of more decorum might have worn a shawl, and indeed she had considered one when exiting the house. But then, she'd realized who the incident involved, and changed her mind. The shawl, she believed, wasn't her most flattering colour.

Turning a pair of severe almond eyes on Lyle, a useful inheritance from her father and a match for her freckles, she said in a voice like glaciers rolling over a particularly difficult hillside, 'Horatio, is this true?'

For a second, his indignation almost overwhelmed all power of speech. 'Do you really believe that . . .'

'Please, miss,' sobbed the girl, 'please, miss, don't let him hurt me. I'm so hungry and cold and scared and he's such a brutish man, he hasn't heard of Christian charity, miss, please . . .'

'Horatio!' The woman flushed. 'I demand that you come down here at once and assist me with this unfortunate waif!'

'*Waif?*' exclaimed Lyle. 'Miss Chaste . . .'

'Horatio, I shall summon the police!'

Pigeons were startled out of their roosts at the indignant squeak in her voice. Lyle flinched, sighed and said humbly, 'Yes, Miss Chaste.'

Mercy Chaste knew her duty. As the local vicar's daughter, she took an immense pride in her Christian heritage, and had an evangelistic streak in her which had led to a new and interesting reinterpretation of the verb 'chastened'.

A minute later the front door opened and Lyle appeared, dragging a large metal box as if it was very heavy, and after it a tube connected to a large pile of what looked like leather sacking. This he spread out under Miss Chaste's furious eye to a rough square beneath the pipe and kicked the box moodily. There was a hissing sound and the leather square expanded slowly into a small inflated mattress. The girl craned her neck to see the mattress and squeaked, 'I'm not falling on to that!'

Lyle's eyes flashed. 'It's that,' he snapped, 'or the pavement.'

She thought about it, even as Miss Chaste barked, 'Horatio!' Lyle's expression was unshakable.

Sullenly the girl muttered, twisting to see her destination more clearly, 'I think I'll let go now.'

'Why not?' he sighed.

The girl closed her eyes and let go. She fell, and bounced up from the mattress several times. It was almost fun, she thought, and wondered if she could bounce some more. Then she saw the two adults' faces peering down and hastily she crawled off the mattress and picked herself up, putting on her most endearing expression of innocence. Lyle scowled. Seeing this, the girl launched into emergency procedure. She threw herself at Miss Chaste, wrapping her arms around the woman's waist and bursting into tears. 'Please, miss, don't let him hurt me. Miss, please, I'll do anything . . .'

'Oh, for goodness' sake.' Lyle pulled a plug in the mattress, which slowly started to deflate. As the girl sobbed into Miss Chaste's nightgown, Lyle stalked up to his half-open door, disappeared inside, reappearing a second later. With a whirring sound, the section of dangling pipe started to wind back against the wall, locking itself in place, as if it had never moved.

'Horatio.' Miss Chaste's voice had a tone of determined finality.

He wished he could simper as well as the girl was doing. 'Yes, Miss Chaste?' he sighed.

'What do you have to say for yourself, Horatio?'

He thought about it.

'Erm . . .'

The girl chose this hesitation as a chance for prolonged sobbing.

'You realize I can't possibly permit the child to go home in a state like this?'

Something of the Lyle family spirit flared up in Horatio. Though he prided himself on being able to deal in a rational manner with any crisis from chemical fires to electrical overloads, *some* things were beyond reasonable expectations, and he snapped. 'This child damn well *broke into* my hou—'

'Language, Horatio!'

'Please, miss, I never, I never, miss, I . . .'

'Horatio,' snapped Miss Chaste, 'I think you owe this young lady an apology.'

Lyle realized the girl, between sobs, was slyly watching him through her fingers. She grinned slightly behind her hands. His scowl deepened. 'Miss Chaste, I have reason to believe this young lady may be a thief.'

'No, miss, t'isn't true, miss, I swear! T'isn't true!' And then, fulfilling a plan which had been brewing from the moment she'd labelled Miss Chaste a busy-body, and better still, a *rich* busy-body of total gullibility, Teresa Hatch, pickpocket and burglar by trade and notorious up and down Shadwell, fainted.

And in that part of the city where the fate of continents is decided over a glass of port and a game of bridge, in a room with a ceiling appreciable only by giraffes and a width that would certainly appeal to a small blue whale, if it ever had occasion to see it, a room hung with pictures of fine old men with large moustaches, a man sits at the end of a long, polished table topped with black leather, and says, 'Well?'

'We've just had confirmation of the break-in.'

'And?'

'And . . . we can't say how it happened, sir.'

Silence.

'What do you wish done, sir?'

'I wish to know where they have taken it, and what they are planning.'

'Would Her Majesty approve, sir?'

'Her Majesty,' the man replies quietly, 'need never know.'

CHAPTER 1

The sun rose on the city, and the city rose with the sun.

And someone was shouting, 'What do you *mean*, it wasn't there?'

'I mean the object was not in the vicinity.'

'You have failed?'

'We will find it. Investigations are already underway.'

'Meanwhile, we'll have lost precious time. They will be looking for it as well. By this time we could be in the streets, we could be drowning in the power and dragging this city out of the smoke and metal back into the clean, pure light rather than this black *abyss* . . . and *you* . . .'

'I appreciate that, my lady.'

'See that you do, my lord.'

And in the house of Lord and Lady Elwick, young Master Thomas woke in a large soft bed to the sound of heavy footsteps in the corridor outside. The door burst open and his governess rushed in and said from behind the bed curtains, before he'd even hauled himself up on his elbows, 'Master says you're to be downstairs immediately.'

'What?' he asked, swinging himself out of bed a little bit too fast for his groggy head. 'Why does Father want me now?'

'The whole house is mustering, Master Thomas. Everyone says it's because of the bank. I've never seen the master so angry.'

'The bank? Which bank?'

'*The* bank, Master Thomas! Your parents are going down there immediately to check the vault. You must be up quickly, they'll want to say goodbye!'

Thomas didn't hesitate. No Elwick *ever* hesitated. He stood up and made for the giant mahogany wardrobe on the other side of his large room. 'If they're going,' he said determinedly, 'then I'm going too!'

His governess rolled her eyes when he wasn't looking, but didn't ask what a fifteen-year-old boy thought he could do. He'd just say what he always did. 'If I don't try, I'll never know.'

Which wasn't an answer at all.

The sunlight spread from east to west and crawled through high windows and low windows alike, trickled across floors and ceilings, and brushed the eyes of the sleeping.

Tess Hatch woke, and was instantly alert. *I know it's early in the morning, and I'm pretty sure the house must be asleep, so . . .*

She tried to work out her moves, piece by piece. She was lying on her side, staring at a tall window through which faint sunlight crept, as if embarrassed to call itself morning.

She was in a bed. This caused her sudden alarm, and she sat up, feeling the unusual softness. A *bed*. Not just any bed, but a big bed, with sheets and blankets and . . . *feather pillows* and . . . She looked round the room. Miss Chaste must have been more of a fool than even *she* had suspected. She slipped, utterly silent, out of the bed.

The room wasn't particularly big, the only features in it, apart from the bed, being the large window, a stool in one corner, a shelf laden with books, and a small desk with a mirror above it whose centre had an unlikely and slightly alarming, perfectly rounded scorch mark. Tess was wearing what she always wore – the only clothes she owned: a pair of worn trousers that were starting to give way at the knees and a shirt several sizes too large. Looking around, she saw her padded jacket with holes at the elbows, lying on the stool, neatly folded. She scampered across the room, snatched the jacket up, and for a second saw her face in the mirror above the desk. She hesitated. Her dark brown hair stuck out around her face in every direction, and her dirty pale face, long and knowing, stared back with a surprised expression, unused to seeing itself.

She crept to the door. It was unlocked, which was a surprise. She pushed it open and stepped out into the cold corridor beyond. Floorboards covered with a red carpet, a candle burnt down on a table, thin curtains open across the window at the end to let in more light. She padded in what she thought was perfect silence to the end of the corridor and pushed open a door that led to a flight of stairs. Slowly, she took them one at a time, testing each to avoid creaks. Halfway down, she became aware of a distant rumbling and speeded up, anxious to find the imagined loot and get out. She went past two landings and into the cold of the basement, where she crept along a corridor, listening for any sounds of life. She heard a fire burning behind a nearby plain white door to her right, hesitated, then pushed it open a little. There was a large stove, open to receive more wood, and a figure in shirt sleeves, black trousers and bare feet, bent over to toss on a log. Without looking up he said, 'Good morning' in a tone of polite disinterest.

For a second she thought about running, but then . . . He was cooking *breakfast*.

Tess stepped carefully inside. The man straightened up, pushing the stove door shut, turned to her and grinned. She saw a pair of grey eyes and sandy hair, reddish in places. He looked terribly, terribly familiar, but she knew, *knew* that this couldn't be, well, *him*, because that wasn't what was in her plan, that wasn't how it worked, not *her* plans, especially not with the bigwig who had paid, not if she was . . .

Tess heard the cracking of eggs and the hissing of oil. She took in a row of neatly tidied desks, a low wooden kitchen table, and a dog bowl marked 'Tate' in large letters.

'Sit down, lass, make yourself comfortable.' His voice was unusual. If she'd been back on the streets with her friends she would have said it belonged to a bigwig, except there was a familiar stop on the 'd's and the 't's, something that was common in the slums of Shadwell and the rookeries of Soho.

She sat down cautiously. 'Are you Miss Chaste's butler?'

'Me?' He looked slightly alarmed. 'Goodness, no.'

This was possibly a good thing. She drew herself up to her full, and less-than-impressive height. 'Do you know who I am?'

He smiled brightly, and said in a conversational, light-hearted tone, flipping a slice of bacon, 'Who are you?'

'I am . . .' her mind raced and her voice changed slightly, rising a little in pitch and slurring the vowels, 'Lady Teresa of France. I am a guest of your mistress. She's given you instructions as to how I should be looked after an' all?'

To her surprise, the man started grinning, as if in on some secret. He broke another egg into a frying pan. 'Well, I hope you're hungry.'

She folded her hands in her lap and tried to look ladylike, saying primly, 'Tol . . . toler . . . yes.'

'Tell me, Lady Teresa,' he continued in the same jovial tone, pulling a couple of plates out of the cupboard, 'do you always break into the houses of the people you're going to visit?'

Tess hesitated. Then, 'How dare you say that!'

He scraped the eggs off the bottom of the pan and tossed them onto her plate. To this he added a couple of slices of bread, two rashers of bacon, a glass of orange juice and a knob of butter, setting the whole lot in front of her on the low kitchen table. Pulling up a chair he sat down and stared thoughtfully across at her. Finally he said, 'Your fainting was very good last night. Well, you fell . . . went the wrong way – gravity was clearly not the only force at work – but still, the sigh was very effective, the rolling of the eyes, the little theatrical gasp. Have you ever considered giving up a life of larceny for an age of acting?'

She hesitated only a fraction of a second. 'I was all overcome, see?'

'Miss Chaste was very insistent that you were brought into her house for good treatment and a decent meal. But it would have been wrong to let her be taken in by that trick.'

'If you—' she began.

He ignored her. 'I was impressed, though. More than I've been in a long while by any thief.' He held out his hand. 'Horatio Lyle.'

She was off the seat and had her back to the wall in a second, terror buzzing in her skull.

He rolled his eyes. 'Please don't be like that. Have breakfast.'

Very, very carefully, never taking her eyes off him, she sat.

Lyle sighed. 'I'll keep this simple. I don't like my home being broken into. But when you get a reputation for inventing things, people keep thinking, "Yes, I'll have that", and there's only so much you can do about it.'

'You seem to have done summat, sir.'

'Thank you.'

'Probably got too much time on your hands. In fact, if I can say . . .'

'Thank you,' he repeated. Tess was aware of Lyle's eyes upon her, thoughtful. Finally he said, 'This is going to sound unusual.'

'Is it unusual for things to sound unusual in your house, sir?'

His eyes narrowed. 'That's incredible. Abject terror to insolence in less than thirty seconds. I have a proposition for you.'

She sprang back indignantly. 'That's horrid!'

'Believe it or not,' he pointed out mildly, 'I'm offering you a chance not to go to prison.'

Her shoulders hunched slowly and suspiciously. 'What kind of chance?'

'I was thinking about this after you fainted. That really was impressive, you do know that? I mean, the way you managed to fall at just the right angle to sustain minimum bruising. I wish I'd been less distracted . . . an almost perfect example of moments around a pivot. But then, I suppose, no one really considers the medical consequences of the centre of gravity in—'

'You havin' that bacon?'

'What? Erm, no, I suppose not.'

'Okay. Keep goin'.'

'Erm . . . yes, what was I talking about?'

'How you was not sendin' me to prison.'

'How I was *hypothetically* not sending you to prison.'

'Oh. Like that.'

'You don't know what hypothetically means, do you?'

'You havin' that toast?'

'What? Yes, I am!'

'Oh.' Tess pushed it back on to his plate with a guilty expression.

'The truth is,' continued Lyle, looking slightly flummoxed, 'I could use an assistant.'

'That's nice.'

'Lass, I think you're missing the point and *don't even consider going for my egg, understand?*'

'You sure? Only it'll get cold.'

'I need to keep my belongings safe. I'm also running a series of experiments that could require the assistance of someone with a very dexterous touch. The problem is,' said Lyle, warming to his theme, 'that in order to measure resistivity in proportion to surface area and density – not together, obviously, because,' he laughed, 'that would just be absurd – but the problem *is* how small you have to get the wires for comparison and the delicate nature of the equipment . . .'

'It really is gettin' cold.'

'And since you proved last night that you are very good at dealing with delicate things – *I can see you watching that egg* – I thought I wouldn't send you to prison and make you for the rest of your life an embittered professional thief with a reputation and long-term grudge against the laws of society . . .'

'That's nice.'

'. . . I'd make you my assistant for the week.'

The words settled over the table like a blanket. Tess sat, fork laden with bacon, and thought about it. 'Uh . . .'

'Lass, I could have turned you over last night. I could still.'

Tess broke into a strained, bright grin. She knew that, in situations like this, you didn't think. You didn't worry about what you were getting into, you didn't agonize over possible repercussions, you just took the easiest way out that you were being offered. 'You've made the right choice, sir. I'm the best in the business, I am.'

'Good.'

'An' at the end of the week?'

'You can go. And I'll give you back your very fine collection of lock picks.'

Tess's mouth dropped open. 'You *pinched* my picks?'

'I relocated them.'

A glower settled over Tess's face. 'You don't try big words like that with me; I know what that means – it means you went an' you pinched them!'

'And you can have them back at the end of the week.'

'That ain't fair!'

'It ain— it *isn't* prison, lass.'

'Fine.'

'Good. *Fine.*'

'So,' she said, brightening with the thought, 'how much was you goin' to pay, sir?'

He spluttered. '*Pay?*'

'Well, seein' as how my services are *so* skilled . . .'

'I'm sorry, I think I must have misheard. I could have sworn I heard you ask *me* for money.'

'At least I *asked.*'

'How moral.'

'I thought as how you might app . . . appre . . . might be all impressed an' everythin'.'

'I think you should probably stick with thieving rather than spiritual appeals to mankind's better nature. Although I do have *one* question.'

Tess's eyes narrowed suspiciously, her fork halfway to her mouth. 'Yes?'

'What is it about my house that made you want to break in in the first place?'

She hesitated, then started to grin. 'You'll pay me if I tell you?'

Lyle rolled his eyes. 'I don't know why I try. All right.'

'It were this gaffer what had a silly name.'

'What silly name?'

'Havelock.'

A sad smile spread across Lyle's face, opening his mouth to speak . . .

And above, there was a knock at the door.

Naturally, Tess thought of large policemen and small prison cells. Then she chided herself for too much imagination, and told herself it was more likely to be the Palace than the police.

As it turned out, she was absolutely right.

The dog got to the door first. He sat there barking, and when Lyle and Tess came up the stairs from the kitchen, he gave them a look of utter contempt that suggested, if they hadn't heard him then they were deaf, and if they had, then why hadn't they run?

'Thank you, Tate,' Lyle muttered, as he walked briskly to the door. The dog lay down very firmly in the corridor and stared at Tess with big, brown eyes in a long brown and white face, his ears sagging on to the floor. Tess stared back at him, keeping her distance. He didn't blink. She wasn't sure if she'd ever seen an expression of such intelligent despair at the stupidity of humankind.

Lyle opened the door a crack. Two men stood outside. They wore long black cloaks, tall black top hats, and the expressions of people with a very specific task who hadn't even *considered* the possibility of not fulfilling their aims.

'Mister Lyle?'

'Yes?' There was a suspicious edge to Lyle's voice that immediately put Tess on guard, and made Tate sit up.

'You must come with us, Mister Lyle.'

'Why?'

'The Palace wants to see you.'

Lyle looked surprised, then pained, then downright upset. 'I'm a little busy. I've got an experiment all set up downstairs, and if I don't do it soon the tubes will be completely useless . . .'

'Sir,' repeated the man in a tone of disbelief, 'the *Palace* wants you.'

He hesitated. 'Uh, well . . .'

'*Sir.*' The word took on a pained quality, suggesting that here was a man who, though about to break Lyle's legs, was at least polite enough to recommend a good doctor afterwards.

Lyle smiled tightly, seeing this, and said, 'Ah.' He raised his shoulders in defeat, put on a feeble attempt at an innocent expression and said, 'May I bring a friend?'

Later, Tess, wearing a dress, sat in a carriage driven by two men wearing royal rings, next to a man whose house she had tried to break into. She tried to work out what she was doing. Next to her Lyle muttered, 'Please don't fidget.'

'I'm nerv . . . nervy? That's a word, right?'

'No, and you're making me nervous.'

'You ain't never been to the Palace before?'

'Have *you*?'

He had a point. She shifted uncomfortably. 'Uh . . . why am I coming?'

'Because I'm not trusting you alone in my house.'

'Can I have my lock picks back?'

'In a week.'

'Why am I in a dress?'

'Because I'm not letting you go to the Palace looking like an East End thief.'

She thought about this. 'But I *am*.'

His look cut her off, and she sat back in sullen silence. The carriage had blinds across the windows and she couldn't see where they were, but the sound of the street was strange, with cobbles instead of dirt. She could hear voices calling out in unfamiliar accents and the hubbub of a distant market.

Finally she said, 'Sir?'

'Yes?'

'Who is Miss Chaste?'

Lyle shifted uneasily. 'A very . . . proper lady.'

'Sir?'

'Yes?'

'Does she . . . you know . . . and you . . . ?'

'Teresa, are you always this quick to dispose of respect and discretion?'

She thought about it. 'Nah. Usually get there faster. But you had me scared for a second, sir.'

He looked slightly glassy-eyed as he intoned, 'She and I are not engaged in any mutual bond.'

'Oh. Thank you, sir.'

He shot her a sly glance and said, 'You don't know what any of that meant, do you?'

'No, sir. But I thought how it might be best not to ask.'

'Does the phrase "repressed vestal virgin" mean anything to you?'

She thought about it. 'Nah.'

He let out a little sigh. 'Thank goodness.'

'You goin' to explain, sir?'

'Absolutely not.'

The carriage rattled through the streets of Mayfair, round the green-brown edge of Green Park where lovers walked in the cold autumnal air and the trees were coated with the soot of the city, towards a black iron gate tucked away in an endless yellow-brick wall, guarded by a pair of black iron dragons, and so across the smooth, worn cobbles of an inner courtyard towards the stables of Buckingham Palace.

They got out of the carriage and walked in silence through a tradesman's door and up a plain stone staircase. Corridors grew wider, staircases became carpeted, pictures appeared on the walls. Beyond a mahogany door, they suddenly found themselves in the very heart of the Palace itself, following a butler who looked as if he'd been mummified.

Tess stared, her eyes flickering from vase to clock to painting to silver candlestick to the butler's gold buttons and back round again. Lyle too looked about him. He reflected on the apparent height of the royal family, that it needed such lofty rooms for its daily living, and whether they'd let him try some of his inventions on their doors and windows. Next to him, Tess had fallen into a suspiciously deep silence. He said mildly, not looking at her, 'They probably change the patrol paths of the guards every month.'

'Why do you say that, sir?'

He glanced down at her. She was trying to smile innocently, and in that neat blue dress — nothing too fine but nothing that would shame a lady — with her unruly hair curled away from her washed face, she *almost* got away with it.

'And if you're considering the rooftop approach, you'd require a stronger grappling hook and tougher gloves than you possess. I hope.'

'Actually, sir, I was considering going to the back door with a basket of oranges and asking for the nicest cook in the place.'

He tried to hide his smile. 'That might work too.'

The door ahead opened, and Lyle was announced by a man in a large white wig who had the expression of one who'd been shown a nit underneath a magnifying glass. There didn't seem to be anyone there to announce them to. But if it made the man happy, Lyle wasn't going to question his purpose in life.

The room beyond was poorly lit and hung with huge red curtains and further portraits, all wearing a Colonel-of-the-Empire-I-kill-barbarians-for-breakfast expression. Lyle squinted down its length as the door shut behind him, saw a grandfather clock clicking away in a corner and, in the absence of any other object of interest, went towards it, fumbling in his pocket for something.

Behind him Tess said thoughtfully, 'Problem is, nothing much can be carried in a hurry, see?' Lyle didn't answer, and Tess walked up to his side to peer at the clock as well, trying to see whatever it was that fascinated him. He pulled out of his pocket a small object that looked like a cross between a compass, a pair of protractors and a fob watch, but like no watch she had ever seen. The needles, as far as she could tell, read '3.23 N 70'. Lyle squinted at it, then at the clock and sighed. 'It's slow.'

He didn't hear the sound behind him, wasn't even aware that someone was standing there. Then when he thought about it, perhaps the man had been there, but so neatly folded away in a chair that he simply hadn't noticed.

'Good morning, Constable,' said a quiet, precise voice. 'Might I offer you coffee?'

They turned. Tess attempted a bob that might have been an illusion of a curtsey. Lyle tried a polite nod, not sure what else he was expected to do. The man nodded in acknowledgement, a tight smile across a tight, bony face. He was short, neat and grey-haired, wearing a black three-piece suit, with the chain of a silver fob watch threaded through his waistcoat. His eyes were so sunken into his pale face that Lyle wondered if there was room in his head for anything else. As the man's gaze swept the two of them, Tess drew nearer Lyle, then realized what she was doing and straightened up to stare defiantly back.

The man looked at them for a long moment, seemed to reach a conclusion and gestured at the long table that ran the length of the room. 'Will you both sit down?'

Lyle led the way to a place near the head of the table, and Tess scuttled round to sit by his side, furthest from the man. Sitting opposite Lyle, the man placed a file on the table and rang a small bell. The door opened, and a butler glided in holding a silver tray laden with coffee, rolls and jam, on a silver plate. Tess eyed this latter thoughtfully. Lyle, eyes not moving from the man, kicked her under the table. She said loudly, 'Ow!'

The man turned an icy stare on her. 'I beg your pardon?'

'Uh, nothing, sir. Cramp.'

'Oh dear. I do wish you a speedy recovery.' He sounded as if he was announcing an execution.

Lyle cleared his throat. 'Forgive my bluntness, but why are we here, my lord?'

The man raised his eyebrows slightly, and a smile like canvas that didn't want to be stretched tugged painfully at his white lips. 'What gives you the impression that I'm a peer of the realm, Constable Lyle?'

'Not a Constable, sir. Special Constable on a good day, which today isn't.'

'What do you believe to be the difference between a Constable and a Special Constable, Mister Lyle?'

There it was, thought Tess. Even this person – whoever he was – said *Mister* Lyle.

'The hours and the pay, Lord Lincoln,' Lyle replied, utterly deadpan. Tess wiped her own face clean. If Lyle wasn't smiling there had to be a reason. She tried not to fidget.

Lord Lincoln nodded in acknowledgement. 'You have me correctly, sir. May I enquire how?'

Lyle hesitated. Somehow 'inspired guesswork' didn't sound as if it would appeal to Lincoln's calculating mind. 'A process of elimination? Your clothes are of the finest cut, there are inkstains on your right hand, a ring bearing the royal seal on your left hand, and your shoes, albeit well made, are worn down hard at the heel, though not the toe. Uh . . . you're carrying a pair of reading glasses in your right-hand pocket and there are a series of slight abrasions on your jacket, suggesting that you frequently wear medals. Erm . . . anything else? . . . you are clearly highly decorated and honoured, yet involved in daily administration. You're *here* and so are we, therefore you are Lord Lincoln, personal aide to Her Majesty.' He smiled, looking nervous. 'Is that right, my lord?' Tess realized she was gaping, and quickly closed her mouth.

'Perhaps. Although it equally may have been an inspired piece of guesswork.'

Lyle's smile grew thin. 'We'll never know, my lord.'

Silence. Then, 'You are a man with a reputation, Mister Lyle. I have a proposition for you. In the Queen's name. How would you feel about serving your country?'

Lyle's expression became a little frantic. 'Well, actually, and please don't take offence, I've got this rack of test tubes waiting back home which will be ruined in a matter of minutes . . .'

Lord Lincoln cut him off with a look. 'Then, Constable Lyle, I will be blunt. There has been a robbery, and an object very personal to Her Majesty has been taken. The circumstances are, to say the least, mysterious. The item which is our chief cause of concern was taken along with numerous other valuables from a theoretically impenetrable vault and is—'

'Not the crown jewels?' asked Tess eagerly. 'Not again?'

'No, madam. Not the crown jewels.'

'Not India?'

'What?'

Lyle tried to hide his grin. Tess said primly, 'I was askin' if someone pinched India, sir.'

'Indeed no, India is very firmly locked in Her Majesty's heart.'

She looked up at Lyle. 'Is that possible?'

'It's not healthy,' he conceded.

'Constable,' said Lincoln, sounding exasperated, 'the artefact—'

'Is it the Fuyun Plate, sir?' asked Lyle sharply.

Tess held her breath. In a voice that reminded her of the men in a darkened alley with garrotting wires explaining that you hadn't seen nothing, Lincoln said, 'Whatever gives you that impression?'

'The file under your elbow, sir.'

'I see. How much more do you know?'

'Pass me the file and I'll tell you.'

Lincoln's voice could have made salt water freeze. 'The Fuyun Plate is of immense cultural and historical value to Her Majesty. It was given to Her Majesty as a gesture of goodwill by the Chinese government, being a native artefact of Tibet. Legend around it abounds. Its loss is a cultural tragedy. I require that it is found again, and the thieves brought to my attention.'

'Don't you mean Her Majesty requires that it is found again, and the thieves brought to the law's attention?'

'Quite.'

Tess shifted uneasily. The two men were staring, trying to read each other. She wondered why Lyle didn't just say yes, and then they could get out of there. But he didn't even blink. Softly, Lord Lincoln said, 'There is the matter of a salary.'

'Money is of no interest to me. In fact, if it's all the same, I've got a lot of chemicals any minute now burning through a table of which I'm immensely fond, so if you don't mind . . .' Lyle made to stand up.

'And membership of the Royal Institution.'

Lyle didn't move. He looked as if someone had just hit him. At length he said, '*Lifetime* membership?'

'Naturally.'

Silence. Then, '*Really?*'

Lincoln sighed. 'Very much so.'

Lyle reached out for the file. Lincoln put it carefully into his hand and Lyle flicked through it without stopping to read, then said, 'A pleasure to serve, sir. Might I ask – this impenetrable vault – where is it?'

Lincoln's smile could have scared rattlesnakes. 'Where you might expect, Constable. In the Bank of England.'

'*Ah.*'

Taking the case was probably, Lyle would later admit, his first mistake.

CHAPTER 2

Elwick

The file, Lyle grudgingly muttered as the carriage bounced its way through the grey, cobbled streets, was impressive. He flicked through the pages of notes on the Fuyun Plate, its history, its makers, how it had ended up in the hands of Her Majesty, in the Bank of England, and said finally, 'Good grief.'

'What?' asked Tess, resisting the temptation to chew her fingers nervously, a habit she'd developed at an early age and never quite kicked. The carriage rattled through the high, narrow streets of the City towards the towering edifice of the Bank of England, stopping and starting among hordes of carts, and cabs carrying the rich and the richer to and from their wealth, while on the river ships rang their bells to summon the sailors, and the factories warmed up for the day, spewing out steam and black soot into the sky.

'Listen to this: "The Plate was believed by the natives of Tibet to have been forged in the making of the world by and for the 'Tseiqin', an ancient and powerful race, some call demons, some angels. On drinking holy water sanctified by the gods and mortal magic, the Tseiqin were said to acquire the powers of gods, and to this day are believed to roam the jungles and forests of the world, in search of their lost magic. The Plate has been valued at two hundred pounds."'

'Two . . .' she squeaked. 'I've never even seen a sovereign!'

'Teresa,' he said mildly, 'with respect, you're in an irregular occupation. You've got to try to understand the context. You break into the most secure bank in the world, into a vault said to be impenetrable by mortal man, merely to steal a stone plate valued at the kind of sum that would sustain no more than a single, small industrial family with no servant in moderate comfort for a year.'

'Perhaps I knew 'bout the whole cultural malarkey.'

He gave her a look. She raised her eyebrows and said indignantly, 'Well, it's *possible*.'

'You want to make odds?' He flicked through the file again. 'Ah. This is more like it. Also stolen – three gold goblets from the Hindu Temple of Camdoon, valued collectively at one thousand pounds; a silver ornamental plate presented by the last King of France to the Duke of Buckingham, valued at seven hundred and fifty pounds; a series of ornate gold swans gifted to Her Majesty's Ambassador in Peking by the Manchu Emperor,

35

valued at one thousand three hundred and fifty pounds. *These* would appeal.'

Her mouth was hanging open. 'That's . . . that's like . . . like . . .'

'Three thousand one hundred pounds.'

'That's . . . that's . . .'

'Enough money possibly to justify a break-in. The Fuyun Plate is an anomaly – an item of apparently no value.'

'Well, that's good, though, ain't it?'

'Then why did Lord Lincoln ask *us* to find it?' Lyle looked worriedly out of the window at the dirty streets.

Tess said in the silence, 'Actually, sir, he asked *you*. That's probably a bad thing, right?'

'Thank you for reminding me.'

'Any time, sir. Are we goin' to the Bank, now?'

'Yes. But first we'll pick up Tate.'

As Tess and Lyle rattled through the streets of London towards the Bank, the Honourable Thomas Edward Elwick stepped out of the family carriage into the grey, filtered daylight of the City. Dressed in a dark morning suit precisely tailored, complete with deep green waistcoat and black leather shoes, he felt ready to take whatever the world could throw at him. He had combed his thin, straight blond hair back from his face, stared into the mirror and wondered how much longer before he'd have to start worrying about shaving, and hoped it was soon. They'd all said how well he was growing, what a fine young man he was, how proud the family would be. They said it a lot.

Behind him his father got out of the carriage and stared up at the Bank with a grim expression. It towered over the street, all dirty white stone, decked with statues of strange ladies holding spears with slightly odd expressions on their faces, as if wondering exactly what they were doing and why. It was a huge raised slab of stone that dominated the road. The body of the bank, far too large to be meant for ordinary humans, was a mix of stone pillars, iron cages and giant black iron doors. It looked as though it could accommodate an angry mammoth, and in the maze of corridors and halls inside, it might well and no one would ever know.

'You see this, boy?' demanded Lord Elwick sharply.

'Yes, Father?'

'It's supposed to be the most secure vault on the planet, a symbol of Britain's greatness. You know why we've been robbed?'

'No, Father?'

'Because the people of this day and age don't give a damn about their fellow Christians!'

'Yes, Father.'

And only a few hundred yards away, the tide turned by Blackfriars Bridge, and as it did it dragged something up from the depths of the slop-black Thames. It bumped against a bridge support and stayed, too heavy to be dragged further round, too buoyant to sink.

It would take a bored, slightly depressive sempstress several minutes of staring out across the waters to identify the corpse for what it was. By then, of course, it would be far too late.

Lyle had said that Tate needed his daily walk. Tate looked no more excited to clamber dutifully into the carriage than he would have been to stay at home. He sat on one of the seats with his nose between his front paws and looked, to Tess's mind, far too disinterested to be real.

Arriving at the Bank of England, they climbed the stone steps up to the concourse and walked through two giant green-black iron gates to a hall buzzing with confusion. Policemen in their peaked helmets, blue uniforms and capes were looking uncomfortable and hoping no one would ask them for opinions, investigators in long overcoats were trying to radiate authority and the Bank's clerks were in various stages of panic-induced breakdown.

One man was a picture of calm. He stood in front of a group of clerks, brandishing a pair of callipers, a ruler and a little note-book. To one cowering woman he said, 'Are you aware that you have the skull of an adulteress?'

Lyle saw him and scowled. Before Tess could protest he grabbed her arm and dragged her behind a large white marble statue of some Greek warrior. Tess peered out between its legs across the room. The man, a precise gentleman, had an unhealthily sweaty white face, topped with greasy thinning black hair running to a pink bald spot. When he spoke, every syllable was pronounced sharply through his nose, as if he felt the listener was too slow to understand his words in any other way.

'Who is it?' she hissed.

'Inspector Vellum,' Lyle answered bleakly. 'Satan's answer to scientific advance.'

'What's he doin'?'

'Measuring people's skulls.'

'Why?'

'Because he believes in phrenology.'

'What's that?'

He looked at her crookedly. 'For a thief, you don't know much about the police, do you?'

'And that's surprisin'?'

He sighed. 'Phrenology is where the size and shape of your skull determines whether you dunnit or not.'

'Oh.'

Her reaction didn't seem nearly as outraged as Lyle felt it should be. He said, in a slightly strained voice, 'Teresa, the size of your skull is *not* proof of murderous tendencies.' He thought about this statement, and then added, almost to himself, 'Especially not if it's been sat on.'

An indignant voice said, 'Will you move on, please?'

The speaker was a flustered man with a huge gold fob watch suspended from his waistcoat, a scarlet face, a beetroot nose and thin grey hair. He looked like someone with an itch in the small of his back that he couldn't scratch, and had a constant pained twitching in his eyes. Waving a sheet of paper at them, he exclaimed, 'Unless you have business here, please move on!'

Lyle and Tess exchanged looks. Tate, as if sensing that here was someone who developed allergies, snuffled busily at his feet. The man paled. 'It's a dog!'

'Well, actually, if you kinda look at him out of the corner of your eye . . .' began Tess.

'Teresa,' said Lyle in a low, warning voice. He turned to the clerk and put on his best smile, which wasn't very good. Horatio

Lyle was not a very sociable person, and lacked practice. 'Sir, I am Special Constable Horatio Lyle and this lady is . . .'

'Her Ladyship Teresa of . . .' began Tess brightly.

'She's my assistant. And the canine in question is my loyal bloodhound . . .' he hesitated, '. . . "Smells McNasty", famed throughout the known world for his ability to track a thief through flood, storm and fire, responsible for the capture of Daniel "Devil" Derbish, notorious murderer of the axe school of psychopathy.'

The clerk just stared. Tate rolled on to his back, legs in the air, tongue lolling slightly in expectation. Not knowing what she did, Tess bent down and scratched his stomach. Lyle's smile stretched just a little bit further, wrinkling his eyes from the strain. 'We're on special commission from the Palace. Might we inspect the vault, please?'

They were led down a flight of stairs into a corridor which grew ever narrower as it wound through the building. Within a few turns Tess had lost all sense of direction and her attempts to count steps from place to place, doors and turns, had failed. The first door to the vault was a square iron thing, black and solidly constructed, which the clerk unlocked with a fat iron key. Lyle glanced at Tess, who shrugged and said, 'Might be able to do something with it.'

Beyond this door there were no lights except for a few orange lanterns burning in a cold, dead air, at intermittent points along the corridor. A door led off halfway down, to a small room divided in two by a large iron cage. On one side crates were piled up wall-to-wall, and on the other a single stall and rickety wooden table sat, a guard standing just behind it looking like a man trying to impress. They passed to a large, circular room, against which a half dozen large, circular doors were butted, five of them locked tight. The sixth, directly at the end of the corridor, stood slightly open, and above it a wooden placard declared that this was 'V18E'. Outside it a constable stood, looking uneasy. Lyle put his head on one side and looked very long and hard at the door. On the front was a large central wheel, with two keyholes on either side of it. Inside, three heavy round bolts ran across the door, hinged together on the same iron arms, which, when the wheel turned, locked them into grooves in the wall.

Lyle said briskly, 'Who has the keys?'

'There are only three copies . . .'

'Who has them?'

'I have one, the manager has another and the duty manager on shift has the third for the primary lock . . .'

'Can you account for your movements last night?'

The clerk flushed indignantly. 'Absolutely.'

'And the manager?'

'Definitely.'

'What about the secondary lock? I assume you need both keys to open the door.'

'Well, *quite*.'

'Who has both keys?'

'The duty manager on shift – the guard, if you like, although personally I feel it is such an imprecise definition of the many complexities of—'

'Who was the guard last night?'

'Bray.'

'I'd like to talk to him.'

'Constable Lyle,' he said indignantly, 'if you are in doubt as to the loyalty of my—'

'I'm not doubting it, sir, I'm just a little . . . curious. How was the crime discovered?'

The clerk, feathers ruffled, muttered, 'V18E is shared by the Elwick family, representatives of Her Majesty's Government, and the Molyneux family, both of upright repute and . . .'

'Yes, but how was the crime discovered?'

'Lord Molyneux arrived this morning to retrieve an item of personal value from the vault. On examining the door, we discovered that it was unlocked and that several items of immense value were missing.'

'Including the Fuyun Plate.'

'Uh . . .'

Lyle raised his eyebrows. 'The Fuyun Plate? Stone bowl, cultural significance?'

'Quite possibly, the item was never of principal concern in this matter.'

'Really? Why not?'

'Sheer *financial* considerations, Constable Lyle,' the clerk said, managing to imply that such matters were probably above the understanding of the uninitiated. 'The Plate is not valued to nearly such an extent as many items which were . . .'

'You never received any special instructions regarding it?'

'Never.'

'Who put it in the vault? Is it Elwick or Molyneux property?'

'I believe the object was placed on behalf of Her Majesty's Government by Lord Elwick.'

'I would like to speak to Lord Elwick.'

'I'm not sure if . . .'

At the clerk's feet, Tate sneezed violently. Tess hid her smile. Lyle's expression could have frozen a small volcano. Seeing it, the clerk tried to hide in his own shoulders. 'I'll see if his lordship is available.'

He scurried away.

Lyle and Tess stood looking thoughtfully at the door. Finally Lyle said, 'Teresa, I'm perplexed.'

'Oh dear, Mister Lyle. Sit down and see if it goes away.'

'Teresa . . .' He shook his head slightly. 'No. Maybe not.'

'What?'

'Have you ever read a book called . . .'

She scowled, cutting him off before he could finish. 'A *book*?'

Silence. Lyle had frozen, a man whose world has just been shaken. 'Teresa?' he murmured dully after a long, long while. 'Can you even . . . ?'

'What?'

Silence. He half-turned away. 'It doesn't matter.'

She opened her mouth to answer rudely, but Tate, having grown bored with this conversation, had pushed his way through the small, half-open space between door and wall and padded into the darkness of the vault. A sudden barking erupted from inside it and Lyle rolled his eyes. 'Nag, nag, nag,' he muttered. He pulled the heavy door back a little further and stepped into the gloom, unhitching a lantern from the wall. The dull orange light fell in a little pool around his feet, and the shadows peeled back to reveal, gleaming very faintly, gold.

Tess's eyes widened, her mouth dropped. 'There's . . .'

'Yes.'

'I mean, no one could possibly . . .'

'They could.'

'But it ain't *fair*! We could just . . .'

'No.'

'But it's so shiny.'

'Yes.'

'But no one would ever guess.'

'Teresa,' he said reproachfully, 'we are here on a matter of law.'

She pulled herself together. 'Yes, Mister Lyle.'

They picked their way along shelves lined with countless treasures, the majority of them doubtless stolen in the first place and locked away for posterity. The light bent and split inside jewels, shimmered off bronze, flashed off gold, slithered off silver, to all of which Lyle seemed oblivious. At the end of the shelves stood delicately painted giant vases from China or heavily adorned ones from India, and along the far wall stood huge statues of people with too many arms to be comfortably thought on or too few clothes to be practically viable in the English climate. Lyle and Tess wove their way back and forth through these shelves until Lyle muttered, 'It's a little vulgar, really.' Tess said nothing, and stared.

They found Tate barking indignantly at what looked to Tess like a large stone box. He gave them a look that said, 'What took so long?' Lyle raised the lamplight a little higher to let it fall on the old yellow stonework, and Tess saw symbols carved all around it, strange eyes and birds and people who looked as if they didn't know which way they were going. On the top the box curved to form a crude face and a pair of crossed arms, the blue, red, gold and brown paint chipped and peeled by ages. She whispered, feeling that it would be wrong to talk loudly in front of something this strange, 'What is it?'

'A sarcophagus,' replied Lyle.

She nodded sagely. 'Oh.'

He looked sideways at her and added, 'From Egypt.'

'Ah.'

'It's a box where people a very long time ago put other dead people.'

Her face split into an expression of delighted disgust. 'That's horrid!'

He brightened at seeing something nearing enthusiasm. 'What they did was remove all the internal organs and put them in canopic jars for preservation, including the brain which was removed through the . . .'

Her face wrinkled up, but her eyes glowed. 'Why did they do that?'

Delight lit up Lyle's eyes, as an opportunity to enlighten the ignorant on a favourite topic presented itself. 'Well, they believed in the afterlife, and thought that if you weren't properly prepared you couldn't get into paradise. At the gates of heaven, Anubis would weigh your heart against a feather and . . .' He stopped, his expression frozen. He put his head on one side and stared at the sarcophagus. He said quietly, 'Oh.'

She hopped in irritation as Lyle's voice trailed off. 'What is it, *what is it?*'

'Uh . . . would you hold this?' He handed her the lantern. She took it uncertainly and tried to hold it up to her full, unimpressive height as Lyle squatted down by the side of the sarcophagus and rummaged in his pockets. From the depths of his large grey coat he pulled out a roll of blue cloth, opening it carefully on the floor in front of him. Strange tools, the use of which Tess couldn't even begin to guess at, rested in little sewn compartments inside the cloth. Lyle twiddled his fingers expectantly in the air and, like a falcon diving for its prey, picked out a long, thin blade. Turning it so it was parallel with the slit between the top of the sarcophagus and the main body, he ran it very carefully through the gap. The tip of the blade came out stained with a very thin, bright red dust. Lyle rubbed it between his fingers and started to grin.

Tess squeaked, trying to hide her excitement, 'Mister Lyle, what is it?'

'Wood rot.' He straightened up, prodding the sarcophagus with his toe. 'This bit's stone.' Then, to Tess's astonishment and dismay, he slammed the palm of his hand down on the top of the sarcophagus. It boomed emptily. 'This is light, hollow wood.'

He tried to get his fingers under the lid and pull it up. Something inside gently clicked. Tess brightened. 'It's locked on the inside, ain't it?'

'Yes.'

'Well . . .' She chewed her lip. 'There ain't no hinges, so it's probably got two locks on either side what click in place when the lid comes down – the release would be on the inside . . . uh . . . have you got acid?'

He stared at her. 'You . . . want *me* to give *you* acid?'

'What? You ain't never burnt your way through a difficult lock?'

'Erm . . .' He patted his pockets with a dazed expression, as if only just beginning to remember who he kept company with, and only just beginning to wonder why. Things clinked inside them. Then he unbuttoned his coat and patted two inside pockets. He sighed. 'Nothing that I could easily administer.'

'You got another knife?'

He blinked, as if seeing her for the first time. 'You want me to trust *you* with a sharp object?'

'Yes.' She made it sound as though he was asking a stupid question.

Lyle hesitated. Then he raised his hands in defeat. 'All right,' he sighed. 'I'm probably aiding and abetting as it is.' He handed her his blade and, after searching through his pockets, pulled out another, wrapped in greasy leather and slightly chipped. Wordlessly Tess walked round to the other side of the sarcophagus and ran her blade between lid and body. Lyle did the same on his side and, glancing at each other for confirmation, they slowly started sliding their blades along the sides until, almost together and directly opposite, they hit something solid inside the lid which prevented their passing. Tess grinned. Lyle rummaged in his bag until he found a slim hook.

Tess said, 'Why do you carry that kinda thing, Mister Lyle?'

'Oh, you never know when you might need a bent bit of metal or a piece of string or a pair of scissors or a spring or a spare bottle of ammonia nitrate,' he replied easily.

'Mister Lyle?'

'Yes?'

'Do you go out ever?'

'It's been known.'

'With Miss Chaste?' she asked, grinning slyly.

'Miss Chaste is a vicar's daughter,' he said with a scowl. 'What more can I say?'

'I could think of . . .'

'No! If you must know, I have a fondness for the fireplace and early nights.' Glowering across the top of the sarcophagus, Lyle slid the hook between the lid and body, and carefully bent it side to side, until something clicked. The lid jerked slightly and he hastily turned the knife, pushing the lid up half an inch, when it would go no further. Wordlessly he passed the hook over to Tess, who slid it under the lid and wiggled it until, on her side of the sarcophagus, a like mechanism gave a similar click. The lid jerked slightly and Lyle slid his fingers under, pulling it up lightly and holding it open. The two of them looked down into the dark rectangle of the sarcophagus. Tess said thoughtfully, 'Shouldn't there be somethin' there?'

Lyle looked surprisingly cheerful, carefully putting down the wooden lid and brushing his hands clean, a severe expression mingling with an excited look in the eyes. 'There should be a mummy.'

'A . . .'

'Dead person in bandages.'

'Oh.' She looked utterly disinterested.

Lyle sighed, disappointed that she wasn't sharing his enthusiasm, and said almost reproachfully, 'I think I know how it was done.'

'Oh. So does that mean we can stop workin' now and have lunch? I mean, not that I ain't curious an' all, but . . . lunch . . .' Tess's eyes bulged in what, on any other species from injured puppy to pining kitten, would have been a desperate cry for emotional support, and on her gave her young face a slightly gerbil-like quality.

Lyle glowered and rolled up his bundle of tools, slipping them back into a pocket. He strode towards the door with the confidence of someone who knows what he expects to find and isn't prepared to tolerate anything else. Tess followed dutifully. Tate yawned. At the door, Lyle paused to examine the hinged bolts that ran across it and towards the wall. The hinge ran, by a complicated series of bolts and turns, into an arm that extended into the iron door itself, and moved up and down in a carefully cut groove. Lyle peered inside, but with just the low lamplight, could see nothing but darkness, smelling of oil. He sighed again and dug in his pocket, pulling out a small globe of tinted glass that fitted easily in the palm of his hand. He said, businesslike, 'Pass the lantern, please.'

Tess handed him the lantern and watched in fascination as he held the globe carefully over the flame until the bottom started to blacken, and carefully slid a tiny glass shutter off the top of the globe, so that the top was open to the air. Almost immediately, it blossomed into burning white light, too bright to look at directly, and only slightly filtered by the tinted glass. Tess jumped away hastily. 'What the holy hell is that!'

'Language.'

'Sorry, sir. What *is* it?'

'Magnesium.'

'Oh, you should've said it were *magnesium*, sir, that makes everything clearer. I mean, it were all we ever talked 'bout down at Shoreditch, sir, how they ain't makin' magnesium the way they used'a do, how it ain't never blowin' up and fizzin' and goin' all scary and bright without warnin' like we always said it should. If you'd said it were *magnesium*, sir, I would never have lost five years of my life just then, sir.'

He shot her a sideways look, and said nothing.

Holding the globe carefully between thumb and forefinger, he peered into the groove once more, the white light falling on internal gears and bolts that lined the inside of the door in small armies. He said brightly, 'Ah. There it is. Teresa?' She took the lantern back and, with some trepidation, the burning globe, holding it at arm's length while inside it the metal blazed white, occasionally sparking in the process and leaving a bright after-burn ingrained on her eyeballs. With a strained expression Lyle slid his knife into the small groove under the protruding metal arm and twiddled it. There was a click. Something inside the door went *thunk* in a loud, decisive manner. Lyle drew back his hand quickly as the arm slowly descended, sending the bolts shooting across the door. Tess jumped. Lyle grinned, and, reaching into the groove, turned the knife the opposite way. The arm lifted and the hinges retracted to the open position again. Looking smug, he wrapped the knife up. 'I think I'm getting interested in this. The old brain has started to work once more. If we're lucky, it'll be over in time for Brahms at St Martin's.'

In Tess's hand, the little sphere of burning light flickered and died. Lyle sighed and plucked it from her nerveless fingers, wrinkled his nose at the little wisp of smoke coming off it, wrapped it in a handkerchief and dropped it back into his pocket.

'Sir?'

'Yes?'

'What the . . . uh . . . I mean, what's happenin'?'

'I know how the thief got in. Actually, I know how the thief got *out* having got in, which is by far the trickier question. I'm just a little concerned that he came so well prepared. Come on, Teresa, let's go and pester the aristocracy.'

She brightened at this prospect. 'I've never pestered a bigwig, sir.'

'It's a wonderful pastime.'

They walked side by side up along the corridor, past the guard's room to the iron door just beyond. Tess said, 'How'd he get past this?'

'One of two methods. No – one of two *rational* methods.'

'Yes?'

'Either he picked the lock, or the door was already unlocked.'

She frowned. 'The last one seems easiest.'

'You *are* economical, aren't you?'

'It's my best quality, sir.' She paused, then said, 'So . . . how'd he do it?'

'I'm afraid of telling you.'

'Why?'

'Because you're already far too good at what you do without me giving you ideas.'

Tess beamed proudly, and nudged him, trying to look sly. 'Go on, sir. You want me to help you with security, right?'

They walked on through long dim corridors, until Lyle suddenly reached out and grabbed Tess by the arm. 'Shush.' At his feet Tate started growling.

From the end of the corridor, they heard a voice, the same precise voice that Tess had been introduced to earlier. Lyle paled.

'Damn,' he muttered, eyebrows drawing together. The voice grew louder. Then the owner appeared round a corner, saw Lyle and stopped dead. Lyle's face had contorted into something resembling a dentist's smile, all teeth and pain.

'Special Constable Lyle,' said the man at the end of the corridor in a low, clipped voice. Tate's eyes narrowed, and his nose wrinkled in an expression of doggy dislike.

'Inspector Vellum.' Lyle's voice could have announced a funeral.

'I wasn't aware that you were involved in this investigation.'

'Well, you know, I don't like to make a fuss . . .'

'Do I know that?'

'I hope so.'

'I fear you will find me ignorant. I see you still have that pet of yours.' Tate growled. Lyle very gently nudged him towards Tess with an ankle. Tess squatted down and scratched behind Tate's huge ears.

'And who is this individual you're with?'

'Uh, Teresa, this is . . .'

Tess bounced forward hastily, held out her hand, and declared, 'I am Lady Teresa of Prussia. In fact, of Russia *and* Spain.' She saw his eyebrows go up and wondered if she'd pushed a little bit too far. 'Only by marriage.'

'Indeed.'

'Yes. Indeed.'

'And what, pray, does your ladyship feel she can bring to this undertaking?'

She hesitated. 'Uh . . .'

Lyle's hands fell very firmly on her shoulders and through

gritted teeth he said, 'Inspector Vellum, I trust your literary exploits are successful?'

'Indeed, yes. I will reserve you a copy of my latest undertaking. Four shillings only, I believe.'

'What journal is it published in?'

'No journal, *Constable* Lyle. Published by the house of Hooker and Son.'

'Mr Hooker is your publisher?'

'That is correct.'

'Isn't he your wife's brother?'

Tess could see a slow darkness spreading behind Vellum's bland expression, hear an edge entering his nasal voice. 'Constable Lyle, I was always fascinated by the frontal lobe development of your skull, symbolic, I believe, of your whole engaging persona.'

Lyle felt his forehead. 'I can't feel any kind of frontal development.'

'Quite.'

He glared. 'Inspector Vellum,' he said, in a voice etched with steel, 'perhaps you would like to oversee my commission. It comes from a certain Lord Lincoln, at the Palace. Perhaps, having seen my commission, you could be so kind as to find the security officer called Bray who was supposed to be on duty last night, as well as all documents appertaining to a certain sarcophagus in the vault.'

Vellum started to turn beetroot. 'I think,' he growled, 'you may find that *I* am the senior officer here and I say that . . .'

'Inspector Vellum, I know how the crime was committed.'

'Then I trust you can inform us.'

'Yes.'

'Then pray do.'

Lyle put on a pensive expression. 'No, thank you. I'd like to see Bray.'

CHAPTER 3

Bray was nowhere to be found. A messenger sent to his residence discovered that it didn't exist. Confident people began to grow sheepish. Vellum became increasingly noisy, snapping at his constables like a sergeant major determined to keep order. Lyle just grew quieter and quieter, until Tess began to worry.

'Mister Lyle?'

'Um?'

'You still know how it was done?'

'Yes. Teresa, do you think you could have picked that lock down there, between the vault and the exit?'

She screwed up her face. 'Is this some kinda test?'

'All I need is an honest answer.'

'Uh . . . *well* . . .'

'That's a no, isn't it?'

'No! I didn't say that!'

'I couldn't pick that lock,' Lyle muttered, more to himself than to her, half-turning away and looking thoughtfully at the busy hall. 'Which means there's only one alternative.'

'Genius?'

'The door was already unlocked.'

'See! Eco . . . econ . . .'

'Economical.'

'. . . is good!' She shifted nervously. 'Uh . . . and the open door.'

'Must have been unlocked by whoever was on duty.'

She grinned. 'Bray, right?'

'Right.'

Bray wasn't found. From Shadwell to Shoreditch the bobbies searched, knocking on doors and scrambling through markets, from Bethnal Green to Bloomsbury, in the darkest rookeries and under the bridges of the wide open marshlands that flanked the Lee Valley they searched.

And Bray still wasn't found.

'So . . . if we know how it was done . . .'

'Yes?'

'Who done it?'

'I'm hoping Bray will know that.'

'Oh . . .'

'*What?*' hissed Lyle finally.

'Nothing!'

'You're *thinking*. It's very distracting.'

'I'm not thinking!' Silence. 'But . . .'

'What?'

'. . . why they dunnit?'

Lyle seemed taken aback. 'Well . . . money.'

'And the Plate thing?'

'Cultural curiosity?'

Tess looked reproachful. Lyle put on a determined face and said, '*Right*. That's it. We are going to . . .'

'Yes?'

'We are going *to* . . .'

'*Yes?*'

'Ask someone for assistance.'

'Excuse me?'

The man Lyle addressed was called Mr Sland, and despite an unfortunate taste in sideburns, whiskers and monocles, he wasn't a particularly harmful individual, and couldn't really cope with all the excitement taking place that day at his usually sedentary job in the Bank. 'Mmm . . . yes?'

'Special Constable Lyle,' said Lyle in a rush, hoping that the 'special' would compensate for the 'constable' part of his address, and give him an authority which his general demeanour utterly failed to project. 'I'd like to see your records.'

'My records?'

'Of valuable items placed in and removed from the vault within the last week.'

'That is . . . mmm . . . special information.'

Lyle faltered. 'Erm, well . . .'

'Mister *Lyle*!' hissed Tess.

Lyle hesitated, then reached a decision and blurted, 'I see. *Obstruction*, is it? Do you know that your skull is precisely the same shape and size as Napoleon's? I know that the Bailey doesn't take kindly to Napos, as they're known. Wouldn't you agree, Te . . . Special Officer . . . Teresa?'

'Oh yes,' she chimed, nodding enthusiastically.

Mr Sland paled beneath his sideburns. 'I'll see what I can do.'

They were given a small office of their own. The heavily studded doors and high, small windows made it feel cold and grey, and Tess itched to get out of it. The ledgers were put down on a large, polished table and Lyle flicked through the heavy pages with a frown drawing his eyebrows into one.

'So?'

'*Yes*, Teresa?'

'What are we lookin' for?'

'Whoever deposited the sarcophagus must have been in on the scheme, because they would have known there was a thief handily hiding inside it. Since the vault is jointly used by the Elwick and Molyneux families, only one or the other of them could have issued the correct authority for an item to be deposited.' He looked up at a sudden thought. 'Perhaps they hate each other passionately and one hired a thief to get in and steal the other's goods to annoy him . . .' He hesitated. 'No. No, that doesn't work.'

'At least you tried, Mister Lyle.'

He glared. 'Just keep looking for that sarcophagus.'

'Erm . . .'

'What?'

'This book . . . it's English, right?'

He stared down at the ledger, then slowly back up at her, realizing. 'Yes.'

'Oh. All right, then.' She studied the pages diligently. As she did so, she turned them from right to left. Lyle hesitated, and then said in a soft voice, 'Teresa?'

She looked up quickly, already starting to flush. 'Yes?'

'Tate is probably lonely. Why don't you see if he needs attention?'

'Is that an order, sir?'

'Uh . . . yes. Yes, it definitely is.' He took a deep breath. 'That's right. It's an order. Well done.'

She bounded away, and didn't look back.

Time passes. In the streets of London, the early-morning cress-sellers and hawkers have sold the mass of their wares and are retreating to the inns to spend the day's profits in relative luxury. Out at Deptford, the sailors are watching for the tide to change, in Westminster the two sides of the House are trying to outdo each other's witticisms, down in the opium dens of St Giles smoky oblivion is crawling under the doors, and at Blackfriars something is about to be discovered. On the rackety wooden piers that hang precariously over the water's edge by the crowded Blackfriars Bridge, Rosanna Doyle, sempstress, a basically well-meaning soul who hasn't done anything to deserve the shock she is about to get, looks down at the muddy waters of the

Thames where they lap against the thick pillars of the bridge, choked with traffic rattling across the old stones over the old river, and sees something floating in it, bulbous with trapped air beneath muddy cloth. At first she thinks it is a sack that has fallen off a barge shipping freight up from the deeper docks to the shallow western wharves. Only after she sees the contorted dead fingers tangled in the body's own drifting hair does she start to scream.

'Here it is.'

'Where?'

'The sarcophagus was deposited by "Mr C.R. Wells, special aide to Lord Elwick", yesterday afternoon. He came with a letter of reference, signed by Lord Elwick, written on paper engraved with Elwick's monogram, and wearing, as ultimate proof, a ring bearing the Elwick family crest. He was then taken down to the vault by Mr Bray. The sarcophagus contained the thief and was locked in, then the plate was stolen and the vault door unlocked from the inside, and the thief escaped with the insider of the Bank, Bray.'

'That's not very interestin',' said Tess, sounding disappointed.

'Tess, it's a bank robbery. Making it interesting probably wasn't a priority. But why the plate? Why steal the Fuyun Plate, and then why should Lord Lincoln want it back so urgently? It's just a bit of stone.'

'Cultural sig . . . signif . . . significa . . .' Tess gave up. 'Perhaps the thief weren't seein' straight after all that time hidin' in the sar . . . sarcoph . . . the wooden box.'

'Mr C.R. Wells,' muttered Lyle, more to himself than her.

'Perhaps we ought to talk to Lord Elwick. Yes, I think—'

And the door opened.

'You!'

The voice had an imperious tone suggesting a lot of good breeding designed to obliterate any actual politeness that might have been inherent. Tess and Lyle turned. Tate lay down, paws over his nose.

Lord Elwick swept into the room, Inspector Vellum looking smug at his side, and in the rear, Thomas Edward Elwick, trying to seem as if he knew what he was doing, though his glare fell far short of his father's. Tess and Lyle stared at them with mute incomprehension, which darkened Elwick's expression even further: he was used to being recognized and, more important still, acknowledged. It didn't matter where he was: Lord Elwick would expect to be important in the smallest, most rural island community, and you'd better know it.

'Are you Horatio Lyle?' he barked.

'Erm . . . yes.'

'The Inspector informs me you are here on authority from the Palace.'

Lyle shot a look at Vellum, who put on the determined expression of every jobsworth just doing his duty as he thought fit, and relishing it. 'That's basically true.'

'I resent Lord Lincoln thinking he can intrude into my affairs! Assure him that the Plate *will* be recovered and that the situation is fully under control. You and your . . .' he seemed to see Tate and Tess for the first time, '. . . *companions* may leave.'

Lyle took a deep breath as Elwick's ringing tones died away. 'No, sir.'

Elwick started to turn red. Behind him, Thomas cowered, thinking, *Not the right thing to say* . . .

'Did you *speak*, sir?' The words bounced around the room like bullets.

'Yes, sir. I'm not going. I wish to know the significance of the Plate. Why is it that Lincoln thinks only of the Plate? And why is it the first, as well as least valuable, object you mention on coming in here?'

Elwick hesitated, starting to feel confusion seep in. 'I do not need to answer your questions!'

'You don't, sir, but please do, because I've got a rack of test tubes that are probably spoilt by now, but the sooner I solve this the sooner I can clear up and prevent the nitrates from . . .'

'Are you deaf, man? I gave you permission to leave! Tell Lincoln that the situation is being dealt with.'

'Is it? Who's C.R. Wells?'

'What? I've never heard anything more absurd in—'

'You don't know Mr Wells?'

'Absolutely not!'

There was a faint shift in the room, a change in the air. Tess realized she was staring at Lyle, who took a deep breath and leant back on the table, rubbing the bridge of his nose. No one spoke, not even Vellum.

'Sir,' said Lyle finally, in a weary voice, 'Mr C.R. Wells was the individual who deposited a sarcophagus in your family vault, using a letter with your signature on it as proof of his origins. That sarcophagus contained the thief who stole the Plate, opened the vault door from inside by triggering the bolt mechanism within the door, and then disappeared with your property.'

'A pleasant idea,' said Vellum smoothly, stepping forward, 'but quite implausible. How would he get past the other vault doors? They are locked on *both* sides.'

'Have you found Bray yet? The missing guard?'

Silence. Elwick's eyes were burning. 'Mister Lyle, did you say?'

'That's right.'

'Son of Harry Lyle and a lady of . . .' his smile was tight, 'dubious parentage?'

'Dubious? Clearly not dubious enough to stop them fulfilling their necessary biological function.'

'A police constable, are you?'

'Yes, sir.'

And then, to Tess's horror, Lord Elwick laughed. It was a cruel laugh that denoted some joke only he could see. 'A *policeman*?' he sneered. Tess looked, appalled, from Elwick's twisted face to Lyle's utterly impassive one, then on to the boy standing behind him. His eyes were fixed on Lord Elwick's face, and his mouth hung slightly open, as if unable to comprehend what he was seeing and hearing, utterly unaware of his own physicality in the horror of the moment. Elwick blurted between malicious peals of merriment, 'I see now that the Bible was correct – the mighty *are* fallen.' He took off his top hat in a sweep. Spinning on his heel he called, not even looking back as he did so, 'Good day, *Mister* Lyle.'

Young Thomas Elwick turned to follow his father, and saw the girl looking at him with her head on one side. He hesitated. He heard his father's laughter. He glanced back at Lyle. The man was standing with his hands in the pockets of his long coat, chewing one side of his lip. Thomas stopped. His father kept walking, bellowing at anyone who'd listen, Vellum sweeping along in his shadow, 'I demand to speak with a Superintendent . . .'

And Thomas turned, and faced Tess and Lyle. 'Excuse me?'

CHAPTER 4

Tate

Lyle was never sure whether he chose Tate, or Tate chose him. He hadn't meant to have a pet, reasoning that an animal was a hazard in any occupation where chemicals were involved. He didn't hunt, and regarded most members of Tate's species as an accessory to shotguns, tweed and inbreeding of the most genetically ill-advised kind. When he had opened the door, therefore, one cold winter's night, and found a puppy with a huge nose and a bored expression slumbering on his doorstep, his instinctive reaction had been to find it some warm fireplace where people who believed in hunting and string quartets and dog food could look after it.

The first dog expert he'd questioned had informed him flatly that he couldn't begin to guess what Tate's parentage had been, but didn't think it could have been healthy. And as soon as Tate had woken up and looked at him, Lyle had had the overwhelming feeling of being regarded by an intelligence that could solve eleven-figure natural logarithms in its head and still have room for a biscuit afterwards. So he'd taken Tate in. There didn't seem any real choice.

Now Tate sat to complete inattention by Lyle on the steps of the Bank while, below the huge white walls blackened with dirt, the carriages rattled by, and Lyle said, 'Your name is Thomas?'

'Yes, sir.'

'Tell me about your family, Thomas.'

'We . . . own things, sir.'

'What kind of things?'

'Houses, parks, horses, dogs and counties mostly, sir.'

'What about the Fuyun Plate?'

'I'm unfamiliar with the object, sir.'

'It's in the Elwick household's possession in the name of the royal family. It was put into the vault under the Elwick name, and then stolen.'

'Yes, sir?'

'How about a sarcophagus? Does your family own a sarcophagus?'

'No, sir.'

'You seem very sure of that.'

'My mother refuses to have truck with anything that might once have been organic, sir.'

'No sarcophagus?'

'Absolutely not.'

'That's interesting. And you've never heard of C.R. Wells?'

'No, sir. But I've heard of Harry Lyle, sir, I mean of Mr Lyle, and I read all the papers and I think that . . .'

'Tell me about your family, Thomas. I want to know *everything*.'

As they talked, Tate looked at other things. The smells that dominated this part of town were grease from the axles of the carriages, manure and sweat from the horses, and the river. Only a few years ago, Lyle wouldn't have been able to take Tate anywhere near the river because of the overwhelming stench that rose from the stagnant, scummy waters, but now, somewhere behind the waste and oil and dirt and slime, there was just a hint of salt. Tate could smell the coal burning in Liverpool Street just to the north; and at Blackfriars to the south the leather drying in the tanners' shops, the steam in the weavers' factory, the tar on the rigging of the ships, and through it all, something else. Tate sat up, and instantly Lyle's eyes flickered to him. Tate sniffed the air, trying to place that strange, alien smell. Then he started to bark. He stood up and trotted away. Lyle stood up too, cutting Thomas off in mid-flow about his sister's arranged marriage to the second Count of Ihnaticz and how good the trumpet players were in that part of the world, and muttered, 'Hello.'

The three of them watched as Tate trotted over to a segment of wall below the towering edifice of the Bank, stood next to it and irrefutably claimed a small part of London as Kingdom Tate. Thomas's face involuntarily twisted into an expression of disgust. Tess looked bored. Lyle just stared. 'That is *interesting*.'

'Ain't you never seen it before?' asked Tess in an incredulous voice.

'Yes, but you wouldn't expect to see it here.' He started to walk along the pavement towards the wall, while the traffic rattled by and overhead the grey sky threatened rain. Thomas realized that Tess was looking at him with exasperation, and he straightened up and tried to force a polite smile on to his face, as he had been taught to do with all ladies, no matter what their social origin.

As the first drops of drizzle started to fall, Lyle walked straight past Tate and knelt down carefully on the edge of the pavement. He dug into a pocket and pulled out a long pair of tweezers and a rough paper bag. Reaching down, he completely ignored the stares of passers-by, and picked up the stone lying alone and discarded. It was wrinkled, old and dirtied, with scraps of some kind of fruit, all strands of damp brownness, still clinging to it. He turned it over and over thoughtfully. '*Hello.*'

'Mister Lyle, are you feelin' well?' asked Tess, starting to feel exposed as people stared.

'Teresa, doesn't it occur to you that in this part of town it's extremely uncommon to discover a fruit of this variety?'

She thought about the question, put on a sage expression and nodded fervently. '*Yes.*'

There was a long silence. 'Teresa . . .' began Lyle.

'Yes, Mister Lyle?'

'Teresa, remind me why I employ you.'

'I got *charm*, Mister Lyle.'

Silence. 'Good grief,' muttered Lyle finally. 'I'm examining fruit remnants in central London with a thief and – no offence, lad – a bigwig, having just been to the Bank of England and the Palace in short succession, if not that order, on the one day of the week when I really felt ready to tackle copper anodes and a nitrate solution.' He thought about this. 'How did that happen?'

The arrival of an answer was forestalled by the arrival of a policeman, running up from Blackfriars Bridge.

In a white-marbled mansion on the edge of town, surrounded by red-leaved trees in green-grassed grounds, a man with white gloves over long hands and a voice like black leather says, 'The situation is being dealt with.'

'Where, then, is the Fuyun Plate?' The speaker is a woman, and when she breathes, the air shimmers with delight at its motion in her vicinity.

'We have nearly located the associate – Bray. Mr Dew has been very effective.'

'I am informed that Lord Lincoln,' a name spat in the same voice that might describe a particularly long, slimy, orange-grey slug, 'has engaged the services of a detective to locate the Fuyun Plate.'

'A *human* detective?' The voice like black leather has an inherent sneer, ugly and cruel.

'Horatio Lyle.'

Silence. Then, 'It doesn't matter.'

'Son of Harry Lyle. The son is very like the father, they say, but more so. He breathes the iron, it's in his *blood*, his heart. He was born out of hot coals and dirty smoke. Do you believe Mr Dew can be so effective against such an . . . *abomination*?'

'My lady, the matter *is* in hand.'

'My lord, please see that it is.'

*

Thomas Edward Elwick was confused. He had been confused enough when informed that the strange man with the stranger girl as his assistant was the son of Harry Lyle, the man who had welded more strange and wondrous tricks out of a bit of iron than anyone on the planet. He'd become more confused when he'd found himself trying to explain to Lyle why his family was trusted with artefacts by Her Majesty and how it was more about prestige than *money*, really. Now he was most confused of all by the sudden and unexpected arrival of a breathless constable who was shouting, 'Where's the Inspector? There's a body down at the bridge! In mysterious circumstances!'

Lyle had been inexplicably annoyed by the statement 'in mysterious circumstances'. He'd spent a good five minutes trying in vain to explain to the unfortunate constable how precision was important, especially if you got such words as 'kill' and 'mill' confused in a society of capital punishment and sent the wrong people to the wrong places, but had given up when it became apparent that no one cared.

Now Thomas was finding himself being carried along by a crowd, whose inexorable passage was taking him down the tight winding streets of Blackfriars, towards the river through a maze of slippery docks, warehouses and factories belching soot across every rooftop. He wondered whether it hadn't been a mistake after all to try and help.

But if I don't follow now, he thought, *I'll never know what happens.*

He saw faces black with grit staring at his fine clothes as the crowd of policemen, and general onlookers eager for a spectacle, swept on down towards the bridge. He could hear the rattling of trains, hear steam being let off in huge billows, spewing down from the local yards in a thick, hot, damp fog that burnt his eyes. With the figure of Lyle for guidance, he kept going along the uneven, muddy, salty ways.

And suddenly the crowd slowed and thickened, until he was crushed between Teresa, who ignored him, and a constable trying in vain to push his way through. He could see how many dirty looks the coppers were getting from the locals, especially the costermongers, traditional enemies of the police, and wondered why. Thomas had always been taught to respect the police force as a tool against revolution, a wall of steel against any insurrection that might come from the lower orders. He looked at Lyle, and wondered if he thought the same way.

Lyle, meanwhile, had elbowed his way to the front of the crowd and was climbing over the parapet of the bridge on to a flight of creaky stairs that led down to the mud, greenish in places, of the river at low tide. The flight was missing some steps, and Thomas held his breath as he watched Lyle cautiously move each foot, sometimes pausing for thought, and then carefully avoiding a tread that looked particularly unsound.

At the bottom of the stairs was a shape almost impossible to see with the mud that caked and camouflaged it. Around it was a small crowd of filthy boys in rags, shoeless, and several policemen with their trousers pulled up around their hairy knees for fear of having to pay for a new uniform. Lyle stepped into the mud, which rose up around his ankles. He seemed oblivious, picking his way over to the body.

'Who found the body?'

'Miss saw it,' said a raggedy boy, pointing up at a young, handsome woman standing by the top of the bridge and looking pale.

'Did you touch it?'

'No.'

Lyle glanced at them suspiciously, but a constable said, 'We heard a commotion so we came running. They couldn't have got to it till low tide, sir.'

'So it hasn't been moved?'

'No.'

'How long ago was it found?'

'Half an hour, maybe?'

'How long till the tide comes back in?'

'Maybe an hour or two, sir.'

'Right. Help me turn it over.'

The constables looked at each other uneasily. Lyle saw their expressions and tutted. 'Come on, don't fuss.'

They took an arm each and dragged the body unevenly round. Thomas saw mud settled on a shape in the man's throat that shouldn't have been there, and felt bile rising. Next to him, Tess looked on with a disinterested expression. Thomas heard Lyle say distantly, 'A very clean cut. Entry from the left, right on the artery, dragged straight across to the other side. A lot of force behind this. Good, sharp blade. And a second stab wound to the lower abdomen.' He saw Lyle scrape green-brown, probably toxic mud away from the man's wet clothes without any sign of a second thought, and again felt nauseous. He turned his face away. At his side he heard Tess say excitedly, 'Look! Do you think he's goin' to poke it? That's *horrid*!'

Down in the mud, Lyle bent further forward over the body, oblivious of the brown squelch which crawled at his knees. 'This abdominal wound would probably have bled heavily, but not enough to kill.' He looked thoughtfully up at the nearest constable. 'Did it rain last night?'

'Don't think so, sir.'

'Right. I want . . .' He froze. 'Constable?'

'Yes, sir?'

Lyle bent down and carefully picked up the corner of the man's muddy sleeve, dragging it and the limp arm within it from the mud with a slurping noise. A white hand sagged heavily in the sleeve. It had only four fingers. 'C.R. Wells,' sighed Lyle. 'Egotist.'

'Sir?'

'Carwell. This man's name is Gordon Carwell. He's a thief. You'll find an indecent tattoo dedicated to "Inga" on his back. He lost the middle finger of his left hand during a fight in Limehouse last year. He's notorious for small-time burglaries in the more expensive suburbs – Hammersmith, Chiswick, Putney and Hampstead mostly. A master of the "humble workman" ruse, along with his brother, Jack Carwell. He knocks on the door saying he's come to repair a shelf, and doesn't leave until his pockets are full. His brother plays look-out, or distracts people while he does them and their property over. They always work together.' He straightened up and looked down sadly at the body. 'Get it to the mortuary – and make sure only Nurse Marie is allowed to touch it, all right?'

'Yes, sir.'

'And . . .' Lyle hesitated, then shook his head. 'No.'

'Sir?'

'You might want to think about searching the rest of the river.'

'Why's that, sir?'

'As I said, Gordon Carwell never worked alone.'

A little later, Lyle climbed back up from the river looking weary, and at the top stood slowly dripping damp mud from the bottom of his trousers on to his filthy shoes. For the first time he seemed to become aware of this. He gave a deep sigh, then put a hand on Tess's shoulder and on Thomas's and said, 'Come on.'

'Where we goin' now?'

'The Bank broken into and Carwell dead in the river? Too much of a coincidence.'

'So where *are* we goin', Mister Lyle?'

'To find a blood trail.'

The crowd opened around Lyle, Tess, Thomas and Tate without a care, the living not as interesting as the dead, and closed again behind them, absorbing them without a thought. Tate wove through a forest of shoes and feet, aware that his ears were in peril, his nose twitching nervously, overwhelmed by the smell of the river, the fish in the wharves, salt and tar and soot and coal and, oddly, just a touch of ginger biscuit.

It took a good five minutes to find a cab, Lyle protesting all the way that there's never one when you want one, and things weren't like that when he was a lad. The inside of the cab smelt of old leather, battered wooden seats and too much time in stables, until, finally, the tired cab horse raised its head, turned, and they rattled away from the almost heedless crowd.

Almost heedless, because it takes just one exception to disprove a rule.

Someone watched them go.

CHAPTER 5

Canwell

It took them forty minutes to find what Lyle was looking for, in a quiet side-street near the church of St Anne. In the middle of the road, too narrow for the press of traffic that swarmed around St Paul's, and overshadowed with bakeries and tailors competing for space to serve the local merchants' hall, Tate suddenly stopped and began to bark. Lyle picked his way through the horse manure that liberally littered the centre of the street, and smiled when he saw what was causing Tate so much dismay. 'Here it is.'

Thomas scurried over, eager to see. He looked at the cobbles and saw only a darker brown stain that reminded him of spilt cough mixture. 'What is it?'

'Blood,' said Lyle with some satisfaction.

Tess sniffed suspiciously. 'Could've come from the meat goin' to market up at Smithfield, Mister Lyle.'

'Good thought, if unwelcome,' he sighed. 'I can prove it, though.' He squatted carefully next to the stain in the street, while passers-by gave him looks of deep mistrust. Thomas started to feel uncomfortable, hoping that no one in this mixture of hawkers, and merchants going to the halls, would recognize him or, worse, report him to his father.

The thought of his father brought a brief pang of guilt, followed by a sharper pang as he realized this was the first thought he'd had of his father since he'd followed Lyle. For a second he wondered if he would ever see his father again, or if he was going to be kidnapped, dragged down to the docks and sold into slavery or murdered for his wealth or replaced by an evil twin who would steal his fortune while he was condemned to a life of servitude and . . .

'Thomas, you might be interested in this.'

Lyle had produced from his pocket a small handful of tubes. He chose one that looked no different from the others, except for a small red dot on the top of the glass, shook it vigorously, thumbed the cork off the top and carefully tipped a few drops on to the brown stain. Immediately, the cobbles beneath it started to hiss. A thick, smelly white smoke rose up from the ground and all three backed off quickly as it drifted up, sizzling on the stone. Lyle coughed. 'Yes, well, I think that settles the issue, don't you?'

Thomas waved smoke out of his eyes and managed to croak, 'What is it?'

'A little compound that came to me one day while I was trying to repair the privy. Only what's *special*,' said Lyle, instantly warming to his subject, 'is that it only works on human blood, because when you leave blood to settle, or even better whirl it round and round at very high speeds on a piece of string, you can get a separation effect which isolates certain unique components and . . .'

'So it's human blood,' coughed Tess.

'Erm, yes.'

'Well done. What are we goin' to do now?'

'Follow it, of course.'

Lyle flapped his hand at the smoke until it finally cleared, and looked down at the cobbles. A small, neat hole had been burnt in the stone where the drops had fallen. He coughed and looked away innocently. 'I think there's another stain over there,' he said, taking the fascinated Tess and the appalled Thomas by the arm and leading them further on.

There was indeed another stain, in fact the trail ran intermittently on and off in larger and smaller droplets and pools all the way up the road, disrupted here or there by the erosion of feet or the intervention of traffic, or that traffic's digested meals. Lyle stood above the largest, most conspicuous line of blood and muttered, almost to himself, 'All right. I'm stabbed about here,' indicating with two fingers on his abdomen, 'I'm bleeding heavily, I'm trying to move, so the blood is falling behind . . .' For a second his lips moved soundlessly, then he grinned and pointed down the street. 'He ran in that direction. Towards the river. Which, I suppose, makes sense.'

'So?'

'So we follow the blood trail and find out where it began.'

They followed it through winding streets, occasionally losing it, to where the traffic became thicker and thicker around the great cask of St Paul's cathedral, one half of which was covered in scaffolding that ran right up to the dome as emergency repairs were carried out on the dirty white stone and tarnished green roof. Here the stain was obliterated beneath the press of carts in the street, the drivers yelling at each other to move out of the way, horses neighing and wheels clattering. But by that point, they could guess where it was heading, and Tess ran on ahead, darting and dodging enthusiastically between carts to shout back occasionally, 'I've found another stain! It's goin' the same way!'

Close behind her, Thomas made a great effort to study each particular stain that Tess found, bending over and looking as thoughtful as he could, without actually disgracing himself by running. Lyle and Tate followed slowly after, Lyle with his hands buried in his pockets, Tate with his paws buried at least in a pair of hypothetical pockets.

The blood led directly to the Bank of England, and suddenly stopped. So did the group. Tess pouted. 'Is this *it*?'

Lyle studied the smeary pavement, and said, 'I think I can see a larger stain here. Very faint. And . . .' He hesitated, suddenly aware that there were other things in the world apart from him and the thoughts in his head.

Tess said impatiently, when Lyle didn't move, 'And? You were sayin' somethin' an' then you all sorta stopped.'

'I *was* going to say that this much blood in one place is more than I would have expected from the injuries Carwell received.'

'What does that mean?'

'I don't entirely know.'

They waited. Finally Thomas said tentatively, not wanting to sound like a fool, 'Didn't you find the fruit thing here, sir?'

Tess stared at Thomas as if he was mad, and for a second Lyle did too. Then Lyle started to laugh, a sudden, quiet sound that grew to a delighted roar. They both stared at Lyle. Even Tate looked a little surprised. Lyle clapped his hands together. 'Of course! They waited here and stabbed him the second he brought the goods! It was cold last night – they probably got hungry and bored! Why not eat something?'

'Sir?'

'Come on!' He turned and started marching back the way they'd come.

'Where are we goin' *now*?'

'To find the other end of the bloodstain!'

Tess groaned. But Thomas, all thoughts of his father gone, felt more excited than he had in a long time.

And down by the river, in the thick, green-brown mud that bends and rises around each footprint, smothering ankle and knee in essence of squelch, the passage of the sun across the sky burns away a shadow that has fallen beside a docked boat.

And the cry goes up: 'Sarge! There's another body over here!'

They found the far end of the stain in a quiet, dark street just above Blackfriars Bridge. They also discovered a larger pool of blood which, Lyle declared gleefully, was 'Probably straight from the jugular.'

Then, to Thomas's horror and Tess's exasperation, he said,

'Right, children, I want a volunteer to go and ask people what they heard last night, sometime between midnight and three a.m.'

'What do you mean, *ask* people?' sighed Tess.

'As in knock on their doors and be pushy.'

'Must we?'

'Yes.'

'They'll laugh at me.'

'They might laugh at *you*,' said Lyle sagely, 'but I'm sure they won't laugh at Thomas.'

Thomas realized they were staring at him. And they were grinning.

Left with Tess in the gloomy street that stank of mouldering laundry, stale water and tar, Lyle stared at the dark brown stain on the ground that indicated Carwell's last living point in space and time, and felt something rise up in him bordering on anger. He was surprised at himself – usually these things were just scientific anomalies to be studied, and others could be angry. But as people jostled past him, some even walking on the bloodstain darkening the pavement without realizing what they did, he felt a certain anger at the world, not just at the murderer. He wanted to stand up and say, 'Don't you realize a man has slit another man's throat in cold blood? Don't you realize what this says about people in general?' He didn't. He stared at the ground and thought furiously.

'What you thinkin', Mister Lyle?'

He didn't answer. He thought, *Carwell and Bray. Bray and Carwell. And Jack Carwell too, the younger brother who always fol-*

lowed Gordon Carwell into whatever venture, whatever peril. Was he a part of it too? The bloodstain by the Bank was large, the direction of the blood not quite right for a disabling wound, something like that would kill instantly, but Carwell ran . . . where Gordon Carwell goes, Jack always follows . . .

They agree it between them — Bray as the inside man with the keys, on a take of the percentage, Carwell as the thief. Bray wouldn't have access to the vault itself, but Carwell gets round that, gets into the vault.

'Mister Lyle?'

'Yes, Teresa?'

'What you thinkin'?'

'I'm thinking . . .' *How did he manage to get the letter of approval from the Elwick house? The right seal, the right stamp?* 'A letter from the Elwick family would be hard to forge. You'd have to have an original to work from, the right paper, the right seal, the right signature.'

'You think the bigwig knows?'

'The bigwig?'

'Thomas,' she said with a shrug. 'The bigwig.'

He frowned, and shrugged half-heartedly. Something was itching at the back of his neck, something stirring deep inside that made him want to find a dark doorway to hide in. He scanned the street distractedly, and thought, *Carwell must have been acting on orders.*

'Mister Lyle?'

'Would you break into the Bank of England without a specific target?'

'Not bl . . . not likely, Mister Lyle.'

82

'And inside you wouldn't steal a stone plate?'

'Hell . . . uh . . . no. Not if someone weren't payin' me.'

'That's *it*. Carwell had to be paid, someone had to *pay* him to steal the plate, otherwise why would he do it? Someone had to be out there to take the plate, someone who can pay a lot, risk a lot for a plate.'

'Like Lord Lincoln?'

'Like Lo . . . Teresa, that is not a helpful comment.'

'Sorry, Mister Lyle. But . . . if Mister Lincoln wants it, then you said it's gonna be important, ain't it?'

'If they want the Plate badly enough to break into the Bank,' murmured Lyle distractedly, 'perhaps they wait outside?'

She shrugged.

'Besides, no one eats exotic fruit in this part of town – few people eat it at all. Luxury, decadence, money, eating while you wait for Carwell to come out with the Plate, at night when no one else is watching.'

'Coo-ee, Mister Lyle?'

'Teresa?'

'Yes, Mister Lyle?'

'If someone paid you a sovereign to steal something, and asked you to hand it straight over, would you?'

'Depends how big that person's knife were, Mister Lyle.'

'If you thought you could get two sovereigns instead of one, would you go to the drop-off with the item?'

She thought about it. Finally she said, 'I might've given it to someone. To hide, an' all. So that they couldn't hurt me. 'Cos I wouldn't have it.'

The silence dragged.

'They killed Carwell. But Carwell might not have been carrying the Plate.'

'Maybe not.'

'They let him run after they'd stabbed him and then they *killed* him, like . . .'

'Mister Lyle?'

'Something must have gone wrong, that's the only reason Bray would have gone so quickly underground. Carwell was clever, he knew that Bray going under would have drawn unnecessary suspicion to him, so something must have gone wrong. Carwell got stabbed by the people who paid him to steal the Plate and Bray's probably still got the Plate and . . .'

'Mister Lyle!'

He jumped, looked round and realized people were watching him. He coughed uncomfortably, and turned away to study the nearest wall, trying not to whistle nonchalantly. There was no proof, he knew that. There was instinct, and it was *right*.

And just behind that instinct, he had another, more uncomfortable feeling: of being watched. He turned and scanned the street, but those who had stared at first were now drifting by again, uninterested in anything except their daily lives. Still the itchy feeling persisted, like something he couldn't scratch at the back of his neck. He looked down at the pavement and saw, in the gutter, a small flash of orange. He hesitated, then slowly squatted and picked it up carefully by the corner. It was orange peel, dirty and hard. It lay a few feet away from the pool of blood, and was discoloured by something more than just natural processes. He put it carefully into the paper bag, next to the fruit stone.

Someone, he decided, had a taste for fruit.

'Mister Lyle?'

'Teresa.'

'You seen him yet?'

'The man in the crooked top hat hiding in the doorway?'

'Oh. You seen him.'

'Teresa, I have a little job for you.'

Thomas was elated, for a number of reasons. Firstly, because the second he'd walked into the bakery and said, 'Excuse me, ma'am?' the lady behind the counter had assumed he was the Heir Apparent, and started gushing over him in a cockney dialect so unintelligible it had been all he could do to keep nodding and smiling. This nodding and smiling had so delighted the employees of the bakery that they had begun clapping and rejoicing, saying that at last fortune had come to them with an aristocratic jacket and an aristocratic accent, and so buoyant had they been at receiving, for the very first time, a 'client of breeding in our 'umble store' they had insisted on showing him their full selection.

And he had bought a hot cross bun.

A *hot cross bun*. Never in his whole life had he been allowed to buy such a treat, never had he *bought* something with his own hands, and now it was between his fingers and he could just eat it, in the street, taking large, undignified mouthfuls and *Father would never know*! This triumph had swelled him with confidence and, as a result, he had knocked on a whole five doors with half the bun still in his hand and demanded in a voice booming with authority, 'Ma'am, I am here to enquire about a murder.' '*Enquire about a murder.*' It was a phrase he'd never thought he could say. The words felt mature and weighty, big fat words that you could toss on to a barge and watch chug upstream with stately grandeur. It was the 'enquire' and it was the 'about' and it was the 'murder'. In fact, it was probably the 'a' too. He had been so full of satisfaction at the sudden rush of responsibility that when he got to the sixth door and the woman who answered it said, 'Really? Was that what the carriage was about?' he hardly noticed.

This led to the second cause of his elation. He scampered back to where Lyle was leaning against a wall, staring up at the thin elusive break of sky in the dark street with a thoughtful expression, and immediately began his report in as adult a voice as he could. His chest heaved, his shoulders bulged, his voice resounded with authority as he barked, 'Sir, I have information, sir.'

Lyle looked at him out of the corner of his eye. 'Good,' he said in a tone that, even to Thomas's ears, sounded slightly too bright to be true. 'What is it?'

He recited it carefully. 'Mrs Farse, who lives by the butcher's, said she heard the sound of a carriage late last night. She couldn't sleep because of a toothache and claims she roused herself to find a drink. Well, sir, she says she remembers the carriage, sir, because it was so late, and because you rarely get many objects that sound like that down here, at least, she thinks you don't, and she remembered hearing the horses, sir, and running feet. Personally I think that if she really did have a toothache then . . .'

'Did she look out?'

'Yes, sir, but it was very dark.'

'Well, what did she see?'

'She saw a carriage, sir.'

'Really.' Lyle's face was unreadable.

'Yes, sir!' Thomas blurted, aware that he was starting to lose some of his authority. 'She saw a four-seater, sir, with two horses, standing there, but the driver wasn't sitting on it and the horses weren't moving.'

'What colour was it?'

'It all looked black to her.'

'Including the horses?'

'Yes, sir.'

'Did she see any people?'

'No, sir, but she says the window was down on one side of the carriage and there must have been someone inside because there was a white-gloved hand resting on the window!'

'It might have been someone's disembodied hand,' suggested Lyle mildly. He saw Thomas's hurt expression and added, 'This is very useful. Do carry on.'

'Well, after a minute she saw the driver return, dressed up formally, sir, in livery.'

'Black?' suggested Lyle.

'Yes, sir. And he was carrying a bag. She said she saw the driver look through it, then whoever was in the carriage also looked through it. And she says she saw *gold*, sir.'

Lyle brightened. 'Just gold?'

'Yes, sir.'

'No stone bowls radiating cultural significance, by any chance?'

'No, sir. She was very specific. Just gold, through and through. The man inside the carriage seemed to get angry. She thought she heard shouting.'

Lyle was by this point grinning ear to ear. He slapped Thomas on the shoulder. 'Excellent!'

'Then the carriage drove off, sir.' It seemed, to Thomas, like a bit of an anti-climax.

Lyle, however, looked ecstatic. 'This is excellent news, lad! Well done.'

'Thank you, sir.'

'You ever think of being a detective?'

And Thomas thought of another world, foggy and vague round the edges, that he knew existed, but had never seen; and after all those hunts and all those dances and all those evenings sipping tea to the gentle patter of rain and polite conversation, he remembered sitting up in bed when everything else was asleep, and swearing that *he* would make a difference. 'All the time, sir,' he whispered.

Lyle wasn't listening. He detached himself from the wall, smiling broadly, wrapped a fatherly arm round Thomas's shoulder and said, 'Come on. Let's go and find ourselves a carriage.'

'Shouldn't we wait for Miss Teresa, sir?'

Lyle's smile turned slightly evil. 'Miss Teresa is doing a very special job at the moment.'

Tess was bored. She had been looking forward to traipsing round with Thomas, in order to ridicule him a little when he couldn't understand what the locals were saying, and possibly to pick his pocket while he wasn't looking. The boy, she was convinced, would be a mark for any decent thief, despite his burgeoning height and strength. However, as she had moved to follow Thomas, Lyle had put a restraining hand on her shoulder. Her talents, she knew, lay in different areas.

And now she was lurking in a doorway, watching everyone, and feeling bored. She had done this since she was old enough to tell the difference between bulging pockets and sagging pockets, and the pockets in this place were, generally speaking, bulging. And she wasn't allowed to touch them. So she had watched Lyle. For a while he'd just stood there, staring at the blood. Then he'd leant against a wall and stared at the sky, not moving, Tate lying dutifully across his feet, where he seemed to be most comfortable, also not moving. Then Thomas had come back, and by both his and Lyle's expressions, the news had been good from the people around the bridge. Then the two of them had started walking.

Tess had moved out of the shadows when they were thirty yards ahead of her and, keeping a shoulder to the wall, drifted along behind them, now very much alert. She had followed them up towards Cheapside with its bustling shops and shouting hawkers, joining the flow of people, ducking top hats and walking canes and leather boots and tweed elbows, keeping in sight as a guide Lyle's sandy-red hair, brighter than the black top hats that moved through the streets, and when not searching for that, watching the people. Sailors, smelling of salt and tar and fish and sweat and grease, businessmen with white silk handkerchiefs and ivory-capped canes that they swung with a deadly ease, women with trays slung from their shoulders bearing steaming packets of nuts or fruit or vegetables or biscuits or tins of mushy peas or soup or flowers, or girls selling handfuls of ribbon, or burly men setting up their coffee cauldrons under the nearest bedraggled and blackened tree, or the priest scurrying to the service at St Paul's or at the Guild Church with the gold dragon sitting on top of it, facing perpetually north despite the wind, or the man with the music box and the money, or the Dutch singers, or the bobbies in their blue top hats and capes, who she strained to avoid out of habit, or . . .

For a second she saw someone who was immediately swallowed up by the crowd, and she felt a momentary flash of recognition, not sure where she'd seen him before but trusting her instinct that she *had* seen him before. There again, a man all in black, coat collar turned up high about his face, a red scarf wound tightly across his mouth, neck and chin, brown leather gloves on his hands, a tall top hat looking somehow incongruous on his head, dark hair sticking out under it. Gone again. She kept following Lyle but now she was looking for the man with the dark hair beneath that hat, sitting at a rakish angle that didn't really fit, supported mostly by his ears. As Lyle turned again into Gutter Lane, taking the most complicated route he knew, all the way up to St Alban's Church and the red-grey stretch of the City Wall half-incorporated into the local building where it ran past the gold-rimmed marble-walled Goldsmiths' Hall, *he* followed, that man in the lopsided top hat, eyes fixed on Lyle. And as Lyle ducked and weaved, making it harder with each inexplicable turn, so the man turned, and Tess soon was following him only, not Lyle, because he was following Lyle.

Still she couldn't see his face. Once she saw him raise something wrapped in a dark red silk handkerchief to his mouth, and in his footsteps she noticed a small spattering of ginger crumbs, but he never turned his face towards her. At last they were at the giant edifice of the Bank, and Lyle and Thomas were walking towards the tall, thick black-iron doors opposite the Merchant Exchange. Tess took a deep breath and ran forward. She barged straight into the man who had followed them all the way there, bounced off him, muttered a quick 'Sorry, guv', and ran on past, catching up with Lyle and Thomas just as Lyle put his hand on the door.

Lyle turned expectantly as she ran to him, gasping for breath. 'I seen him!'

'And?' asked Lyle mildly.

She heaved in lungfuls of air before she managed to blurt, 'He's a chink!'

'A . . .' began Thomas uneasily.

'And I went for his pockets!' blurted Tess.

'And?' suggested Lyle, his voice kept tactfully away from disapproval.

'He's got a gun!'

'A . . .' Thomas tried stammering again.

The door burst open. '*Thomas Edward Elwick, what do you think you are doing?*'

Lord Elwick erupted on to the scene. And he was *angry*.

CHAPTER 6

Night

Evening settled on the streets of London. In a carriage clattering back towards his dull mansion with its dull books on dull
counties full of dull people, Thomas had already shut his ears to
the rantings of his furious father, and was watching the blind
drawn down over the window. He didn't know whether it was
there to prevent the world contaminating him, or to stop him and
his family contaminating the world. He thought of the last thing
he had seen or heard before his father had practically lifted him
off the street and thrown him into a carriage. Lyle had put a hand
on his arm and said, 'How could a thief get hold of your family
seal and father's signature, Master Elwick?'

The question buzzed in his mind. The servants would never have given out the seal, used for all formal documents, nor any of the family papers bearing Lord Elwick's signature. He could guess what Lyle was worried about; he didn't need to be told: the documents used to get the sarcophagus into the vault had to be signed by his father. Thomas looked at Lord Elwick, and felt his own anger settle into a seething resentment. He knew in his heart that his father was a fool; nonetheless, he realized that he might be a loyal fool, and that he was, for whatever reason, genuinely angry and upset at the loss of the Fuyun Plate. Thomas knew Lord Elwick would not have contrived to give someone, anyone, the means to get into the vault.

How could a thief get hold of your family seal and father's signature, Master Elwick?

They rattled on, through growing darkness.

When the sun set, Tess noticed, it didn't reach the horizon, but shimmered out in a dirty brown pool before its light could touch the ceiling.

'Water vapour,' Lyle said, coming up behind her where she stood in the window of his house, watching the red evening. He thought about this. 'And general dirt. You know, there are some people who suspect it could have a detrimental long-term effect on the climate.'

'What?'

'Dirt.'

'Will it?'

He looked sheepish. 'It's not really my field.'

She grinned. 'You don't know, do you?'

'Well, no.' He added, before her grin could grow any wider, 'Come on. There's more work before supper.'

Night settled, thick and dark and suffocating. As the temperature dropped, the fog rose, drifting up into the emptier sky and rolling across the town in a choking green-grey wave that slithered into every pair of lungs and tickled them with dirty blackness. In the street, a policeman swung his rattle, and the theatre halls started to drain out for the evening.

In the Elwick mansion – a new, ugly white stain on a large swathe of green land encased by high red walls – the family sat down to supper, and Lady Elwick began the conversation. 'My dear, I am concerned for Thomas's Latin.'

'It is not the only blemish which should concern us, Lady Elwick!'

On the other side of town, in a house too small for Tate, too large for Lyle and perfect for dark goings-on, someone struck a match in a dark, cold cellar, and someone else blurted, 'For Christ's sake, not in here! Wait until I've opened the vents!'

The match went out. There was a scuffling sound. 'Ow! That's my foot!'

'Well, what are you doing standing *there*?'

Something clicked. Cold air started to flow, taking away an oppressive smell. '*Now* can I strike a match?'

'No. Take this. It's safer.'

'What is it?'

'A magnet and a bit of wire.'

'That ain't helpful, Mister Lyle.'

'Just turn the handle, Teresa.'

A sound like a cricket. Light slowly blossomed in the room, illuminating Tess's astonished face. She stared at the single bulb stapled to a small piece of wood, on which was attached, simply, a short coil of tightly wrapped wire and a magnet, which spun inside the wire as she turned the handle. The faster she turned the magnet, the brighter the bulb glowed. She whispered, 'Jesus Christ.'

On the other side of the room, Lyle was fumbling with a pair of levers. 'You believe in God, Teresa?'

'I'm gonna say sorry just in case.'

'Watch.'

He pulled a lever. There was another click. Somewhere beyond the wooden door in a corner of the room, something started thundering. Across the room bulbs lit up, flooding it with white light, illuminating desks lined with bits of bent glass and metal and strange liquids of every colour and thickness, and tubes and tools and bits of wire and gears locked together in a monstrous mountain that somehow, through the chaos of metal teeth, seemed to be connected by rods to more gears that disappeared into walls or cupboards or metal contraptions waiting for a use. She stared, speechless. Lyle, grinning proudly, unlocked and pushed open the small wooden door at the end of the room and the sound of distant thunder grew a whole lot louder. 'Look.'

She crept to the door, no longer turning the handle on the magnet in her hand, and peered through. The room beyond was covered with tubes and gears and felt hot and dry and smelt *terrible*. Central to it all a huge coil of wire, sparking and hissing, spun around a single metal core attached to wires that ran into every wall, nook and cranny, huge heavy wires hanging across the ceiling while pistons pumped up and down below, driven from the pipes that seemed to rise out of the floor itself.

'How the *hell* . . .' she began.

Lyle looked like a child with a toy. 'Natural gas,' he chuckled. 'Burnt natural gas drives the pistons which push the wire which spins round the magnet, cutting the magnetic field, which creates –' his grin was huge – 'electricity. Magnetism makes electricity, electricity makes magnetism – you can't have one without the other. Faraday is the new God, and he explains his universe in lines of force around a wire.'

'Where do you get the . . . the . . .'

'Natural gas to burn?'

'Yes.'

In a distant, reverent voice, he said, 'The sewers.'

She stared at him in horror. He shrugged. 'Wonderful natural source, right under us. I'm thinking of calling it something like "Lyle's gas", but then that means my name will be forever associated with sewage, and I'd much rather it was associated with . . . oh, I don't know . . . coffee or a new and better kind of light source or sugar or something like that.' He chuckled to himself. 'Perhaps I'll call it "Vellum's gas". But no. That would give him too much credit. I'll think of something.'

Out in the dark street as the fog and the night wash over the world, a man with a lopsided top hat and a mysterious bulge in his coat pocket that might just be a gun casually breaks the end off a neatly wrapped ginger biscuit, and chews thoughtfully, watching the house across the road and wondering about its inhabitants. A woman goes by, nodding at him in the dark, and says, 'God bless you, good sir.'

'Ma'am.'

He watches her go into the house opposite Lyle's, but not before she casts a longing glance at the gloomy windows. He thinks that he really must try and break the bad biscuit habit. He has to stay in shape. Especially now.

A carriage rattles by. It slows as it nears Lyle's house, and the watcher ponders on how grand the carriage seems to be, how really it is too well oiled to be in this part of town, and how dark the livery of the driver is, before it picks up speed again and drives quickly by.

He doesn't move, doesn't blink.

After a while, he looks down at the pavement, and wonders whether it should be humming under his shoes or not.

'So how long have you had a . . . a . . .'

'Electricity-magnet generator?' prompted Lyle, carefully dipping a slim piece of wire into a glass pot of blue liquid.

'. . . in your basement?'

'My father started building it when I was a child,' he replied. Satisfied with his work, he started digging in his pocket. He found a paper bag and tipped its contents out on the table. 'My first memories are going to the Royal Institution to listen to Faraday's lectures on the principles of electric and magnetic interaction. My father built the original coil, but had to power its rotation through the magnetic field given out by the magnet via an old-fashioned coal engine, adapted from a railway locomotive. The gas was my idea. The second I heard that Bazalgette was going to build a new sewer system I went straight to him for the plans. A good man, Bazalgette.'

'Your father . . .'

'He died several years ago. Harry Lyle. He believed in metal and machines, thought that if you just knew how, you could make a machine do anything – even think. People said he was a heretic. The letters he got were unbelievable – he was told he was betraying Britain by giving over all of life to iron and steel.' He sighed, frowning. 'It's a little sad, really.' Then shook himself, snapping back to attention. 'Right!'

From the paper bag he took the fruit stone and the orange peel, examining both under a magnifying glass and tutting to himself. Finally he sighed, and dropped them into two separate, foul-smelling jars of clear liquid, which he hastily capped and locked away on a shelf.

Tess watched, suspecting that she was starting to get interested, but trying to keep a bored expression. 'What you doin'?'

'Just trying to narrow down the search area,' Lyle replied gaily. 'How do you feel about fish?'

She blanched. 'Fish? You do things to fish here too? Like you have all these things what you power with fish, like how you do things with gas an' all? How do I feel 'bout *fish*?'

'Supper.'

And somewhere, behind the steel and iron and smoke and dirt and fog and dust and dark, something just a little bit magical was about to happen, and something evil was about to extend a tentacle towards the light.

*

'I really do feel that fear of a Chartist revival at this stage is absurd, although if Disraeli continues with . . . Charles!'

Thomas rarely saw his father so animated, and more rarely still did he hear him address anyone by their first name. Everyone in the drawing room rose to their feet, including Thomas, who had been attempting to cultivate a taste for port, and failing. The man who entered was tall, elegant, with fine features carved on a white, bony face above a bony, handsome body clad in black silk. As he came in, he pulled off a long white glove, and Thomas noticed keenly the tiny pinprick of blood on one of the fingers. For some reason he felt his stomach turn.

'My lord,' said the man with the white gloves, and his voice was like black leather, and his eyes were emerald green and . . .

'Lord Moncorvo,' said Thomas's father, recovering himself, 'welcome.'

Lord Moncorvo glided towards where Thomas stood and draped himself into an armchair. Though the man had given him just a glance Thomas felt his green eyes boring into him.

'You had some discomfiture today, my lord.'

'A robbery, no less!' Elwick's face hardened as he looked at Thomas. 'My son can probably enlighten you. Today he went gallivanting by himself without a word to me. Children today have . . .'

'Gallivanting?' Moncorvo stared straight at Thomas, who couldn't look away from those green eyes.

Elwick seemed to take no offence at being interrupted. 'With the son of Harry Lyle, no less.'

Moncorvo's eyes filled Thomas's world. 'Is that so?'

Something turned in Thomas's stomach, something old and

dry like leaves rustling across the forest floor. He could feel the coldness of the iron door into the Bank, he could see the green eyes filling his own, burning down on him as if they read his mind, and he heard a distant voice, almost in a dream, saying, 'And how much does Constable Horatio Lyle know, boy?'

And he's speaking, he's *speaking*, and his father just sits there, his mouth slightly open, eyes fixed on some vacant point, spittle slowly accumulating in one corner of his lips, like a madman in an asylum staring at something else, and there's just green eyes and . . . and a feeling like . . . or rather a sound like . . . or a smell like . . . black leather leaves rustling over an emerald forest floor and . . .

'What did he ask you to do, boy?'

'Sir, he wants to know how someone could get my family seal and my father's signature in order to put the sarcophagus into the vault.'

'Does he indeed?'

'Yes, sir.'

'Does he know what the Fuyun Plate is?'

'I don't know, sir.'

. . . and he felt like sinking, drowning, falling and . . .

'Boy, perhaps it is time we discussed Horatio Lyle in more detail.'

He's sitting with his father, reading about the fall of the Roman Empire, and his father is saying, '. . . this absurd reform nonsense then I fear the Party will decay into a Gladstonian state!'

'Yes, Father.'

'Thomas? Are you paying attention?'

'Yes, Father.' And there's something he needs to remember. 'Father?'

'Yes, boy?'

'Did . . . did Moncorvo . . .'

'A damn good fellow. What of him?'

'Where is he?'

'Where is he? What do you mean, boy, where is he? How is this relevant?'

'I . . . where is he?'

'Do you mean is he voting for Disraeli?'

'I don't know. I don't know.'

. . . and there were eyes and . . . nothing else . . . except, perhaps, just on the edge of smelling, the faintest scent of decaying leaves falling in an autumnal forest, that blows out with the wind.

The night settles on the city, and somewhere a man with a black leather voice and a white glove pricked with old blood that is not his own says, 'The boy is a fool, my lady, and so is his father.'

'That does not concern me, my lord. What of the Plate?'

'Lyle does not have it. Even if he does, he cannot use it.'

'If blood is spilt in it before it is repaired . . .'

'It will make no difference! Mr Dew has almost found Bray, *Bray* has the Plate and he will give it to us, and we will repair it, and we will be restored. We will bring back the power, my lady. Lyle cannot stop us.'

'Can he hinder us? I know Lord Lincoln is watching, and we cannot afford mistakes now.'

'Lincoln is a fool too! They are all fools, they are just *human*!' The echoes die away.

'My lord?'

'Forgive me, my lady. I . . . have lived in iron too long.'

'It is understandable. I think, if Lyle gets too close, we should have him killed. Just to be sure.'

A shrug. 'I see no reason why not.'

'Very good, my lord.'

And the night settles, and the city sleeps, a deep, cold, dozy sleep as the furnaces idle in their halls of steel and the day's dirt slowly rains out of the black sky on to the black roofs. And the carriages fall silent and the horses start to snore in their stables and the dirty clothes flap in the dirty wind and the fires slowly start to burn out. And somewhere, a boy dreams of emerald eyes and running through a forest of dead black leaves, falling from a dead black sky, and wakes in a cold sweat, not knowing why.

CHAPTER 7

Fruit

Tess woke with the sun. It was her habit: in winter she could sleep sixteen whole hours just waiting for daylight, in summer she could get by with barely six hours' sleep. For a second she had difficulty remembering where she was, but when recollection slowly settled like feathers on her mind, she was surprised to realize that she felt almost pleased at the thought. Her stomach was full, her feet were warm and the room was all hers.

Having got up, she drifted around the house, trying door handles, a lot of which were locked, before wandering down to the kitchen. No one there. She peered into a few cupboards looking for anything that wasn't in mysteriously unlabelled jars, before finally pulling open a large wardrobe door. The wardrobe itself was empty, but her eyes fell on its back wall, which seemed to protrude at a very slight angle. She ran her hands thoughtfully over it, wondering. Something clicked. She pulled gently at the wardrobe door and behind her a voice said, 'Erm, you ought to know about the mantrap inside.'

She very slowly let go of the detachable door. 'You ought to disguise it with coats, Mister Lyle,' she said, backing away.

'No, no, no! That's not the point at all! If I disguised it with coats, people wouldn't start looking inside it for a hidden compartment.'

She frowned up at him. 'But, an' this might seem slow, but ain't the point of a hidden compartment to be . . . *hidden*?'

'And if anyone opens that up, they'll not be able to look for another compartment for a very long time, will they?'

She scowled. 'You're horrid, Mister Lyle.'

He looked almost embarrassed. 'Yes,' he muttered. Then he brightened. 'More positively, I think I've found something.'

'Miss Laskell?'

'Yes, Master Thomas?' Miss Laskell, Thomas's governess, waited patiently.

'If . . . have you ever seen my father write a letter?'

'Of course I have, Master Thomas!'

'I mean . . . on the paper with the family crest, with the family seal?'

'Yes. When he wrote references for Violet he wrote it on the family paper.'

'And signed it?'

'How strange of you to ask, Master Thomas!'

'It's important.'

A sigh. 'Yes, of course he signed it, Master Thomas.'

'Where does he keep the paper?'

'Now why would you be . . .'

'It's important. Please?'

Another sigh. 'Locked in his desk. Only he has the key to it. And only he ever uses the family seal for special documents, things from the Palace, you know.'

'None of the servants could get to it?'

Her voice darkened. 'I don't know what you've been thinking, young Master Thomas, but *no* one except your father gets into that desk.'

'Oh. I see.'

'Is that all, Master Thomas? If so, I'll just——'

'No. Wait! I . . . I need your help.'

Lyle put his elbows on the desk in the dark basement and said, 'It's boiled.'

'What?'

'The orange was boiled before it was sold, to make it look bigger and juicer.'

'Oh.' She saw his expression. '*Oh.*'

He looked back down at the two pieces of fruit on the table and said in a slightly less enthusiastic voice, 'There were also traces of formaldehyde on the orange peel, a drop of rabbit's blood and some salt, so I'm assuming it came from somewhere near the meat markets. And I found out what the fruit is.' From a shelf near a giant wardrobe that looked, to Tess's eyes, even more suspicious than the one upstairs, he pulled down a large encyclopaedia, and opened it on the desk. 'It's something called a "lychee". An incredible delicacy. I think there must be about two men in the whole city who'd be able to sell something like this, and to a very specialist clientele. The tooth marks on the stone are remarkable – razor-sharp teeth, very pointed, one of those sets of teeth you'd recognize *anywhere*.'

'Anywhere?'

'Have you ever seen a stuffed predatory fish, a freshwater trout, perhaps?'

'Uh . . .'

He scowled. 'A dead fish with big teeth?'

'Urgh.'

'So you'd better get your shoes on.'

'What?'

'You're going to find the people who sold these pieces of fruit.'

'Why?'

'Because they were found too close to the bloodstains in an area where no one eats that kind of food to be coincidence.'

'Why *me*?'

'Because of your charitable, helpful character?'

Now she scowled. 'What are you goin' to do?'

'I'm going to take Tate for a walk.'

A man wearing a crooked top hat, who turned up his collar in all weathers and had a taste for ginger biscuits, still watched Lyle's house, but now his narrow, alert eyes were tired in his face with its unusually almond-dark skin that was once yellow but had been baked and lined by exposure to all elements, including the worst of humanity. He had been standing and waiting too long, relieved on his endless watch for but a few hours by a colleague, who long ago left him to his task. He stretched, tight shoulders bunching under the thick coat, and yawned.

The door opened on the other side of the road, and the girl, who he knew was called Teresa but about whom he knew nothing else, slipped out, looking furtively around. She didn't see him as he drew back into the shadows, and he smiled. For a moment yesterday, he'd worried that she had.

He didn't follow her. He watched the house expectantly.

It took Lyle fifteen minutes more to emerge, with Tate padding at his feet, then look around thoughtfully, eyes flickering over where the man stood but not focusing on him, before turning and marching in completely the opposite direction from Teresa. Lyle today was wearing an anonymous grey overcoat and a broad-brimmed traveller's hat that was very distinct indeed. In the shadows, the man almost smiled.

He followed Lyle.

He followed him up to the Strand, through the throngs of people and carriages, up the bustling, shoulder-to-shoulder wide streets of yellow Regency houses nestling against each other, through Covent Garden where the stall holders called out, 'Pineapples, ha'penny a slice'; 'Penny a bunch turnips'; 'Oranges, two a penny'; 'Cherry ripe, two pence a plate'; 'Wild Hampshire rabbits, two a shilling'; 'Fine ripe plums, penny a pint'. And then on, elbowing past the hawkers and the buyers and the penny-gaff clown with his penny gaffs and the Silly Billy chanting 'Eh, higgety, eh ho! Billy let the water go! . . . Nicky nickey nite, I'll strike a light!' – and on, up Long Acre.

He followed Lyle as he skirted the St Giles rookery, a maze of dark alleys and dens that huddled round the church of St Giles and the brothels of Seven Dials. Avoiding the looks and eyes of the blackcaps and garrotters hiding in the shadows of the cheap boarding houses, twelve to a room, seven rooms a house, five houses a privy, he followed Lyle around St Martin's Lane, past the shut doors of the dancing halls and the music halls where each night the crowd pressed in on each other's feet to hear the lady in the red rouge scream and the man with the fake nose howl. He followed Lyle into Trafalgar Square and then down towards Charing Cross Station, where steam billowed up in huge gusts that shrouded the seedy hotels around it and drove the men waiting with their hansom cabs to shout out loudly, 'Cabby, cabby' to draw attention to themselves. Briefly, in this mêlée of crushing human life, he lost sight of Lyle, but almost immediately saw that distinctive hat and, more telling yet, Tate's paws and ears contending for which could pick up more dirt from the cobbles.

He followed Lyle up towards Green Park, but at Haymarket Lyle seemed to change his mind and cut north again up a wide road adorned with heroic statues and stately clubs, a clean, far cry from the brothels that co-existed just a few blocks away under roofs held up with strategically perched planks and mouldering below gutters of stagnant green water. He followed him all the way back up to Piccadilly Circus, starting to wonder when Lyle was going to tire of his sport. Suddenly, in front of a new building that narrowed to a desperate point on one corner, Lyle stopped, bent, scratched the dutiful Tate behind the ears, straightened up, surveyed the clattering jungle of streets hung over with the perpetual smoke and haze of London, and briefly took off his hat to swipe a finger along the sweatband across his forehead.

Underneath his hat, Lyle's hair was black.

The man with the crooked top hat and taste in ginger biscuits stopped dead, almost in the middle of the street.

Underneath his hat, Lyle was not Lyle. But Tate was definitely Tate, and as the man watched, the dog turned and started trotting away back towards Covent Garden seemingly without a care. He tried to follow the dog through the crowd, but quickly lost him, and before the man knew it he was standing in a heaving mass of people pushing and shoving towards Regent Street. He stopped again, and scanned the crowd with a slow, intense gaze.

There was no sign of Lyle. Anywhere.

He started walking, nearly a run. He doubled back, avoiding the dangerous narrow streets to the west of Regent Street that led into the notorious, cholera-ridden, smoke-drenched, crime-ruled dens of St Giles, and marched determinedly back towards the wide expanse of Green Park. The second he stepped on to the grass, oppressed by the blackened trees that dotted it here and there, he stopped again, and his gaze swept the park. No sign of Lyle.

He marched quickly through the park, stopping every now and again to turn and scan every face that passed. Then he walked again, almost running, sending ducks scattering around the stagnant brown lake, as a smelly, acrid rain began to drizzle, that spattered the damp mud and sounded like a distant muffled drum.

He stopped one last time as the rain thickened to a grey

blanket, and people started scurrying for shelter, collars turned up. He saw couples sheltering under coats and running for trees or gazebos; workmen trudging on with the same resolute expressions; children, filthy, black with soot and grime, dancing under the water as the dirt flowed down their faces and into their brown clothes. He saw a woman in green; a man in a black overcoat, his collar turned right up against the rain, darting under a tree with a newspaper over his head; a man in corduroy; a man in tweed; a woman in plain wool; a horse in harness. He thought, for a second, he saw a dog of uncertain parentage, ears trailing in the mud, rolling over and getting himself thoroughly dirty in glee, but when he moved towards the dog it saw a pigeon and started barking, galloping away through the rain and sending up a spray of water behind it, overwhelmed with enthusiasm for this new cause.

The man gave up. He turned and started to walk west.

Lyle watched him go.

When the man was more than forty yards away, just a vague shape in the rain, Lyle shook the water off the newspaper he held over his head, did up the last button on his black coat, pulled his collar higher around his chin, and followed. Tate, turned brown with the mud, padded along behind him.

At its very north-western corner, Green Park joins Hyde Park's south-eastern corner, after which Hyde Park bends sharply north up Park Lane, where the carriages with the padded seats and expensive ladies of taste and tastes clattered around, looking for someone to keep them company. And just behind Park Lane, tucked into a surprisingly well-kept street that bordered the slum of hidden factories mazing the narrow byways behind the wider, more popular arteries of the city, was a mews. The stables were empty, the horses being out on their long day's work. Above the stables and occasionally in them were the homes of the horses' owners: messengers, cabbies, and coster-mongers with their carts. Beyond these stables was a house that might once have been luxurious, but now was crumbling, old red bricks cracked from neglect, windows half-covered by tatty curtains. Through a small door below these windows darted the man. He bounded up a flight of stairs that shook and warped under him, pushed open a loose door and went into a room, empty except for some furnishings covered over with dust cloths that would never be moved and a few mats on the floor. Sitting around a small fire set in a cauldron in the centre of this floor were a group of Chinese men. They paid the man no attention as he strode in, unwinding his long red scarf to reveal his worn face in full, and stripping off the coat, to toss it lightly into a corner.

A man with a fat pigtail almost down to the bottom of his back, looking out of place in an overlarge waistcoat, said serenely in near-accentless English, 'Why are you back so early?'

'He knew I was following.'

'Are you sure?'

'He went to great pains to lose me.'

'That is unsatisfactory, Feng Darin. What are you going to do to remedy the situation?'

Feng Darin stared thoughtfully out of the window at the rain. As he watched, a shadow, greyed in the rain, sandy-red hair soaked dark brown and clinging to its scalp, looked back up at the window. At his side, brown mud trickled off a dog. In the rain, the man seemed to smile, then turn slowly and walk away.

'Feng Darin,' repeated the man with the pigtail from inside the room. 'What are you going to do to find him again?'

'I won't have to do anything, *xiansheng*. He has found us.'

The other man smiled faintly, and nodded. 'If he can find us, Feng Darin, he can find the Plate.'

'Before the Tseiqin?'

'We can only hope.'

Feng sighed. 'But hoping is too passive, *xiansheng*. The Tseiqin have no hesitation about taking matters into their own hands. I think we should not hesitate either.'

'Well then? What are you doing standing here?'

CHAPTER 8

There was one other place Lyle wanted to take Tate that day, and it was on the other side of town. He found a hansom cab and sheltered inside, shivering from the rain pelting the loose cab window and drying on his coat, while water slowly pooled around Tate at his feet. The wet weather brought premature darkness down on London so that, even though it was still morning, the whole city had the feeling of dusk, before a long night.

The driver of the cab wouldn't take him closer than half a mile, and even then he took convincing. The Bethnal Green rookery was cold, dark, damp. Out of dark doorways dark faces leered; from the broken crooked windows in blackened crooked walls, tattered rags serving as curtains flapped wetly. Under each passage and arch across each street, pipes dripped on to mildewed surfaces; at the end of each street refuse mouldered; between each courtyard and alley there was a cellar through which people passed as a common thoroughfare, dipping in and out of a darkened doorway that opened up through a smoky wall. Not even the most intrepid costermongers ventured into the heart of the rookery with their wares or carrying anything more than a few pennies. Children gambled on the edge, hiding behind shattered crates dumped on ruined muddy streets. In the heart of the rookery, boarding houses boasting no beds and only a partial roof hid scowls that lurked around each bubbling wrought-iron pot where strange concoctions slowly burnt black and each inn was full of the silence of broken men taking their tankards too seriously to be safe.

Lyle padded through all this, hands deep in his pockets, chin buried in his coat, avoiding the glares that flew his way, Tate trying to pretend he wasn't with Lyle at his side. Barely the only people attempting to ply their wares were the patterers, who leapt out of doorways to thrust in Lyle's direction pamphlets with titles like 'The Serving Girl Surprised!' followed by a suggestive picture that promised worse inside. Lyle scowled, shook his head and scurried on.

There was one place inside the Bethnal Green rookery that resembled civilization, and even then it was a civilization in decline. Lyle found it through a half-open crumbling door a few steps below street level, above which someone had hammered a sign reading 'House of Pr' before someone else had come along and broken off the other half of the sign for some other purpose. He pushed open the door and stepped into a darkness that stank of tobacco, opium, sweat and cheap make-up made from ground lead. Faces lurked in the shadows, and those that weren't lost in some other world glared at having their rest interrupted. A stair at one end led up to an unseen fiddle player whose instrument possessed no more than three strings. The sounds of drinking and pattering feet accompanied him in occasional loud gales of shouting that lapsed again into an alcoholic silence. Lyle walked to the stairs, but didn't climb them, turning instead to a small door tucked just behind them, bolted, with a sign crudely written on it in charcoal, 'kep owut'. He knocked on the door. After a second it opened and a very large man with a crooked nose that hadn't healed properly from when it last broke, and a pair of lips so cut and bruised they barely resembled a mouth any more, glowered at him. 'Keep out,' he growled, indicating the sign with a huge, bulging finger.

'I need to see the Missus.'

'Keep out!'

'Just tell the Missus Mister Lyle is here, please.'

The door slammed shut. Lyle waited, leaning into a corner, trying to look unobtrusive in the smoke. Someone lying on a pallet by the opposite door was starting to whine in a high-pitched, if undeniably happy voice that sounded like a frightened cat mewing. The door unbolted again and a new face appeared. It was round, possessed more chins than its owner had fingers – of which three were missing on the right hand, just stumps remaining – above a large red, low-necked dress stained in more mysterious ways than Lyle wanted to speculate on, and was topped by a huge yellow wig that in low-ceilinged houses presented something of a fire hazard. It beamed at Lyle.

'Horatio! Come in, come in.'

He sidled uneasily into the room. The woman glanced at the large man skulking in a corner and said imperiously, 'Go.'

The man lumbered out, his face impassive. The door closed behind him. Lyle looked round the room. A huge, dirty and cracked mirror dominated one corner, a sofa another, the stuffing showing, and another wall was obscured by equally damaged dresses of a similar low-cut nature, and wigs to match. His eyes fell on a desk in front of the mirror, laden with pots and brushes. He picked up a pot at random, sniffed it, frowned and said, 'This smells of belladonna.'

'Mistress of the night,' replied the Missus with an overdramatic flourish.

'Hallucinogenic,' replied Lyle reproachfully, putting the pot down again. 'How are you, Mrs Gardener?'

She drooped herself over the end of the sofa, waving a long white hand airily. 'As well as can be expected, darling boy. And you? Are you *still* trying to cure society's ills?'

'Only as a hobby, Mrs Gardener. But I do have a favour to ask.'

'*Favours?* Horatio, dear, I thought we established that all debts are repaid.'

'All right – an exchange.'

'You're not going to be so vulgar as to offer *money*, are you?'

'Ma'am,' he replied with a faint sigh, 'I couldn't compete.' Lyle dug into a pocket, rummaging around deep inside before he found what he was looking for. He pulled it out triumphantly, held it up and said, 'Burn one teaspoon in your room whenever you have an attack, inhale the fumes and it'll temporarily reduce the breathing difficulties.'

She took the pot, lifted the lid and peered suspiciously at what was inside. 'It's a powder, not a herb.'

'Yes.'

'What's it made of?'

'It's chemically derived.'

She frowned. 'Have you tested it?'

'Yes.'

'On *people*?'

'Once, yes!'

She sighed, and the pot disappeared somewhere into the desk next to her. 'Well, I trust you, Horatio Lyle. More than the quacks who call themselves physicians, at least. And what do you desire in return?'

'Information, please.'

'It's *always* information with you, Horatio, my darling boy. How do you expect our relationship to develop like this?'

'I need to know about Bray.'

Her expression darkened. 'Bray?'

'Yes.'

'Why do you want to know about him?'

'I'm looking for him.'

'For yourself, or for *them*?'

'If by "them", you mean the bobbies, no, not necessarily. It depends what he has to say.'

'Horatio, wouldn't it be simpler for us all if you let him be?'

'Why, where is he?'

She sighed expansively, leaning back and away from him, to study his face from an angle. As the silence stretched, he shifted uneasily and said, 'Ma'am, I'm not leaving until I have an answer. A *good* answer, I mean.'

She took a deep breath, and let it out again. 'Bray is an unfortunate. If you'd met his Pa . . . born bad, died drunk. You can't blame the boy for falling into other pursuits.'

'That's not really for me to decide, is it? Where is he?'

'He was staying with a friend of his, a man with four fingers . . .'

'Carwell?'

The sharpness of his question surprised her. 'Yes, it might well have been the same.'

'Where was he staying?'

'A boarding house owned by Mrs McVicar, a Scottish lady of some repute.'

'I think I know it. Is he there now?'

She waved her arms in expansive ignorance. 'He and Carwell both appear to have dug themselves into the shadows. Carwell – and his brother – used to be a common client here, but I hear from those who know such things that he and Bray were both working on something –' she waggled her eyebrows meaningfully at Lyle – 'substantial. Is that what brings you here, Horatio? Something "substantial"?'

'I'd rather not talk about it.'

'It must be sensational, then.'

'Will you contact me if you see Bray?'

Her eyes narrowed fractionally. 'Perhaps.'

'He might be in danger.'

'From who?'

'The people who killed Carwell.'

She didn't blink, and though her smile remained fixed, there was a tiny, imperceptible tightening as she hid her reactions behind a mask of stone. 'In that case, it may well be that I will contact you.'

'Thank you.' He smiled, nodded politely at her and, without another word, turned and left the room and that house as fast as he possibly could, trying not to breathe on his way out.

Mrs McVicar's boarding house was a leaning tomb around a small courtyard which had, over the years, filled up with other smaller houses, sheds of wood tied together with bits of damp rope, that turned the courtyard into a square surrounding yet more houses of mud floors, cloth roofs and walls through which the light crawled in each long, crooked crack. In the kitchen there was a small group of footpads and thieves carefully sipping thin soup, the colour of which derived more from the orange-brown water that sloshed out of the pump than from the ingredients carefully sprinkled in it. Several glanced at Lyle as he entered, with a calculating look. Tate growled at them. Lyle did his best to ignore them, and asked in a voice increasingly inflected with the accents of that part of town where the Madam was. It was a habit he'd acquired when young, and never managed to lose, so wherever he went, Lyle found himself speaking in the local accent. Though it could often be embarrassing, it was occasionally useful too, and Lyle was almost grateful for it now.

The Madam was outside, washing. Lyle found her bent over a stone trough by a wrought-iron pump, hammering sheets so thin he could see through them the colour of her eyes. He waited until she had finished and was hanging them out to drip dirty brown water on to the dirty brown earth, before saying, 'Mrs McVicar?'

She turned quickly, fists instinctively bunching up, saw him and didn't relax. 'What d'you want?'

'Erm . . . I'm looking for Bray, ma'am.'

Her eyebrows knitted together. 'Who?'

'Bray. Stayed here with Carwell.'

'Who?'

'Carwell. Short, missing a finger on his right hand? If you have any information about . . .'

'I don't know what you're talking about. Goodbye,' she said in a voice that had a strange drone Lyle hadn't expected to hear. Leaving her washing where it was she turned and marched with a glassy expression into the house. Lyle followed, but she slammed the door shut behind her, without once looking back at him. Lyle stood for a few astonished seconds on the step, then hammered on the door. 'Mrs McVicar!' Silence from inside. 'Mrs McVicar!' He looked down at Tate, who assumed an unhelpful expression even by doggy standards. Lyle groaned, looked at the door, backed off a few paces and charged shoulder-first at it. On the third impact it burst open and he limped in, rubbing his aching arm and hopping slightly, having nearly tripped over his own feet. Inside, Mrs McVicar was mindlessly scrubbing a couple of thin metal plates in a stone sink. He strode up to her and tried again, in his most authoritative voice.

'Mrs McVicar, I am a Special Constable.'

She stared blankly at him. 'Who are you?'

'Ma'am, I need to find Bray. I have reason to believe . . .'

'Who?'

He frowned. Her expression was one of total incomprehension. 'Mrs McVicar?'

'Yes?'

'Are you feeling all right?'

'Of course I'm feeling all right. Who are you? What are you doing here?'

'I'm Special Constable Horatio Lyle, ma'am . . .'

Immediately her eyebrows came together. She seemed to be trying to remember something. Distantly she murmured, 'Lyle? Horatio Lyle?'

'Yes, that's right.'

'Looking for . . .'

'Bray. Friend of Carwell.'

'Bray. Bray?' Her eyebrows flickered and she seemed to be trying to say something, mouth working up and down soundlessly around a trapped answer.

'Ma'am, are you sure you're feeling quite well?'

Without a word of warning she suddenly turned and marched over to a shelf, turning her back to Lyle. He followed her quickly as she opened a drawer and reached in. 'Ma'am?'

Her hand came out, clutching a carving knife. He jumped back quickly. It was a cheap knife, the handle half-fallen off, the blade rusted, but it still had the look of something designed for cutting through meat with the least possible effort. She didn't move, didn't look at him, just stared at the rusted knife in her hand. 'A man came,' she said in a distant voice.

'A man?' murmured Lyle, his own voice shaking slightly as he backed towards the door.

'Yes.' She spoke like someone in a dream. 'A beautiful, kind man. Eyes like emeralds. "Where is Bray?" he said. "Where is Bray?" I hardly dared speak, I sounded so crude and so *weak* compared to him.'

'Yes?' prompted Lyle, his voice barely above a whisper.

She turned slowly, and though her eyes were open and fixed on him, he doubted if she was seeing him at all. 'He . . . he *smelt* of sweet exotic fruits and . . . of leaves in empty forests – such a clean, pure smell, so . . . enticing, so warming. He said, "You are weak" and I almost cried to be honoured by his speech and his looks.'

'"Exotic fruits"? And teeth like a fish?' suggested Lyle, one foot already outside the doorframe, ready to run, one hand wrapped tightly round a glass vial, half-hidden behind his white knuckles.

She ignored him. Perhaps she couldn't hear him. 'He said a man would come, a policeman, Horatio Lyle. He said this man would want to know where Bray was, and that this man was evil.' She raised her head slowly, and now her eyes seemed to drift into focus for the very first time. She saw Lyle. She smiled. She slowly changed her grip on the knife and, without warning, without a cry or a change in her serene expression, without a word or a sigh, she ran at him.

Struck dumb, Lyle doubted his own eyes, and only as she was nearly on top of him, the point angled towards his heart, did instinct kick in. He jumped back, pivoting out of the door and round against the wall, while at his feet Tate barked furiously. Mrs McVicar swung out of the door frantically after him, but was hindered by Tate leaping up and biting at her ankle. Lyle staggered back as she struggled to free herself, face still serene despite the blood flowing around her ankle and Tate clinging on grimly. As she brought the knife up again Lyle threw the glass vial down on to the ground as hard as he could.

It smashed, sizzled and then exploded in foul-smelling thin grey smoke that leapt up instantly and burnt the eyes, making them run and tickling the throat. Lyle felt something brush his arm and pushed hard against it. He heard a little, unpleasant sound like the snipping of scissors slicing rashers of bacon into pieces, and a sigh that seemed to go on for ever. Tate was barking, but if he was doing that, he couldn't be biting. Lyle staggered out of the cloud of smoke, coughing and heaving. Windows were opening, voices were shouting, children were appearing at the mouths of alleys to stare, people were emerging from doorways. Lyle flapped ineptly at the smoke with his hat as Tate limped out of it, and slowly, deadened by the still-falling rain, it drifted away. He looked down at the ground. Blood was slowly pooling. Mrs McVicar lay, breathing heavily, legs twisted under her, head to one side, the carving knife bloody at her side. Blood seeped through her bodice, diluted by the rain. He heard someone start to shout, but it was a long way off. Everyone else just watched in silence. For a second he stood in dumbfounded horror, trying to comprehend what he'd just seen, before instinct once again took over. He rushed over to Mrs McVicar's side, kicking the carving knife away with the toe of his boot, kneeling down at her side and tearing at her clothes while shouting, 'Someone get a doctor!'

A child ran off, but whether to find help or not, he didn't know. In the silence broken only by the drumming rain, the crowd of onlookers edged tighter around the body. 'Someone get a doctor *now*!' he yelled. He tore away at the bodice and saw the long, deep slice in her side. 'Oh God,' he whispered under his breath. Her eyes flickered open and slowly focused on him.

'Who . . .' she began weakly.

Lyle grabbed a wet sheet from the stone trough by the pump and started tearing through the flimsy fabric, while everyone stood and watched. 'Help me!' he snapped at the nearest person, who came forward uncertainly to take a handful of sheet. 'Hold it against the cut, hard,' snapped Lyle, digging through his pockets furiously.

'Who . . .' began Mrs McVicar again, trying to raise herself and see his face clearly.

'Horatio Lyle,' he whispered. 'It's all right.'

'Lyle?' There was understanding there now, a recognition and warmth he hadn't heard before. She reached up with a bloody hand and tried to grab his. He held her hand tightly, feeling the weak pulse underneath it. Trying to move nearer to him, and in a voice that was almost drowned out by the rain, she whispered, '*Don't look at the eyes.*' Then she smiled. And gently lay back, and let go of his hand.

The only noise left was of the falling rain. The man holding the bloody sheets glanced up at Lyle with a question in his eyes, and Lyle looked away. He stood up slowly. He turned to search for Tate, saw him cowering, sodden and cold, in a corner, walked over to him, squatted down, wrapped the freezing, wet dog in his coat, and carried him to the nearest hansom cab without saying a word.

CHAPTER 9

Stone

'You all right, Mister Lyle? You look all pale an' all.'

'I'm fine, thank you, Teresa. Come in out of the rain.'

He closed the door quickly behind Tess as she slouched into the quiet house. Taking her coat, he hung it up next to his own sodden garment, so that the two could drip together, and led her quickly into the sitting room, where a fire was blazing and Tate was lying in a warm basket, snoozing happily. A half-eaten plate of bread and cold meat lay on the table next to a large padded armchair, which was grooved and worn in a shape that exactly matched Lyle's dimensions. Into this Lyle flopped without a word, not looking directly at Tess, but staring into the fire. She had a feeling he'd been doing that most of the afternoon. At his feet was a pile of the day's newspapers, crumpled by intensive reading and careless discarding.

'Good . . . dog walk, Mister Lyle?' she hazarded.

'I found out where our elusive follower is staying.'

'An'?'

'He's staying with five other Chinese gentlemen in a mews off Hyde Park. His neighbour said they'd moved in there about three months ago.'

'Ain't that a bit odd?'

'Yes, a bit.'

She shifted uneasily. She wasn't used to his intense silence. 'An' anything else happen?'

'I read the newspapers.'

Tess brightened at this. 'Well, that don't sound so bad!'

'They've found Carwell's brother, Jack. He was thrown up by the tide a few hundred yards further down the river, after we'd gone. According to the reports, his throat had been cut, with some sort of hunting knife.' Lyle's voice sounded tired and empty. 'The Carwells always worked together. It's no surprise.' And, almost inaudible, '*Such a waste.*'

Tess felt obliged to say something but couldn't think what. 'Oh. But nothin' *else* happen, right? Only 'cos it seems to me how you got this way of sorta gettin' into trouble when I ain't here to make sure that you don't do nothin' silly an'—'

'A lady attacked me with a carving knife. Without provocation. In mysterious circumstances.'

Tess shuffled uneasily. 'Oh,' she repeated finally, when the silence dragged too long. 'Well, you ain't seemin' too dead, so it can't have been *that* nasty.'

Lyle looked up, and seemed to see her properly for the first time. He tried to smile, and said in a softer voice, 'I have never seen anyone act the way she behaved. Mrs McVicar, I mean. It was as if she'd been hypnotized, conditioned to think a certain way by someone who came before me. Conditioned not to talk about Bray, conditioned to attack anyone who asked about Bray. "Don't look at the eyes." I don't believe that hypnotism can induce any effect which cannot be undone again, Teresa, but there was something in what I saw that I cannot explain.'

'Perhaps it were . . .' she shrugged, 'magic, Mister Lyle?'

'That's really very unhelpful.'

'Sorry, Mister Lyle.'

Silence again, uncomfortable and heavy. Suddenly Lyle let out a long breath, looked up briskly, forced a smile on to his face and said in an authoritative voice, 'So, Teresa, what have you discovered?'

Sitting by the fire in the kitchen, Tess ate a hastily prepared sandwich with one hand, drank a thick cup of soup with the other, and talked through the crumbs while Lyle watched with a slightly pained expression.

'I went to Covent Garden first, 'cos I thought how they'd know there where this fruit thing come from, bein' a . . . a . . .'

'Lychee.'

'An' all. And I met this man there what said it come from China an' the best place to ask were down at Clerkenwell where the East India Company had their offices. So I went down to Clerkenwell an' there was this man what said "Hello." An' I said

"Hello" an' he said, "What do you want?", only I think it was slightly different, 'cos I . . .'

'Teresa?'

'Yes?'

'Did you find out who sold the fruit?'

She glowered. 'You got no patience, have you, Mister Lyle? I'd listen if *you* were tellin' a good story.'

'No, you wouldn't!'

'Well, I'd *pretend* to listen.'

He sighed. 'More soup?'

She looked at her half-full cup. 'Yes.'

He poured slowly. She crammed another mouthful of bread into her mouth and washed it down quickly. Cheeks bulging, a mumble came out that might have been, 'It's this fella called Granter.'

'Granter?'

'Uh-huh. Mr Granter.'

'He sells lychees.'

'Well, he's the company's repres . . . man what goes around to the houses of all the bigwigs and tries to get their money for way more than it's really worth and probably gets away with it too, 'cos all the bigwigs are just slow when it comes to business an' . . .'

'Where is Mr Granter?'

'He lodges at . . .' she frowned, ransacking her memory, 'the Angel Inn.'

'I know it.'

'Right. *An'*, 'cos I'm extra nice and really underpaid and really underappreciated an' oughta get a medal an' all, I found out who boils oranges.'

'Lots of people boil oranges before they sell them, Teresa.'

She rolled her eyes. 'I *know*, Mister Lyle. But if you'll let me just speak without all this interruption an' all, I'd tell you that there was this man near the meat market in Smithfield, name of Josiah, an' everyone local knows he boils his wares before he goes on sellin', in order to get more money, but he only ever tries sellin' to the bigwigs.' She thought about this, then added righteously, 'On account of how they're slow.'

'Where does Josiah lodge?'

She eyed the loaf of bread on the centre of the table, and didn't say anything. Lyle sighed. 'Teresa . . .'

'Yes, Mister Lyle?'

'Have you so soon forgotten how I didn't hand you over to the bobbies?'

'I think of it always, Mister Lyle. You'd be right proud of how much I think of it.'

He sighed, leant over and started hacking at the loaf of bread. 'You'll get fat,' he warned.

'Then I guess I'll be less hungry when I go back to work.'

Sudden, embarrassed silence. Tess felt her ears starting to go pink. She slurped soup hastily. Lyle said, in a quick, low voice, 'Look, if you ever get yourself into . . .'

'Josiah,' she blurted, 'lives near the old furniture place round the hospital.'

'St Bartholomew's Hospital?'

'Uh-huh.'

'Right! So all we need to do now is . . .'

Upstairs, the doorbell jangled.

The figure standing on the doorstep was so swaddled in a

black cloak, beneath a hat several sizes too large and a huge beard, that it was hard to tell where one ended and the other began. He hissed in a voice hoarse with the effort of disguise, 'This is the residence of Mister Lyle?'

'Yes.'

'May I be admitted?'

Tess peered round Lyle at the figure and said, 'He looks horrid, Mister Lyle.'

Lyle frowned at the figure, then looked past him at the hansom cab waiting below and the rather chubby woman standing beside it with a nervous expression. He looked back to the figure at the door and said in a brisk voice, 'Thomas, why are you wearing a false beard?'

'Sir!' hissed Thomas desperately, his voice becoming slightly more normal, if shrill with dismay. 'I can't be seen here! My father will be furious! Please, let me in!'

Lyle rolled his eyes, but stepped to one side. Thomas scurried in. Lyle closed the door and Tess immediately reached up and plucked at the beard, dragging it from Thomas's face. She looked at it then at Thomas and started laughing. Thomas flushed red from the bottom of his neck to the tips of his ears.

'Thomas,' said Lyle, 'what are you doing here?'

'I sneaked out!' he declared gleefully, unwrapping himself from the huge cloak. 'My father thinks I've gone with my governess to visit my cousins!'

'Why?' demanded Tess, rolling her eyes in exasperation.

'Teresa,' said Lyle, in a warning voice. Then turning to Thomas, '*Why?*'

'I want to help!'

Tess realized she was holding the false beard, and tossed it on to a table in disgust. 'Well, that's very considerate of you, but I think we can . . .'

'I can help, I know I can! I know my father's handwriting, his signature, I know who his friends are, who might have received letters from him, how they could forge it. Look!' He dug into his cloak and pulled out a pile of letters. 'I took these! And I went to the Bank and said who I was and they *gave* me the letter used to deposit the sarcophagus in the vault! *And* I sneaked into my father's study and looked through his correspondence, and I found something!'

Tess put her hands on her hips. 'Do you really think that—'

But Lyle snatched the papers from Thomas's hands, eyes widening in delighted surprise. 'You stole these?'

Thomas flushed a brighter shade of purple-red. 'I do not *steal*. I think that as they are family property and I am the future Lord Elwick I have every right to . . .'

Lyle was already flicking through the thick sheaf of documents. 'Is this the one used at the Bank?' he asked, holding up a piece of paper.

'Yes.'

'Hm. Come on, children.'

He strode down the corridor into the sitting room, reached behind a bookcase, and pushed something that clicked. It wasn't the bookcase that swung outwards, which disappointed Tess immensely, but just a simple square of wall that blended seamlessly into itself. Lyle jogged down the spiral staircase behind it, and through another seamless wall into the furnace room where the pistons, pipes and coils of wire waited for use. He handed the dynamo with its little bulb over to Tess, who obediently spun the handle and watched light burn, while Lyle picked up a very long metal pole, taller than himself, twiddled a couple of handles so that a slow, pervading hissing sound filled the room, extended the metal pole towards a small niche in the furnace that looked specially designed to accommodate it, and flicked something. There was a whooshing sound. The furnace started burning with a dull orange light seeping through the few slits visible in the metal monster. The magnet in its coil of wire slowly started spinning, and as the electricity began to flow Lyle pulled another lever.

Lights went on in the room, bulbs exploding into almost unpleasantly bright fluorescence. Thomas gaped, his eyes wide with wonder and delight. Tess contrived to look bored.

In this radiance and clattering noise, Lyle picked up another pole and reached up to one of the three big bulbs, the size of a man's head and glowing red-hot, embedded in the ceiling. Behind it, he turned a curved mirror, like the reflector in a lighthouse, until the light was centred on one table. He repeated this for the other three bulbs, so that all the illumination was focused on one place. Into this spotlight of burning whiteness, he put the papers, and pulled out a magnifying glass.

For a long while there was silence, apart from the machinery grinding away, while Lyle examined each document with scrupulous slowness. Finally he tutted, put the glass down and said, 'If these letters are originals by your father . . .'

'They are,' said Thomas quickly.

'Well. That is . . . interesting.'

Thomas tilted his chin up proudly. 'Yes, sir. I thought as much, sir.' There was something he had to remember, he knew.

A voice he had to remember, or possibly forget. His fingers itched. He smelt . . . something like dead leaves on a forest floor . . .

Lyle was reading the letter. *To whom it may concern . . . the following item . . . deposited in my name . . . redeemable upon . . . vault V18E . . . not to be opened under any circumstances . . . yours faithfully, Thomas Henry Elwick, third Baron of that name.*

Lyle was starting to frown, rubbing the edge of the paper, turning it over, looking at its thickness, feeling its texture, scratching at the letterhead, then at the stamped seal on the bottom, then at the signature, his frown deepening each time. Thomas hardly noticed, trying to remember . . .

'Teresa, there's a pad of paper in the desk drawer there. Would you bring it over?'

She nodded, scurried to the desk, and opened the drawer. Inside was a series of metal tools that she didn't dare speculate on, a collection of pens and pencils, a pad of paper, a mousetrap, and several pieces of disassembled metal that collectively resembled a gun. She closed the drawer quickly and darted back with the paper. Lyle took it without looking up and murmured distantly, 'Thank you, Teresa.'

Through the thin paper, which had the rough, jagged-edged look of a home-made item, he then laboriously traced the signature written on the forged letter to the Bank. Tess and Thomas watched in silence, though Thomas kept on finding his eyes wandering to the giant furnace, which dominated half of the room, clattering away with a sound that made his heart race. He looked slowly back to Lyle. There was something he had to remember, something inside that said . . .

He felt inside his jacket, and was slightly surprised to feel something cold and metallic there. His fingers tightened round the smooth wooden handle. He stared at Lyle, busily scratching away at the desk, then at Tess, who was absently bent over, tickling Tate behind the ears. He took an uneven step towards Lyle, trying to remember, or perhaps not to remember, perhaps to forget, and . . .

Lyle looked up and said, sounding worried, 'This letter isn't a forgery.'

'It ain't?' said Tess, mild surprise entering her voice as she straightened up and moved towards the table to look.

'If it is a forgery, it's immaculate. The signature is identical, the seal, the paper, *everything* is perfect. This letter is either an impossibly good fake or the very real thing.'

Tess and Lyle looked slowly towards Thomas. His face was stone, his eyes were slightly unfocused. 'Thomas?' murmured Lyle.

Thomas's hand tightened over the object tucked inside his jacket. He saw . . . *green eyes* . . . he saw . . . he *saw* . . .

'What's wrong with him?' hissed Tess.

Thomas's hand started coming out of the jacket. Lyle pushed Tess to one side quickly and dug into his pockets. They were empty. 'Tess, take Tate and run!' he snapped as Thomas drew out the long, slim knife, sharp and clean. Tess looked from Thomas's empty expressionless face to Lyle's pale one, and didn't need to look again. She grabbed Tate by the scruff of the neck, dragged him towards the door and ran. Tate didn't need much convincing to follow.

Thomas's eyes slowly fixed on Lyle, who started edging away from the desk, towards a chest of drawers. 'Thomas . . .' he murmured, and then realized he didn't have anything to say. He shrugged helplessly. 'Forgive me for stating the obvious, but you're holding a knife.'

Thomas blinked once, twice. He whispered, 'He told me, Mister Lyle. He was so kind, so beautiful, how can you disobey a man of his mastery and power? You are not good, Mister Lyle. You and your family bring iron machines to think iron thoughts and make iron worlds. You look at a flower and see numbers in each petal, you look at the sky and see dust in each raindrop. He told me. He said he was strong, and I was weak. I wanted to cry that he could say so.'

Lyle groped at the chest of drawers behind him. 'Thomas,' he murmured, sliding open a drawer, 'you're not well. You're *ill*, in fact. Possibly drugged. Someone's been getting into your head. Just . . . put down the knife somewhere where no one's going to walk on it and we'll find you a doctor and a nice place to go quietly mad in, what d'you say?'

Thomas slowly drew the knife back into a better grip to kill with. Lyle grabbed something out of the drawer. It was a tube, lightly caked in baked white clay, but from inside which could be seen spiralling sheets of metal that never touched but between them formed the thick bulk of the tube's mass, before narrowing into two sharp, wiry ends which didn't touch, but protruded like antennae. Lyle said, 'Now, Thomas, there are two ways this can go. I might have managed to charge this properly on the static generator, in which case it'll be all right, or the science might be terribly, terribly wrong, in which case it'll be difficult to tidy up. So just before you go mad, tell me what you're seeing that's sending you like this.'

Thomas hesitated. He stared at Lyle, his mouth opening and closing slowly as he tried to think. The words that came were half-choked, forced out harshly. He hissed, *'Don't look at the eyes,'* and ran at Lyle.

Lyle let him come and, as he neared, ducked under the knife and stabbed up hard at Thomas with the wiry ends of the tube. There was a static sound, a smell of burning, and a shower of fat blue sparks as the charge stored in the metal and clay tube discharged, up through Thomas. Lyle heard a scream and tottered backwards, surprised to find himself still alive. The knife fell from Thomas's hand and he staggered back, falling to the ground, screaming endlessly, twitching from side to side and holding his head as if in intense pain, and still he screamed, a deafening, unnatural sound, so loud that Lyle had to clutch at his ears, curling away from it in pain, and still the howling went on as Thomas kicked and writhed blindly on the floor, before going limp, head on one side, hands loose and eyes shut.

Tess exploded from the end of the stairs, Tate in tow, as the silence settled. She held a poker and charged with the headlong determination of someone about to do something heroic. She saw Thomas lying on the floor, dropped the poker and squeaked, 'You *killed* him?' She didn't sound particularly offended – just surprised.

Lyle stared at the tube in his hand. 'It's never done *that* before.'

They put Thomas in Lyle's bed and watched him uneasily. 'What d'you do to him?' hissed Tess in a conspiratorial voice.

'Nothing. I allowed a little stored charge to discharge, that's all.'

'What does that mean?'

'I gave him a little electric shock.'

'I heard screamin'!'

'Yes. No one's ever started screaming when they get shocked before,' he said, frowning in worry. 'Confusion and unconsciousness, yes, maybe a tiny burn mark around the point of discharge, possibly, occasionally prolonged vomiting and nausea, sometimes heart attack for a little while – but never have I seen *anyone* roll around on the ground screaming after being hit by *that*.'

'Will he be back to a bigwig soon?'

'I'd be worried if he was back to being a black-market opium dealer with a criminal record soon.' He saw Tess's expression, and said in an embarrassed voice, 'He should wake up quickly. People get more shocked than actually scarred by electricity.'

'What happened?'

'He had a knife.'

She rolled her eyes. 'Apart from that, Mister Lyle.'

Lyle looked with real worry at the slumbering Thomas. 'It's as if someone is going round hypnotizing anybody who's come into contact with the case. I don't know how. It seems impossible to contrive. But he said the exact same words as Mrs McVicar: *don't look at the eyes.* Same words, different people, both connected with the case and the Fuyun Plate.'

'Oh.' Silence. 'Mister Lyle?'

'Yes?'

'You know you were 'orrid when I said the "magic" thing?'

'Teresa!' he snapped irritably.

She raised her hands. 'I'm just thinkin' about what the file thing said. The cultural signifi . . . ficance thing.'

He stared down at the slumbering Thomas. 'The Fuyun Plate was supposedly made for "Tseiqin", demon-angel creatures. Legend places its origin in ancient Tibet.'

'Is Tibet near here?'

Lyle rubbed the bridge of his nose wearily, eyes wrinkling closed to try and shut out distracting thoughts and fatigue. 'No, Teresa,' he said, sighing, but not unkindly. 'Tibet is a province of China.'

'An' it were a Chinaman what followed us, weren't it?'

'Yes. It was.'

'So?' She waited expectantly.

In a slightly surprised voice Lyle said, 'You know, you're right.'

'I *am*?' She sounded astonished and delighted.

'It's time we knew a little bit more about what we're looking for. I think I know who to ask, too.'

CHAPTER 10

Wakings

Evening in London, a bruised sky turned blue-orange near the
sunset.

Thomas woke in an alien bed, sat up, felt a stab of pain in his
side and lay down again quickly. A familiar voice at his side said,
'You're still not bein' stupid with knives, are you? Only Mister
Lyle weren't happy.'

He half-turned his head and Tess slowly came into focus.
'Where is this?'

She sighed. 'Stupid question.'

'What happened?'

'*Well*, first you were all helpful, in a bigwig way, and then you
got out this knife and decided to be all stupid and kill people,

139

which were just *bad*. And you weren't even very good at it, were you?'

'Where's . . . Mister Lyle?'

'Out,' she said sharply. 'But he says I'm to sock you if you do anythin' bad.' He realized Tess was holding the tube with the sharp wire antennae.

He sat up, carefully, taking his time. 'I won't hurt you.'

'Too right!' She frowned at him. 'Why'd you do it?'

'I don't remember. It was a dream. I saw green eyes, the most beautiful eyes I've . . .' He realized what he was saying and blushed. 'And a voice. It was beautiful in my mind. I couldn't argue with it.'

'You're mad!'

'It's all right!' he said hastily as she stood up. 'I'm feeling better now. It's gone. It's just like a dream. I didn't know it was there before, but when I looked at Lyle and saw him working, the eyes and the voice were just *everywhere*, just . . .'

She leant close towards him, and hissed in a conspiratorial voice, 'You want to know what I think?'

'What?' he whispered in the same hushed, dreadful voice.

'Do you believe in magic, bigwig?'

Horatio Lyle was waiting. He stood, fingers twined together, on a bridge that spanned the purple-black Regent's Canal, watching the dark water crawling towards the nearest lock. A barge passed underneath, laden with coal, black from its cargo. The lampman bumped his ladder across the bridge, pausing to light the lamp that hung on its support above and casting Lyle into a pool of yellow light that showed him to be the only person near the water. Lyle waited. After a while, he became aware of a black shadow standing a dozen or so yards away, keeping out of the light, watching him intensely. He smiled.

'It's you I'm waiting for,' he called.

The shadow slunk into deeper darkness.

Lyle waited. He didn't hear the footsteps behind him, though he had been concentrating for all he was worth, but nor did he jump when the man spoke at his shoulder. 'Mister Lyle.' There was a faint accent there, something foreign and mysterious. He didn't turn to face the man in the crooked top hat.

'You know my name. What's yours?'

'Feng Darin.'

'Very pleased to meet you, Mr Feng.'

'If you are here to confront me, Mister Lyle, you are wasting your time.'

'Why are you following me, Mr Feng?'

'You are looking for the Fuyun Plate.'

Lyle seemed surprised. 'That was easy.'

'In what way?'

'You just answered my question.'

'Why should I not tell you something you already know?'

Lyle smiled politely, and nodded. 'If I turn to look at you properly, will you be offended?'

'Yes.'

'Very well, then. Do you know where the Plate is?'

'If I knew that, why would I follow you?'

'What does the Plate do?'

'What legend says it does.'

'*How?*'

'How legend says it does.'

'Forgive me for scientific doubt, but that hardly seems plausible.'

He felt the shrug behind him. 'Be that as it may, it is the truth.'

'What is the significance of the eyes?'

'I do not know what you mean.'

'I've been attacked twice today, by people acting as if hypnotized. They mentioned eyes. Why did they attack me?'

'People will want to stop you getting the Plate.'

'Why?'

'It has power.'

'Oh yes, the cultural significance. Not to mention legend. Are you a Chinese spy, or is that really just a bit melodramatic?'

'I am . . . *was* . . . Tibetan.'

'Really?' Lyle brightened. 'Was?'

'I serve a cause within China, not Tibet.'

'That's rather interesting.'

'Why?'

'You're the first Chinese man I've met who serves a cause *within* China, rather than the Emperor. Will you stop me getting the Plate?'

'That depends entirely on what you are planning to do with it. If you swear to hand the Plate over to me on recovering it, then I will not stop you.'

'I can't swear that.'

'Then I cannot promise not to stop you.'

Lyle sighed. 'I thought you'd say that.'

Quietly, Feng asked, 'Can you find the Plate, Mister Lyle?'

'Perhaps.'

'It is of paramount importance that you find it before they do. If they can find it and restore it to its original form, they will be unstoppable.'

'They?'

'The Tseiqin.'

'Oh yes, I should have guessed. *Them,*' said Lyle in a dejected voice. 'You don't seriously expect me to believe any of this, do you?'

'You are an intelligent man, Mister Lyle. I hope you can believe whatever the truth happens to be.'

Lyle frowned. 'How do you mean, "restore" it?'

'The Plate was damaged a long time ago – deliberately – to prevent the Tseiqin from using it for their intents. Now the time has come when they can repair it, as the time has never been right before. They will repair it by the iron that they revile. It is vital that they do not achieve this. You must not let them. We will kill to stop this, as they will kill to achieve it. They are watching you, Mister Lyle.'

Lyle stared at the water, and ran his hands wearily through his hair. 'This is horse manure,' he muttered under his breath. Silence from behind. 'Mr Feng?' He turned and looked into darkness. Feng Darin was gone.

'Just let me try to understand this. You say you saw me working and suddenly your head was full of green eyes and beautiful voices and you couldn't resist their exhortations to murder.'

Thomas thought about it. 'Sir, I am so very sorry, I . . .'

'He were bewitched, Mister Lyle,' said Tess brightly. 'Just like that other one.'

'The other one?' said Thomas weakly, feeling his heart trying to jump out of his chest.

Lyle shot Tess a look. 'Why is it I seem to go through life meeting stranger and stranger people who either threaten menace or actually charge at me with carving knives? Who *are* these people who just happen to have carving knives stashed in every pocket and sleeve?'

'Mister Lyle, you carry chemicals and electric things and magnets an' all,' pointed out Tess in the best serious voice she could muster.

'That is beside the point.'

'Well, actually, it really ain't, 'cos . . .'

'Teresa!'

They lapsed into silence. Finally Lyle said, 'You're certain you're not feeling any murderous compulsions at the moment?'

'No, sir!'

'He might be rep . . . repress . . .'

'Repressing, Teresa.'

'Like he were when he come in!'

Lyle stared thoughtfully into Thomas's eyes, and Thomas met the gaze head on, standing up a little straighter and matching his stare with the full force of Elwick arrogance that he could muster, while inside his stomach churned and his elbows shook in his sleeves. At length Lyle said very quietly, 'All right, lad, say I believe you.'

'Lyle never believes no one,' whispered Tess helpfully into Thomas's ear.

'Teresa! You are not assisting the situation!'

'Just thought he deserved to know, Mister Lyle.'

Silence. Thomas swallowed, feeling it drag at his self-esteem. At last Lyle said, 'I don't know what's going on, but I don't like it and it's probably bad. You don't seem like the unstable kind, and nor did Mrs McVicar – and the fact that you both said the same thing is disturbing too. The letter that you brought from the Bank is written in your father's hand, on your father's paper, with your father's seal, and I'm willing to swear that it isn't a forgery. How is it possible that your father would deliberately choose to put into his vault a sarcophagus containing a thief?'

Thomas opened his mouth to speak, but Lyle quickly raised a hand. 'I know. It isn't possible, or at the very least isn't rational. But there have been a lot of people doing a lot of irrational things of late, and perhaps your father's inexplicable action is one of those irrational things. Still, there's a chance I might need you, lad, so I'm going to take the chance that what you say is true and that you're not really a murderer in the making. If, though, you are lying, and if you attempt to hurt Teresa or myself, I swear that a massive electric shock will be the least of your worries. Do you understand?'

'Yes, sir.'

'Good.' Lyle smiled, stood up in a single, brisk movement, clapped his hands together and said, 'Then let's go and do a little detecting, shall we?'

The evening had settled in for good, and now the only traces of light on the horizon were echoes of sunshine, and not the sunlight itself. The office was grand, all strange foreign wood, imposing portraits and, in one corner, a parrot that Tate growled at with unremitting hatred.

'Mister Lyle, your request is an unusual one.'

'Mr Granter, there are pressing circumstances.'

'What sort of "pressing circumstances", might one enquire, Mister Lyle?'

Lyle hesitated. 'Security of the realm.'

'Dependent on the sale of *lychees*?'

'Erm . . . yes.'

Mr Granter looked from Lyle to Tess and finally to Thomas. The last made him sigh and relent. 'Well . . . you are clearly a man of integrity.' Thomas almost preened. When Mr Granter spoke, his eyes had been on *him*. Lyle tried not to seethe, the smile locked on his face.

'You're too kind, Mr Granter.'

Behind the cattle-thronged, chicken-covered, pig-packed streets of Smithfield, paved with the inevitable consequence of pushing thousands of live animals in and out of the market every hour of the day, was a small tenement whose smell of ancient, mouldering fruit immediately identified it. 'That one,' said Tess, pointing a triumphant finger at the smallest, darkest, smelliest door, lit only by the lantern Thomas carried.

'Right,' said Lyle, striding up to it. He hammered a few times on the door, which opened a crack.

A suspicious eye regarded him and a gruff voice said, 'What d'you want?'

'Mr Josiah?'

'Who're you?'

'Special Constable Horatio Lyle.'

The door started closing quickly again, but Lyle had put his foot into it. From behind the flimsy wood, Mr Josiah snapped, 'I ain't got nothin' to do with your kind!'

'Mr Josiah, I'm not here about anything you might have done. I just need to know where you sell your oranges.'

'I ain't talkin' to you!'

Lyle sighed. 'Mr Josiah, I can get authority.'

'And he can pay!' piped Tess helpfully from behind him. The door opened an inch further. The eye returned.

'You *pay*?'

Lyle glared at Tess, but muttered grudgingly, 'I suppose I can offer a couple of shillings for the information.'

'What d'you want to know?'

'I need to know who you sell your tasty, fruity boiled oranges to, which streets and which clients.'

The door opened a little wider. 'Give me the money, an' you can come in.'

'Thank you.'

Half an hour later, Thomas realized he'd never been in London at this hour of night, not without a small army of servants to keep him safe, or unless he'd been to the theatre with his parents or his cousins or the girl from the estate in Hampshire he was supposed to marry. Though it was dark, he had to admit it was, in a strangely haunting way, almost attractively so. Each light seemed brighter and more vibrant for the thick dark surrounding it.

'There'll be fog tonight,' muttered Tess, as the three of them huddled together under the lamps of Smithfield. Lyle didn't answer, but Thomas immediately looked round at the streets leading into the market, searching for an oncoming tide of grey-ness up the narrow passages.

Lyle had a map unfolded and was tracing a route along one of its anonymous black and white streets. 'Primrose Hill?'

Thomas glanced at the sheet of paper Mr Granter had given them. 'Erm . . . no, sir, no clients on Primrose Hill, but there is a Mr Wedderburn on Oppidans Road, sir.'

'No. Josiah doesn't sell to anyone on Oppidans Road. His route skirts the top of Primrose Hill, then up along Fellows Road where he sells to the big estates, and then north all the way up to Lord Crispin's Manor below Parliament Hill, and Kenwood where he's got an . . . *understanding* with the parlour maid.'

Tess nodded appreciatively. 'Some prime slow'uns up that way, Mister Lyle.'

Thomas stared at her with an appalled expression. 'Forgive me, miss,' he finally managed to stutter, 'I don't think I am aware of your . . . disposition.'

Tess stared at him with an intense frown. 'What you do for money,' translated Lyle helpfully.

A grin of delight and revelation split across her face. "Course! I pinch bigwigs' purses.'

Thomas stood in frozen astonishment for a second, then started to laugh, a slightly uneasy laugh made unnaturally loud by its falseness. Tess stared at Lyle again, with another questioning look. 'He thinks you're telling a joke, Teresa,' he translated kindly, not glancing up from the map.

Tess grinned uncomfortably at Thomas. 'Oh. Yes. 'Course.'

'Does Mr Granter go anywhere near Belsize Park?' asked Lyle suddenly, finger still hovering over the map.

Thomas hastily looked down at the map, assuming a serious expression again. 'Erm . . . yes, sir. He has four clients there – Mr Shull, Countess Ascham, Lord Chetwynd and . . . oh.'

'Oh?' said Tess quickly, looking up with alert eyes.

'Same question,' said Lyle uneasily.

'Lord Moncorvo.'

'Who?'

'Same question.'

'He . . . he's a friend of my father's. He . . .' *Don't look at the eyes, boy . . . and how much does Horatio Lyle know, boy?* 'He . . .'

'Mister Lyle?' Tess hissed, as a glassy expression slowly crossed Thomas's face. She edged uneasily behind Lyle as he knelt down in front of the stricken boy and waved his hand slowly up and down in front of Thomas's glazed eyes.

'Thomas?'

Boy, perhaps it is time we discussed Horatio Lyle in more detail . . .

'Thomas, you're not carrying another knife, are you?'

What do you want me to do, sir?

Go to him. And when you are there, kill him, boy.

Yes, sir.

You are weak, boy. But I like you. You have a dream in you yet, boy.

Yes, sir. Thank you, sir.

'Thomas!'

Thomas jerked slightly, stared at Lyle and began to back away. He put one hand in his mouth and said through it, 'Mnn!'

'Thomas, use language!'

'I . . . he came to the house and . . .'

*You won't remember me, will you? I'm a dream, boy, a memory
of a better time when the skies were clear and the trees grew straight
for the sun. You won't remember me. You'll dream of my shadow,
boy.*

'Who came?'

'Moncorvo! He was *there*, but I'd forgotten and . . . mnn . . .'

'Eatin' your hand probably ain't helpin', bigwig,' said Tess
kindly.

'Teresa! Now is *not* the time!' Lyle wrapped his hands round
Thomas's upper arms and shook him gently. 'Listen, just tell me
what Moncorvo said, tell me what happened.'

'He . . .'

'Thomas Edward Elwick, pull yourself together!' he barked
suddenly, sharply.

Thomas snapped automatically to attention. 'Sorry, sir,' he
muttered.

'That's better. What did Moncorvo say?'

'He said, sir, that you were evil, bad . . . that you had a heart
made of iron and blood of iron and that you'd make the world
a machine, sir.'

'That ain't true, is it?' asked Tess in a little, worried voice.

'Think of it as a metaphor, Teresa,' muttered Lyle distractedly, still staring into Thomas's eyes.

'Oh well, if it's a *metaphor*.'

'What else did Moncorvo say, after the evil-aspect was fully
covered?' sighed Lyle impatiently.

'He said . . .' Thomas gulped.

'Thomas, you've run at me with a knife already. Nothing you
say or do might surprise me.'

Thomas's voice was barely above a whisper. 'He said that I should kill you, sir.' Almost immediately he barked, 'But I'm sure, sir, that it's not important now, because I would never, sir, I . . .'

Lyle stood up quickly, without a word. Thomas felt himself starting to burn red again. He opened his mouth to speak, but Lyle got there first. 'Lad, have you ever been hypnotized?'

'No, sir.'

Lyle didn't immediately answer again.

'Sir, I'd never . . .'

'I know, lad. I'm thinking.' Silence. Tess shifted nervously. At her feet, Tate yawned. Finally Lyle shook his head and said, 'I'm out of my depth here.'

'Your fault for takin' the case, Mister Lyle.'

'Teresa, if you say one more unhelpful thing I swear I'll take you straight back to Mr Josiah and offer you as an alternative to the house packhorse!'

Tess wisely closed her mouth, and pouted instead. Thomas hung his head.

Lyle tried not to chew his nails. Finally, he shook his head and muttered, 'There's nothing for it now. We're going to have to go and take a look at Moncorvo's house.'

Thomas paled. A sudden abject terror curled up in his stomach, but he fought it down, telling himself that it was nothing; madness, nothing more. Tess looked thoughtfully up at the sky, then down at the ground. 'Can I say something helpful, Mister Lyle?'

'Try.'

'Do you think seein' that Moncorvo will make us happy?'

'That wasn't helpful, Teresa.'

'But it were an improvement, right?'

He sighed. 'I'll find a cab.'

CHAPTER 11

Encounter

The Moncorvo mansion was part of a new terrace of grand white houses, each one no longer than London Bridge and no higher than All Saints' Church. Lights flooded out of each high window, and the front was busy with carriages. The hansom cab containing three humans and a dog stopped fifty yards away from the front door, which led out on to a green area of pond-dotted grass, across a sparkling new cobbled street, as white and polished and grand as the mansions themselves. The door to the mansion was open, and in and out of it glided ladies in dresses that trailed along in a rustle of silk, men who swept their hats off with the same grandeur with which they swung their canes, liveried servants with impassive expressions, expectant drivers and porters bearing lighted candles.

Lyle, Tess, Thomas and Tate watched this from the window of the carriage. 'A party?' suggested Tess, sounding none too pleased at the thought.

'Perhaps.'

They sat in silence while the night wore on. Somewhere down the hill, an old stone church, lost in a world of urban expansion, struck ten. On the floor of the cab, Tate started snoring quietly. After a while, Thomas realized Tess's head was hanging against one side of the carriage, her mouth slightly open and eyes shut. He looked up at Lyle, and found the man's eyes fixed on his, a slight, almost fond smile around his mouth. Lyle struggled out of his own large grey coat, and Thomas noticed how the pockets bulged and how the inside had its own pockets and was cut just as the outside, but in black, not grey. Lyle laid the coat over Tess's sleeping shape, then sat back against the seat of the carriage and watched the street, still in silence.

The clock down the hill struck quarter past. Thomas said, 'Sir?'

'Yes?'

'May I ask a question?'

'Of course.'

'Why did you decide to become a policeman?'

Lyle glanced at him, saw his sincere expression, and looked slowly back towards the lights of the Moncorvo mansion. 'I needed a job.'

'The Lyle estate has plenty of money, sir. Your father built machines. *You* built machines. I went to one of your lectures. I didn't understand much, sir, but when you talked about what might happen, about how machines might change the world, I understood that. No more pain, you said, no more poverty.'

Lyle smiled wanly. 'I wouldn't take it too seriously, lad.'

'I wish it were true, sir. Do you think it can happen?'

'Possibly. There is a mathematics in the universe, a symmetry in everything on the planet, that leads me to believe machines, tools and devices, are just an extension of nature.'

'Then why a policeman, sir?'

'Perhaps to see if there was mathematics in people?'

'Is there, sir?'

'No.' He frowned at his own words. 'Sometimes. You can say that a wrong plus a wrong will make an even greater wrong, but that's really far too simple. A certain kind of wrong, plus another wrong, can make a wrong. Two "x"s added together makes two x. An "x" and a "y" added together make nothing satisfactorily singular that I can see.' Thomas nodded to himself, and didn't speak. Lyle shot him another sideways look. 'You want to be a detective, lad?' It was hardly a question.

'I want to make a difference, sir.'

Lyle thought about this. 'Good. Good, I am glad to hear it.'

The clock struck half past ten. Tess and Tate slumbered on.

At ten forty, a carriage drove up in front of the Moncorvo mansion. It was pulled by two large dark brown horses, immaculately kept, and driven by a man in a black cloak trimmed with red silk. Lyle sat up slowly and nudged Thomas. The driver finished eating something, and tossed the remainder over his shoulder. It was an apple core. It bounced across the pavement and landed just below the cab. Lyle slowly opened the door and climbed out, crouching in the shadows. He picked up the apple core, patted his sides for the pockets that weren't there, and held it up to the lamplight shining dimly from the gas flame above. Very faintly he saw the tooth marks embedded in the core, sharp and small, like a fish's. He turned to the cab and saw Thomas half-clinging to the doorframe, staring glumly across the street. He looked back to the door of the house. A man and a woman were drifting out in stately pomp. In the dim light all he could see were the green eyes in the almost white faces, and they were *beautiful*. He had never seen anything that expressed so much under-standing, emotion and radiance. He knew that he would trust these eyes no matter what, and that they would repay his trust.

Somewhere, though, something inside said, *But how can you see them in this light?*

'Is that Moncorvo?' he asked Thomas quietly. The boy nodded wordlessly. Lyle turned to the cabby shivering in the cold darkness, grabbing the door open as he moved and snapped, 'Follow that coach.'

The cabby stared at him. 'You trying to be funny, mister?'

Lyle rolled his eyes. 'Look, I can tell you I'm a policeman and be officious, or I can give you another shilling and tell you to follow that coach.'

The cabby frowned. Then he grinned, shrugged and said, 'I'll take the shillin', thanks, mister.'

They followed through dark London streets, and Thomas heard the clock twice as they rattled on, along endless anony-mous ways, bouncing over pot-holed cobbles until, abruptly, the roads were a little *less* pot-holed and, outside the carriage, yellow gaslight began to wash out of increasingly large windows.

And suddenly they were there, and the jerk of the coach coming to a halt made Tess stir in her sleep, open a droopy eye, peer out at the darkness and mutter, 'Are we there yet?'

Thomas looked out of the coach window. 'Oh, my.'

Lyle shot him a look. The couple from the coach they had followed were climbing a flight of white steps up to a pair of large black doors, which were opened ahead of them. 'You know this place?'

'The Norfolk Club,' announced Thomas as they stood at the bottom of the stairs that led up to a building sitting in full Gothic majesty behind St James's Square. 'My father's a member, and his father before him. All gentlemen of repute are.'

'What kind of repute?' asked Lyle with a raised eyebrow that received nothing but blank stares. 'Never mind,' he muttered under his breath. 'What do we need to know?'

'Erm . . . it's customary to leave your sword in a vase by the door with a daffodil motif.'

Tess and Lyle stared at him, dumbfounded. Even Tate started yapping pitifully. 'What?' said Tess.

'Your sword. It's part of a tradition stemming from the time of Richard the Second, when knights of the realm were requested by the Abbot of Westminster to—'

'Never mind!' repeated Lyle. 'Thomas, can you get us inside?'

'Well, membership *is* inherited and you *are* allowed two guests, and today is Thursday . . .'

'So?'

'Ladies' night.'

Tess beamed. 'I'm a lady?'

'I suppose I can get you in.' He grinned at this realization and said, more confidently, 'Yes! I definitely can!'

'Good. Teresa?'

'Mister Lyle?'

'I'll have my coat back now, if that's all right with you.'

The doorkeeper of the Norfolk Club was a man by the name of Cartiledge. As a youth, his heart had been romantic, his head had been poetic and his political affiliations had been conservative to an extreme. He hadn't planned on a life of holding the door open for the aristocracy, and years of bowing to nobility had given him a sense both of what Karl Marx had been on about, and of profound, world-weary depression. Nothing interesting happened at the Norfolk Club.

Until tonight.

The knock on the door echoed through the vast entrance hall of the club, but that was normal. He opened it. The handle was stiff, but that was normal too. He said, 'Yes, sir, may I assist you?'

The voice that answered was youthful and piping, with something that sounded almost like fear. It said at high speed, 'I doubt it, peasant, unless it is to take my hat – careful of the lining! – and assist the lady with her . . . and assist the gentleman with his coat! Come on, come on, you think I wish to wait all day here – I do have business, you know. Are you aware of how much each turning of the tide can affect my business prospects; no, you are not, I take it. Have you heard of me? Well, sign me in then – don't look like that, you can *write*, can't you? Elwick. The Honourable Edward Elwick. "C.K." Not

"C.H." Oh, you *do* know that, do you? Well, perhaps your employment is not such a drain on more deserving purses as I had previously expected. And guests. *That* column. Oh, you know that too, do you? A master of your trade, clearly. Lyle. L.Y.L.E. Mister H. Lyle Esquire. And the lady . . . uh . . .' For a second the boy turned white, and his voice faltered. Cartiledge saw the boy turn in desperation to the taller, older man standing behind him, wearing an expression of surprise bordering on mirth that hadn't left his face from the second the boy had started talking. Then the girl swept forward and said, in a voice spiky with precise consonants, 'Lady Teresa of . . . of Rome.'

Cartiledge stared from the boy, to the girl, to the man, to the guest book, and finally to the picture on the wall of a previous Duke of Norfolk, founder of the club, in the vain hope that His Grace might have some advice to offer. He looked back to the girl. 'Teresa Hatch,' she added helpfully.

The boy, hearing Cartiledge's silence, barked, 'Teresa *de la* Hatch from the French . . . uh . . . *hatcher*, to be very devout. Well, what are you waiting for, sign her in, sign her in, haven't you been taught it isn't polite to keep a lady waiting, let alone a guest of my family. Her ladyship will leave this country for Versailles with such an unhappy impression of English hospitality!'

'And the *pet*, sir?'

'Have you never seen a . . . bloodhound of the Saville-Sachs lineage? Dare you assume to speculate on the breeding of a creature whose left paw alone is worth more than your miserable little lifetime income?'

Cartiledge signed him in, and swore to go back to poetry writing as soon as possible.

Thus, Tate, Lyle, Tess and Thomas entered the Norfolk Club.

'You're shaking, lad.'

'Sorry, sir.'

'It's all right. Just sit down. Teresa, see if you can find Thomas a glass of water.'

'*How?*'

'Use your charm.'

'Is that permission to pinch anythin', Mister Lyle?'

'*No!* Just ask someone nicely.'

'That never works.'

'Teresa! *Go!*'

She scurried away. Lyle sat Thomas down on a low leather-padded bench between a collection of palm trees underneath a huge portrait of Lord Fashion, famously proud owner of the world's largest wig and patron of some of the world's worst plays, and said in a mildly awed voice, 'That was very impressive, back there, lad.'

'Thank you, sir.'

'Have you ever considered going into theatre?'

'My father would never permit it, sir.'

'Well, I was impressed.'

Lyle looked around the club, noticing how full the entrance hall was of exotic plants and trees that pressed into every space where a bust or portrait of some notable hadn't been crammed. Through a pair of black doors left ajar at the end of a corridor, he could hear the sound of polite conversation. The floors were white marble, the carpets were thick and red, and there was, indeed, by the door, a large vase decorated with daffodils and containing at least one, precariously propped, small sword. Lyle wondered whose it was. He said distractedly, 'If you could choose, lad, what would you do?'

Thomas stared at him, feeling his heart start to crawl into his throat. 'Sir?'

'If you weren't the next Lord Elwick, if you could be anything you chose, what would it be?'

He hesitated. 'I want to build a machine, sir.'

Lyle's eyes fixed on him. 'What kind of machine?' Thomas hesitated. 'Lad,' said Lyle with a sigh, 'in my coat pocket I'm carrying a magnet, a set of lock picks and several bottles of highly corrosive and occasionally toxic liquid, just on the offchance I need them. Nothing you say can surprise me.'

'I want to build a flying machine, sir.' He felt himself flush the second he said it.

'Based on the design of a bird, or on the design of a seed?'
'Sir?'

'Have you seen da Vinci's sketches working on the principle of forcing air downwards to create a lower area of pressure above the craft than below?'

'Yes, sir, but I didn't think it was feasible.'

'Why not?'

He took a deep breath. 'The speed at which air was forced down would have to generate a mass hugely greater than that of the craft, sir.'

Lyle looked very surprised, and even more pleased. He opened his mouth to speak, but Tess reappeared, carrying a very large glass jug of water with both arms wrapped around the thing as though it was a child, and she was fearful of dropping it. She put the jug down on the floor next to Thomas without even looking at him, and turned to Lyle. 'The kitchen is *incredible*, sir! If I'd known 'bout this place, I'd never 'ave tried to rob you. They've got way more interestin' things and probably more money and 'sides, they've got better taste than you, 'cos it's all glass and china and everythin', none of them horrid cheap iron things.'

'Thank you, Teresa.' Lyle stood up quickly, and Thomas felt as if something important had just happened. 'Now, Teresa, if you'd be so kind as to take Tate to the kitchens and see if you can find him something to eat, then I think it might be . . . erm . . . *safer* if you stay near the door and see if anyone we know leaves.'

'All right, Mister Lyle.'

'Thomas?'

'Yes, Mister Lyle?'

'I think you'd better come with me. I might need you to do a little distracting.'

Thomas's chest puffed up with pride, as he followed Lyle through the black doors.

Tess wandered through the Norfolk Club, and tried not to look. It wasn't that there weren't pretty and interesting things to see – there were. In fact, there were so many it was a struggle *not* to ogle; so many pretty and interesting things that were so fine and delicate and subtle that they'd just fit into her jacket pocket and then later, when the heat was off, they'd be just right for Mickey to pass on, at a consideration of cost, naturally, to people who'd really appreciate them and if anyone asked she'd point at how she'd been all signed in proper and it would be Mister Lyle's fault really and . . .

She hesitated. In that second of doubt, her eye fell on a small pair of matching porcelain swans guarding a lit candle in the corridor, and she felt her right hand jerk up instinctively and thought, Mister Lyle's fault really . . . and for almost the first time in her life, hesitated in the face of Interesting and Pretty things.

Because that's what they'd say. She'd do her weepy thing (which had been useful more than once) and they'd all say, as they always did, 'Bless the poor lass, she's clearly been neglected; it's that terrible Mister Lyle for not doing his duty' or something like that, and then there'd be embarrassment and arguments and someone else would get into trouble, because someone else always did and though she hadn't really cared before because, in truth, someone else hadn't ever cared about her, this time, the Someone Else was Mister Lyle. And that, for a reason she couldn't understand, mattered.

She wondered when that had happened.

'Excuse me, young lady.'

Tess jumped, hands going into her pockets. 'I weren't doin' nothin'!'

The man who peered down at her had one of those moustaches that made Tess instinctively want to reach for the razor, and the kind of eyes that reminded her of the young men in the street who whistled as the pretty lass selling penny ribbons wound her way past. But these eyes would just stare until they were gorged on the sight. It made her suddenly wish to be at the bottom of a very deep, dark hole, where no one would find her unless she wanted them to.

'I didn't say you were.'

'Oh.' This restored a little of Tess's confidence. 'Then what you doin' starin' then?' she snapped, invigorated by unease.

'You have the most miraculous hair. Quite the finest coiffure I have discerned in this abode.'

Tess snatched instinctively at her hair. 'It's mine!'

'Indubitably.'

The man's grin wasn't the kind of thing you looked at; it seemed to stretch all the way to his ears, making his face an uneven diamond shape, instead of a nice, comfortable oval, and she could *feel* the grin in her spine, an uneven, nervous thing. 'Who're you then?' she barked defensively, in the hope it would make the grin go away.

'You may call me Thomas.'

Tess's face screwed up unhappily. 'Bigwig ain't goin' to be happy 'bout that.'

'Why ever not?'

'He's called Thomas an' all, an' . . .' Tess hesitated. She wanted to say, And if I start calling you Thomas, I'll never be able to call *him* Thomas without thinking of slime and deep, black holes ever again . . .

'In that case, you may call me Mr Hardy, a gentleman out of Wessex.'

Tess squinted at him. There was a way he said 'gentleman', a strange way that made his voice almost squeaky, and that made every finely honed instinct she'd practised with the fraudsters, cons and tricksters of the East End jump up and down, pointing an accusing finger and screaming, 'You ain't, you ain't!' She managed what she hoped was a polite smile.

'What's your name?' he asked. He had the unnaturally soft, lilting voice of most adults confronted unexpectedly by children – the voice of someone who can't believe that he was never sophisticated and suave, and has consequently blanked the memory of youth in any form.

'I'm . . .' She hesitated. 'I'm Tess . . . Lady Teresa . . . of . . . of Derbyville!'

'Of what *mise-en-scène* is Derbyville?'

A small, nervous frown passed across Tess's face. 'Derbyville . . . don't exist, do it?'

'I must confess I am quite ignorant of its location.'

Tess thought about this. 'Well then, you ain't knowin' nothin', ain't you? And I never done nothin'!'

With this proud and happy declaration, Tess turned, swept the two porcelain swans off their stands, dropped them into her pocket with a defiant glare, turned and ran.

Mr Hardy watched her go and breathed a little sigh. 'Miraculous,' he whispered, half closing his eyes and contemplating the burgeoning of womanhood. 'Miraculous.'

The main hall of the Norfolk Club was a jungle. Potted plants dominated each table and chair and the central floor could only be found by navigating a maze of greenery. Ladies in luscious gowns and men in formal frock coats stood talking in low voices. Lyle followed the sound of a distant string quartet, while at his side Thomas nodded and smiled at people and commented out of the corner of his mouth. 'That's Lord Worthy talking to Mrs Forltay, a lady of . . .'

'A certain repute?' hazarded Lyle.

'Uh, and that's Count and Countess Langscheid, who fled to England following the uprisings in Bavaria in 'forty-eight, and liked it so much they bought Yorkshire.'

'What, all of it?'

'The less fashionable half only, sir.'

'My goodness.'

They stepped from a passageway of vibrant green, and looked out at a dance floor laid with wide, dark red boards. Here the crowds of people were thicker, intermingling with each other in a ritual of back-and-forth that was almost a dance in itself, while a thoroughly ignored string quartet played in a corner. Lyle looked around, and found himself staring into a pair of bright green eyes belonging to a lady. She wore a green ball gown the deep, rich colour of leaves in a summer dusk, and her face was diamond shaped. He put his hand on Thomas's shoulder and muttered in his ear, 'Who's *that?*'

Thomas squinted at the lady, and seemed to freeze up. Lyle nudged him harder, sensing something heavy dragging at the boy as he did, and muttered, 'Thomas!'

Thomas swallowed. 'Sorry, sir. That's Lady Lacebark, sir.'

'You know her?'

'She is an acquaintance of my father, sir. And of Lord Moncorvo.'

'Is that . . .'

'Yes, sir.'

Lyle stared at the man standing next to Lady Lacebark, in a way that made Thomas deeply uncomfortable at such unconscious rudeness. Lyle saw a man dressed in black silk, except, he noticed, for the white gloves, only slightly discoloured at the end of one finger with something that might have been blood. His eyes, like Lady Lacebark's, were a vibrant green, and he stood not only taller and slimmer than all other men in the room, but with an authority that Lyle had scarcely seen before. As if growing aware of Lyle's stare, Moncorvo half-turned and glanced across. For a second his green eyes fixed on Lyle's face. Lyle saw a slight jerk pass through the man's expression, in something that might have been surprise. Lyle turned quickly away, guiding the rapt Thomas. 'Come on, lad.'

He dragged Thomas into a corner, refusing to look back, and said, 'Are there private rooms here?'

'Sir?'

'Private rooms! For members to use, stay in, sleep in?'

'Erm . . . yes, sir.'

'Where are they?'

Thomas nodded at a small door on the other side of the hall. 'Through there, sir.'

'Right. I'm going to have a look. Meanwhile, *mingle*.'

'Mingle?'

'Yes. You're better at it than you think.'

'Yes, sir. Thank you, sir.'

Lyle patted him briskly on the shoulder, and darted away across the floor. Thomas stood alone for a second, and wondered what his father would say when he found out.

Lyle padded through the back corridors, looking at the name plates over the doors. Lord Such and Such, Lady Thing, Mr Someone Esquire; he found a doorplate engraved, on brass, *Lord Moncorvo*. He tried the smooth wooden handle. It was locked. He sighed and dug into his pockets, pulling out a bundle which he carefully unwrapped. Glancing left and right, from it he pulled out a set of lock picks. For a minute or so he struggled with the lock before something inside very quietly *clicked*. Lyle opened the door and slid into the room. It was dark, but pulling the dynamo out of his pocket and turning the handle with its low whine, he managed by the subdued glow it gave to locate a lantern. He struck a fat, smelly, smoky match off the sole of his shoe and lit it.

The room blossomed into dim radiance, shadows curling round the walls, and a dull yellow pool of light around the lantern more tiring on the eyes than darkness itself.

A tall window hung with huge red curtains overlooked the nearby outline of roofs and the treetops of St James's Square. At one end of the room a portrait of a man with intense green eyes and an unfriendly expression stared out at Lyle. One hand rested on a sword hilt, the other was wrapped in a suggestive way around a small blue-green Globe. Lyle ignored the portrait and rushed over to the desk beneath it, to try the drawers. Two opened up to reveal merely an empty pad of paper, a small pouch of tobacco and a little loose change. He resisted the urge to steal the money, although he was more inhibited by the thought of Tess's teasing than a moral compulsion. He reached a locked drawer and drew out the lock picks again, wiggling them against the simpler, well-oiled springs in its lock. The lock turned more easily, and he opened the drawer. In it was just one object, wrapped in light blue calico. Lyle opened it up on the desk. It was a knife with a long, slim blade made of lightly tarnished brass. He frowned, holding it up to the dim lamplight, and touched the edge of the blade. It was sharpened to the thickness of a light-ning strike and he thought about the neat slit running through Carwell's neck. There was a faint sound outside the room. Immediately he wrapped the knife up again, slipped it into his pocket, pushed the drawer shut, stood up.

'Why, Mister Lyle, who would have thought you'd be here?'

The voice was almost mocking. It was the voice silk would have had, could it speak. Lyle looked up into a pair of intense green eyes that seemed to fill the room despite the dinginess of the lantern light, and felt something churn in his stomach. He forced a smile on to his face. 'Forgive me, my lady, I seem to have got lost.'

Lady Lacebark carefully shut the door behind her, and stood between it and him. She smiled, tilting her head on one side. The lantern light fell on her hair, the colour of a setting sun, and made it glow. 'Horatio Lyle,' she said in a more powerful voice, and Lyle was surprised to hear his name. 'Are you being diffi-cult?'

He backed away as she moved towards him, and seeing this, she stopped. Her smile became almost cruel. 'Look at me, Horatio Lyle.'

He looked at her. He couldn't not.

'Do you know me?'

'You are Lady Lacebark, m'lady.'

'Do you know *what* I am?'

Lyle wasn't sure how to answer this question. He shrugged half-heartedly. 'I can hazard a guess.'

'I am a lady of great power, Horatio Lyle.'

'That was certainly going to be *one* of my guesses, m'lady.'

'Stand still!'

He stood still. He'd hardly noticed that he'd been backing away. She moved slowly towards him. Ten paces. Five, talking in a low, purring voice. 'Moncorvo wasn't pleased to see you here, Horatio.'

'Well, forgive me for saying so, but it probably reflects his disposition more than mine.'

'Where is the Plate, Horatio Lyle?'

The question took him completely offguard. 'What?'

'Don't try to fight it, Horatio,' she murmured, five paces, three, from him. 'You know we'll find Bray soon, you probably know where the Plate is, a man like you, a detective, who can live in all this iron, *breathe* all this iron, think in iron cogs clicking around iron wheels, you must know where it is now.' Almost next to him now. Lyle realized he had backed up against a wall, and that it wasn't going to bend to let him move. He wondered if he was going to die. He could see both of her hands, but in the dim lamplight, *and with those eyes*, he wasn't sure if that counted for anything. She was right in front of him. She reached up slowly towards his face, a long white hand. 'Give us the Plate, Horatio Lyle. You know you cannot refuse.'

Her fingers brushed his cheek and instantly froze. Her pale face, already standing out in the darkness, suddenly turned whiter, even faintly green. She hissed in a voice that had become filled with shards of glass, 'What is this?'

Lyle grabbed her hand, small in his own. She bent away from him, snatching it away and staggering back, no longer dignified. She stared at him in horror. 'You brought *iron* in here?'

Lyle felt the weight of the dynamo and its small iron magnet in his pocket. 'Iron is everywhere, ma'am,' he heard himself whisper.

She backed off another pace, clenching her hands into fists to stop them shaking. 'You're a fool, Lyle! You're just a weak human like the rest of them; you *cannot* hope to beat us! It is as futile as hoping to stop the river wearing away the stone, the sky passing overhead, the sea rolling into the land, the leaf from falling!' Her eyes narrowed in hatred, and Lyle remembered, *don't look at the eyes*. He thought of Carwell's slit throat, and at once became aware of each drop of blood passing through his own very exposed throat, and the likely use of the knife in his pocket.

Lady Lacebark took an uneven step towards him, fingers opening out like claws. Lyle fumbled through his pockets, brought out a tube, reached up to thumb the cork off and . . .

There was a knock at the door. Cartiledge peered in. He saw Lady Lacebark and he saw Lyle, and turned red. 'Forgive me, sir, ma'am . . . I was looking for her ladyship. There is a Mr Dew at the door to see you, my lady. Shall I admit him?'

Lady Lacebark shot Lyle a look of pure poison, pushed past Cartiledge and swept out of the room. Lyle sagged against the wall, relieved, but not entirely sure why. He saw Cartiledge staring at him.

'Once again, sir, I must apologize.'

To the man's surprise, Lyle strode forward, slipping the tube back into his pocket, and shook Cartiledge firmly by the hand. 'Sir, I owe you an eternal debt.' He turned and ran down the corridor, towards the main door.

*

Tess was waiting outside by the hansom cab in furious impatience as Lyle and Thomas emerged. 'Come on, come on, come on! They've already gone!'

'Which way?' snapped Lyle.

Tess indicated a carriage just disappearing round the corner. Then, to Lyle's dismay, she turned and pointed in the opposite direction, at a carriage hurtling eastwards.

'Which is which?'

'That one's got Moncorvo and Lacebark in it,' she said, pointing furiously at the carriage heading east, 'and *that* one's got this man what was wearin' all this black cloak and red lining and had really horrid teeth, all fish-like.'

'Driver, follow that carriage!'

'You sure? I mean, it's quite late and the lass might be wantin' to get her sleep.'

'What is it about people being so unhelpful – *follow that carriage*!'

The three of them and the dog bundled inside and the carriage trundled off westward, then north as all the while Tess babbled, 'I saw the lady and the lord go into the hall and they talked with this man there with horrid teeth, and I thought Ah-ha – what would you do if I weren't there to think these things, Mister Lyle? – an' I saw 'em go outside and the lord and the lady told the man with the teeth to "Come back with it or not come at all" an' they were the words an' all, an' I thought Ah-ha again, Mister Lyle, 'cos I'm really a lot more useful than your lack of paying me might suggest, an' . . .'

'Teresa! I will give you a whole sovereign to enjoy your proud achievement, so long as you don't enjoy it now!'

Tess, satisfied with this, sat back in the carriage, and looked smug.

'Are you all right, sir?' asked Thomas as they sped through the dark, empty streets.

Lyle pulled an object out of his pocket. It was the brass knife. 'This mean anything to either of you?'

Tess looked at Lyle with a frown. 'Oh yes, Mister Lyle, 'cos I can just look at things, I can, and know that this were the knife what killed the bigwig who hired the horse what ran from the house what caught fire where the lady kept the silver an' why it means you mustn't sit down heavy on a beetroot, Mister Lyle.'

'Thank you, Teresa.'

'No problem, Mister Lyle.'

'Thomas, do you have any insights to add to this staggering conclusion?'

'Sorry, sir. It's familiar but I don't know where I've seen it. I'm sorry that I can't help you. I hope you won't think that I . . .' He realized Tess and Lyle were staring at him.

On the floor the sleeping Tate rolled over, sticking a limp paw uselessly into the air, and snored. Lyle said finally, 'Listen. This is getting a little bit . . . irregular. I'm not sure whether you two shouldn't take the cab home.'

'Sir! Absolutely not!' said Thomas, sitting up straight.

Tess said, 'You got a sovereign on you, Mister Lyle?'

'Not on me, no.'

'Then I ain't leavin'.'

'It would be shameful,' continued Thomas, oblivious of Tess, 'to fail in our duties after this amount of work, and you may have need of us. I can assist you in gaining access and information; Teresa here can also help; and I feel that our duties as citizens of this great nation demand that we . . .'

'He's stayin' too,' said Tess helpfully.

'People are running around with sharpened knives!' snapped Lyle.

No one spoke. Tate snored. Thomas looked down at his shoes. At length Tess, fixing her eyes on Lyle, said in a very quiet voice, 'Then you'll need someone to watch your back, won't you, Mister Lyle?'

The carriage came to a stop.

CHAPTER 12

In a small street behind King's Cross, where the houses on either side of the road squatted like brown caterpillars waiting in vain to turn into butterflies, and where you could look along to see the black sky end before the houses did, at a late hour of this cold, foggy night, an observer might have noted a number of unusual things happen in the clammy darkness.

First, there was the creak of a shoe and someone said, 'Ow! He trod on my foot!'

'*Shush.*'

'You trod on my foot!'

'I'm really very sorry, I didn't mean to . . .'

'*Shush!*'

'Oh. Sorry.'

Then there was a shuffling noise. The sound of metal clinking.

'Are you sure we're in the right place?'

'This is where the carriage went.'

'What about the house?'

'Do you see any other houses with the lights still burning?'

'What's that sound?'

'That's Tate.'

'How can you tell, sir?'

'It's the low whimpering sound of self-pity indicative of someone standing on his ear.'

'Goodness, I am so sorry.'

'Thomas, perhaps you just ought to stand very still and . . . and keep a look out.'

'Yes. Yes, I'll do it!'

'Teresa, you come with me.'

A sound of mud squishing underfoot. A brief shadow darting across the light from a window.

'Teresa?'

'Yes, Mister Lyle?'

'Can you hear anything?'

'Hold on.'

'What *are* you doing?'

'Listenin'! Shush!'

A slightly taken aback 'Sorry.'

And from beyond the narrow yellow gap under a wooden door, another voice, shaking with terror. 'Who are you? What do you want? Look, if it's about Carwell I don't know where he is! He had the goods, find him!'

And then a new voice, dry and cruel. 'Mr Bray?'

'Who are you?'

'I am Mr Dew. You are a very difficult man to find, Mr Bray. Mrs McVicar paid with her mind to find you.'

'No. I don't know what you mean!'

'You have the Plate, Mr Bray. We know Carwell gave it to you. Did you know Carwell is now dead? And young Jack, who hid in the sarcophagus as his brother waited impatiently outside – he was the first to die. Did you know young Jack, Carwell's brother, Mr Bray?'

'No . . . I . . . oh God . . . look, I swear, I . . .'

'What is this? Why is there still iron on him?'

'It's his crucifix, Mr Dew. We are not proud of our weakness. Perhaps with gloves we might . . .'

'Cowards! Fools! You are afraid of a little iron? It isn't even the burning iron, the sickening iron, the magnetic iron, it's just a lump!'

'Yes, sir.'

A faint metallic click, the clatter of a footstep. Lyle looked up sharply and saw a shadow hastily retreating into the darkness on the other side of the street – but too late.

'What was that? Mr Leaf?'

The door opened. Behind it sat the man who had to be Bray, his round face vacant, mouth open, eyes staring at nothing, although he looked unharmed, just sitting passively, in a chair. Three men with bright green eyes stood around him, while behind him stood a fourth who could only be Mr Dew: teeth like a fish, eyes lit up like emeralds, bright red hair stuck straight up, as if he had been born shocked.

Caught in the light sprawling from the open doorway was Tess. She looked up into the surprised expressions of the men. 'Erm . . . hot cross bun?' she hazarded.

And as two of the men drew long brass knives and Mr Dew reached into a nearby drawer, Lyle rose up behind Tess like an avenging angel, grabbed her by the collar, dragged her back from the door and threw a glass tube into the room. It smashed on the floor, then exploded.

Thick black smoke billowed out of the doorway, but the flash powder also went off with a dozen little bangs a second as it hissed and crackled, spitting fat white sparks. Thomas ran towards the door as he heard Tate start to bark and people shouting, and wished he had a weapon. He saw, through the dim light, Tate growl at some unseen shadow and lunge through the door, leaping up gracelessly and pulling back his lips to reveal a lot of white canine teeth. He saw Tess rubbing at her eyes, gasping for breath, and Lyle grab something small and spherical out of his pocket which he crunched between his fingers and lobbed into the smoke, and which immediately started to burn with an intense white light. More shouts from inside, then a man hurtled out of the room, and in the dim light Thomas saw that he had a knife.

The man threw himself at Lyle, who jumped back clumsily, grabbing without any particular skill for the knife wrist, and falling back as the man kicked out at his ankles. Thomas saw Lyle stagger and lose his balance, slipping in the damp mud and falling painfully, the man on top of him. He saw Lyle's grip on the man's wrist falter and then a furious Tess leapt from the smoke and the fog and threw herself on to the man's back, wrapping her hands around his neck and clinging to him. He heard a scream – Tess had bitten the man's ear. He heard another scream – Lyle was holding something small, square and rectangular against the side of the man's face. As Thomas got near enough to see, he realized it was the magnet from Lyle's dynamo. As it touched the man's skin, he screamed and writhed, throwing Tess off and falling to one side, clawing at his face.

As the last of the sparks died, Thomas reached the front of the house – mere seconds had passed. Tess kicked the man lying on the ground, though he didn't seem to notice, while Thomas helped drag Lyle back up to his feet. Lyle shoved the magnet at him, said, 'Take this, and don't let it go!' and drew out of his pocket a pair of test tubes that he held with more diffidence than he had held the others. He hurled one down into the doorway and waved at Tess and Thomas to back away. Tate, smelling the ammonia as it sloshed over the battered stones, whimpered and galloped in the opposite direction. Lyle held the other test tube, ready to throw, and called out to the now dark and silent house, 'Come on out!' Silence. He took a breath, swallowed and called feebly, 'It's the police! You're definitely surrounded!' Silence. 'Don't make us come in there!'

'Please,' added Tess under her breath.

A shadow moved against the dark. Lyle saw the gleam of fish-like teeth. 'Why, Mister Lyle.'

He saw the crossbow swing up, the brass tip on the brass arrow gleaming dully, and threw the test tube at the feet of Mr

Dew. It smashed, the liquid inside met with the ammonia nitrate spilt across the cobbles, and this time the explosion ripped up the damp mud and shattered the wood of the half-open door. In the smoke and the confusion that followed, Thomas charged screaming at the man. He didn't really know why he did it, and later, when he thought about it, was the first to admit it was probably a bad idea; but his hands struck the man full in the chest, and the magnet he held hit him too, and to his surprise Mr Dew staggered back clutching at his chest and calling out in pain. Thomas felt his heart race and bunched his fingers into a fist around the magnet, and swung it for all he was worth at Mr Dew's face. His fingers hurt like hell, and he wondered if he'd broken something, but to his delight and amazement, Mr Dew staggered back, and looked at *him* with fear in *his* eyes.

Outside, Tess hopped from foot to foot impatiently. 'What do we do?'

Lyle peered into the darkness of the house. 'Oh, Christ,' he muttered, and barrelled inside. He saw Thomas swing another punch at Mr Dew, then felt a hand land on his collar and some-one, or something, rise up behind him, and grabbed the knife an inch from his throat. 'Teresa!'

Tess looked around through the smoke and rubble, saw a loose plank of splintered wood, blasted out of the door, grabbed it, turned and swung it for all she was worth at the man who held Lyle. She hit him across the shoulders and saw him stagger, pushing Lyle in front of him against the still shape of Bray. She thought, Hold on, hold on . . .

Then Mr Dew had pushed past Thomas and was running away into the darkness, and his colleague was taking his cue and following him, racing down the dark street as fast as he could. Thomas charged out after him screaming, 'That'll show you! You won't ever mess with England again, will you, because we'll always be here you . . . you . . . you infidels!'

Lyle followed Thomas into the street at a more demure pace, and put a comforting hand on his shoulder. His own face was grimy and, like Thomas's, sheened with sweat. He patted Thomas gently on the shoulder and said in a surprisingly soft voice, 'All right, lad, I think that'll do.'

Tess walked up to join the three of them as they looked into the darkness and to catch her breath. Finally she managed to gasp, 'So . . . uh . . . we won, right?'

'Well . . .'

Behind Tess rose the third and final man. One side of his face was bruised red, black and purple in the shape of Lyle's magnet. His eyes were wild, his hands shaking and his expression one of pure hatred. He grabbed Thomas by the hair, dragged him into the street and laid a brass knife firmly across his throat. Lyle started after him instinctively, but the man tightened his grip and shouted in a harsh voice, 'You want the child alive? Keep back, keep the iron away!'

Lyle froze. So did Tess. The man grinned. 'Your iron will only shed blood, not save it, *Mister* Lyle. A child's blood on your hands.'

The knife pricked Thomas's throat. Lyle said in a soft tone, 'Thomas, when he goes forward, you go forward too, understand?'

And Thomas realized that Lyle wasn't actually looking at him, but at a shadow behind him.

He felt the first bullet enter the man behind him, jerk him forward, and he went forward too. He heard the second bullet more than felt it, but the third one he could feel as the man's chin jerked against the back of his neck. The retort died slowly away as the man toppled forward, and he toppled with him, worming out with each breath a trainload of puffing, each muscle shaking and wobbling, so that he felt as if there was a second skin under his skin which sensed what happened inside, as well as out. He crawled away, shaking and terrified, and Lyle was there, grabbing his shoulders, demanding, 'Lad! Lad, look at me, breathe, you're fine, you're fine, he's dead now, just look at me and breathe . . .'

He saw Tess standing by the wall, staring at the body with an expression of horrified fascination that twisted into something strange and miserable only at the very, very corner of her mouth. Then he glanced up and saw the shadow of a man wearing a crooked top hat, pistol still gleaming in his right hand, looking down at him. Then the man turned and ran in the opposite direction, where the fog and shadows quickly consumed him.

Through his chattering teeth, which he tried to silence but couldn't, he heard himself croak, 'Was . . . who . . . was . . .'

'Feng Darin,' said Lyle in a low comforting voice. 'Are you all right?'

'I . . . I . . .'

'Mister Lyle?'

It was Tess's voice, and there was something in it, a new and frightened edge, that immediately commanded attention. Lyle turned to look at Tess, then followed her gaze down to the body.

Then he reached slowly into his pocket and pulled out a fat match, striking it off his shoe again.

By the dull flame's light, he saw that the blood seeping slowly from the back of the dead man was thick and white.

Lyle looked at this, at Tess, and said nothing until suddenly the match was burning his fingers, when he jerked back to reality and threw it aside. In the silence, the only sound was of Tate barking frantically from inside the house.

'Bray,' he muttered, once, quickly, darting to his feet and running into the house.

It was dark, rubble was strewn across the floor and Tate was barking furiously somewhere in the shadows. Tess followed numbly and lit the lantern that he gave her. The light fell on Bray, sprawled across the floor, expression vacant. Lyle immediately knelt down by him and grabbed him under the shoulders, dragging his head up and into his lap. His hand, where it fell briefly on the back of Bray's neck, came away bloody. 'Jesus,' whispered Tess, her hand shaking. 'Oh God, oh Jesus . . .'

'Tess!' Lyle looked up at her, and there was pleading in his eyes. 'Please, it'll be over soon, *please*.'

She nodded once, sharply, biting her lip.

Lyle looked into Bray's face, heard his strained, choking breath, felt the weakness of his pulse. 'Bray,' he whispered softly. 'Bray, they've gone, you're going to be fine now.'

Bray's eyes flickered and focused vaguely on Lyle. 'Jack?' he whispered. 'You there?'

Lyle swallowed and, his voice only slightly shaking, whispered, 'I'm here, Bray. It's all right.'

'I'm dying, Jack. I'm dying, ain't I?'

'You . . .' Lyle swallowed again. 'Bray, where's the Fuyun Plate? Where did you hide it?'

'Jack? I . . . I didn't have time, you see? I . . . oh God . . . Mary Mother of Jesus, I was going to go to the priest, I was going to, just like you wanted, I swear I . . .'

'Bray? Did you tell them where the Plate was?'

His eyes fixed vaguely on Lyle, but his jaw tightened. 'No. I wouldn't tell them bastards, not for their . . . their tricks and their magics . . . I wouldn't tell them . . .'

'Bray, where is the Plate?'

His eyes started to close.

'Bray! Where *is* it? Where's the Fuyun Plate?'

His eyes flickered on the edge of shut. His voice was barely above a whisper, his skin sodden with sweat, white. The blood seeped on to Lyle's hands, his clothes, but he clung on still, desperately, knuckles as white as Bray's face. 'Bray, where is it?' he whispered. 'Jack's here now, it's all right, where's the Plate?'

'It's . . .'

'Jack's here, just tell Jack.'

Bray's eyes seemed to focus on Lyle for just one, brief second. He almost smiled. 'It's . . . in the hands of justice . . . Jack . . .' He let out a long breath that seemed to deflate every muscle made bigger by the holding of it. He didn't take another breath in again.

Tate stopped barking. Out in the street, windows were opening, doors were slamming, lights were starting to burn at the sound of the gunshots. Thomas leant against the door, grey, clinging to it as if for support. The metal of the lantern rattled as it jangled against itself in Tess's shaking hand. Lyle carefully laid Bray's head down and slumped back against the cold, ruined floor.

In the distance, a church struck the hour. In Covent Garden, the watercress man began to open up his stall by candlelight. On the highway through Archway, a tired messenger paused to water his horse at the trough. In the docks, a sailor called down from the rigging to his neighbour, who snored under a bottle of whisky. In the seas around Dover, the cabin boy snored, in the Channel south of Hastings the captain looked to the south and saw a storm rising off warmer waters. At the Lizard, where the sea lapped sleepily against grey rocks that had seen harder times, a traveller woke to look to the east.

The first light of dawn flecked the horizon, and slowly spread across the land, towards London.

CHAPTER 13

Awake

As dawn spread across London, someone was angry.

'He died before he could speak?'

'It wasn't meant, my lord, there was smoke and sparks and . . .'

'Bray is dead and we do not know where the Plate is?'

'No, my lord. But I am sure that Lyle cannot know either . . .'

'That is irrelevant! If he has it we can take it; if no one has it we cannot use it!'

'My lord, I am sorry, I—'

'Get out! *Get out!*'

*

And in a room too large for its occupants, someone else said, 'My lord? Lord Lincoln?'

'What is it?'

'I have been speaking to the Commissioner, sir. There was an incident last night in the King's Cross area.'

'Well?'

'Horatio Lyle was involved.'

'Has he found the Plate?'

'I do not know, sir. Sir, one of the bodies was Tseiqin. Lyle saw it. He examined it before he left. The other belonged to Bray.'

'Bray? The thief?'

'Yes, my lord.'

'Did Lyle say anything?'

'No, my lord.'

'Well. Well, perhaps it is for the best.'

'My lord?'

'If Lyle is to survive, he must know *how* to survive. The Tseiqin will not let him live after this.'

'Shall I summon him, my lord?'

'If you believe that he will come.'

'My lord, I do not know.'

'Then perhaps you had better find out.'

And as the bells tolled, calling the morning masses to prayer, and the factories whistled, to much the same effect, there was a knock on a door in Waterloo. It opened. A round-faced woman, grey hair loose around a pink face, looked down the short flight of steps to a hansom cab with a near-sleeping driver slumped at the front, a boy asleep in the back and Horatio Lyle holding a small sleeping, bedraggled and grimy girl in his arms, her hands wrapped round his neck. Lyle's face was dirty; blood clung to his clothes and hands.

'Horatio?' said the woman in surprise, not moving, not showing any sign of dismay or horror at the sight before her.

He stared up at her wretchedly. 'I need help.'

And as the washed sunlight spread in pale waves across the city, a door opened in a small mews behind Hyde Park, and closed again.

'Feng Darin, welcome home.'

'*Xiansheng.*'

'You were out longer than we expected.'

'Lyle found Bray. So did the Tseiqin.'

'Has he found the Plate?'

'I do not know. Perhaps. One of the Tseiqin is dead.'

'Then Lyle's life is not worth living.'

'I went to his house to warn him. He wasn't there.'

'Where is he?'

'I do not know. He has gone into hiding. Perhaps he is beginning to understand what he is facing.'

'Feng Darin, how did the Tseiqin die?'

Silence.

'Feng Darin!'

'I shot it. Fire and lead. I killed it. I destroyed it.'

'Do you believe that to have been wise?'

'He would have killed a child.'

'Would that child have found us the Plate? Perhaps fatigue is compromising your judgement, Feng Darin. Now we are all in danger.'

'*Xiansheng.*'

'Once again, it seems, we are waiting on Lyle for the next move.'

And the time passed. Tess woke, in another alien bed. The room was small, but the bed was comfortable and at the end of it she found, to her surprise, a small iron tub full of steaming water that seemed to be heated through some strange, foreign mechanism underneath, and a plate of neatly cooked meat and vegetables, left cold for her. A new, clean dress was lying on a chair in a corner.

Tess thought about it, about it all, sunlight over the scrubby houses of King's Cross, a hand burnt with iron, fires in the night, and made a decision.

For the first time in living memory, she had a bath. To her surprise, it was wonderful.

And the time passed, and Teresa Hatch, newly washed and scrubbed, found herself knocking politely on the door leading to a kitchen hung with herbs. A chubby woman wearing an apron, hands caked in flour, grey hair pinned back from her head, turned, and treated her to a broad grin under her sparkling grey eyes. 'You'd be Teresa, wouldn't you?'

'Yes, m'm.' Something about this lady instinctively made Tess want to be respectful. It was the same unplaceable something that always made Lyle a *Mister*.

'Are you still hungry? I have . . . oh, let's think . . . almost anything you want, really. Nothing too sweet – I don't think children should have too much sugar while they're still growing. Don't linger in the door, dear. I'm Milly,' she said, holding out a large hand. Tess shook it nervously, getting a light dusting of flour in the process.

'Tess. Is Mister Lyle . . .'

'Oh, Horatio dear is in the living room, in Father's old arm-chair, brooding. Just like a sulky boy, really. He gets very embarrassed when I ask him about it – says that I'll think he's gone potty.' She laughed, a deafening sound that made Tess both cringe and smile at the same time. In the same jovial tone she chatted on. 'I assume by the distribution of bloodstains across his jacket he held a man who'd been stabbed no more than an inch from a major blood vessel – probably in the neck, although it could quite easily be the thigh, but not the wrist, and I doubt if it would be the thigh, because then the man probably wouldn't be dead, which suggests somewhere near the jugular. Tea?'

'Erm . . . no, thank you.'

Milly put the kettle on the stove anyway, and continued. 'I'm also assuming by the way he was piecing back together that little dynamo of his that he had need of a magnetic field, which might explain the parallel-plate tube in his pocket. The fact that it had been discharged also suggests he was in a fight, and the mud-stains on the back of his coat – which are very difficult to shift, I might tell you, unless you soak it quickly before it dries – pos-sibly mean that he was involved in a very tight hand-to-hand fight somewhere no more than six miles north or south of the river, probably north by the colour and dirt in the soil, but cer-tainly not north of Alexandra Palace or south of the clay belt.

The faint smell of ammonia means he's been blowing things up, and the vial of white gooey liquid scraped up from a dirty street is something I've never seen in my entire life ever, and which probably isn't a natural compound.' She sighed. 'He does get so carried away.'

Tess stared up at Milly with her mouth open. 'Are you . . . are *you* . . .'

'Yes, dear,' said Milly nicely, patting Tess on the shoulder. 'I wouldn't think about it too much. It tends to upset people. Come on, dear. Let's see if he wants lunch.'

Lyle was indeed sitting in a very old padded armchair, feet up on a table, face covered with his travelling hat, a vial of white liquid sitting on the table in front of him, an anatomical dictionary lying discarded at his feet. Milly strode into the room on surprisingly silent feet, put a tray down on the table by his side, pulled the hat off his head and promptly hit him with it. 'Stop brooding, Horatio! Have you eaten any fish recently?'

He stared up at her with a wan, almost embarrassed expression, and started disentangling himself from the armchair. 'No, not . . .'

'Shellfish? I remember when Pa, rest his soul, ate that plate of oysters and the *mess* was just incredible. I never thought I'd ever find enough charcoal.'

'No, no shellfish either.'

'Hm.' She pursed her lips and peered at his face. 'You missed a bit.' Then to Tess's surprise and Lyle's too, she pulled out a handkerchief from her apron pocket, spat on it and started rubbing busily at an almost imperceptible dirty mark on Lyle's cheek. When she was satisfied she nodded once briskly and said, 'Right. Now stop brooding and eat your greens.'

'Actually, I . . .'

'Horatio, are you *arguing* with me?'

'No, I just—'

'Good.'

'Yes, m'm,' he muttered, picking up the tray with a muted expression. Tess gaped. It was something she was getting quite good at.

As Lyle ate dutifully, Milly picked up the test tube of white liquid and held it up to the light. 'What is it?' she asked finally.

'Blood,' said Lyle.

Milly sighed. 'Oh dear, you haven't been playing with that centrifuge of yours *again*, have you?'

'No, this leaked from a dead person in the ordinary way.'

'Poisoned? Prussic acid, perhaps, maybe with some kind of salt compound in it to react with the pigmentation?'

'Shot.'

'With anything special?'

'With a fairly standard bullet. Three fairly standard bullets.'

Milly's lips drew a little tighter. 'Is there something, dear, that you want to tell me?'

When Lyle didn't immediately answer, Tess bounded forward. 'I can tell, if he ain't goin' to!'

'Teresa . . .'

'Thank you, dear. That would be very helpful.'

Tess grinned smugly at Lyle, then turned and met Milly's kindly gaze and slightly too-pale smile. 'Well, see, first Mister Lyle got attacked by this mad lady what had a knife and were screaming, "Don't look at the eyes" – it were that, weren't it, Mister Lyle? Anyway, *then* he got attacked by the bigwig . . .'

'The bigwig?'

'Thomas,' sighed Tess impatiently. 'What also had a big knife. Mister Lyle, 'ave you ever considered gettin' a suit of armour, by the way? An' he also said this thing 'bout the eyes, and *then* – an' I thought this was really a bit silly of Mister Lyle, but you know what he's like, m'm, don't know what's good for 'im – anyway, he followed this man what's a Chinese man what had the gun what shot the man with the blood and the green eyes. Oh, an' there's this plate thing what's supposed to make these people called the Ts . . . Tse . . . anyway, these angel-demon people become all powerful and it's all really *magical* an' I *told* 'im, but would he *listen*? No, because he don't appreciate me, m'm, an' he owes me a whole *sovereign*.'

Silence. Milly turned slowly to Lyle. 'Do you really owe the lass a sovereign?'

'I might have agreed, in a moment of weakness . . .'

'I thought I told you not to get into debt!'

'Teresa has failed to mention how we met.'

Tess put her hands on her hips. 'What? I showed just how wonderfully good at my job I was, an' now you resent it?'

'You got *caught*, Teresa. I *caught* you.'

'Ah – but you had to admit I was good to get that far, right?'

Milly put her hands on her hips. Standing next to Tess, the two made a surprisingly intimidating pair of annoyed women. 'Horatio, are you paying a clearly highly qualified thief only a sovereign?' Tess grinned happily, and tried to stand up a little taller.

It was Lyle's turn to gape. 'You don't mean to say that you actually think I should *pay* someone who broke into *my own house*?'

'Dearest, you were not raised to be morally presumptuous. I think it might be wise if you tell me *everything*. From the beginning.'

Lyle told it from beginning to end. Halfway through Thomas came in, looking sleepy, and hearing Lyle speaking retreated into a chair without a word, without a look, and sat with his hands folded formally in his lap, and didn't move an inch, eyes fixed on nothing. Tess sat with her knees huddled up to her chin, and idly scratched behind Tate's ears.

Lyle started and Lyle finished.

Silence settled.

'"In the hands of justice"?' repeated Milly quietly. 'The Plate is in the hands of justice?'

'That's all he said.'

'Was that justice with a capital "J" or not?'

Lyle looked up quickly into Milly's grey eyes, the exact same shade of steel as his, and frowned briefly, eyes flickering away again as he thought. 'Oh, goodness . . .' he began.

There was a knock on the door.

Milly answered, looked at the man standing on the doorstep and said, 'Hm. By the manner in which your clothes are of a particularly fine cut, by the inkstains on your right hand, a ring bearing the royal seal on your left hand, the manner in which your shoes are worn down hard at the heel, though not the toe, the pair of reading glasses in your right-hand pocket and the series of slight abrasions on your jacket, indicative of frequently wearing medals, by the fact that you are *here*, I'm going to offer an inspired guess that you are Lord Lincoln.'

Lord Lincoln smiled thinly, leaning on his cane, and nodded just once. 'And by your syntax, appearance and insight, ma'am, would you be the lady of this house?'

'Yes.'

'And is Horatio Lyle in residence at the moment? I sent a messenger to his home, but he appeared to be absent.'

'I think he might be in residence for you, Lord Lincoln. And if he's not now, he will be by the time I've finished talking to him.'

'Mrs Lyle, you are a paragon of virtue.'

'My lord, you don't know the half of the matter.'

CHAPTER 14

Tseigin

Lord Lincoln asked to see Lyle alone. Lyle said not a word, and Milly, wife and widow of Harry Lyle, hurried the children out.

Lincoln pulled off a pair of silken gloves, folded them neatly across the top of his stiff silk hat, looked around for a chair, liked nothing he saw, and stood by the window instead, shoulder turned slightly towards the glass, so that he could watch the street without running the danger of being seen. Lyle stood as far from Lincoln as he politely could, and tried to think of polite things to say. He couldn't.

Lord Lincoln broke the silence. 'You are well, I trust?'

'As can be expected, considering.'

'You are very difficult to find when you don't want to be

found, Mister Lyle. I did not think you would come back here.'

'Yes, well, the happy hearth seemed to be calling.'

Lincoln smiled at the knife-edge in Lyle's voice. 'I suspect you have something you wish to say.'

'Nothing that can pass in polite society.'

'You wish to discuss the Plate?'

'The *Plate*.' Lyle almost spat the word. 'You lied to me, Lord Lincoln.'

'Indeed? How did I so?'

'By omitting the truth!'

'That is not a lie. That is merely a failure to achieve a satisfactory level of communication. It could happen to any man.'

'Tell me the truth! Tell me why I have got a vial of blood in my pocket that isn't human; why people with bright green eyes curse humanity and seem to be able to control minds; why people are *dead* for a stone bowl of "cultural significance"!'

'And if I do not tell you? What can you do, Mister Lyle? One of their number is dead, now. And they will think you have the Plate. What can you possibly threaten to do, Mister Lyle?'

Lyle seethed, but couldn't think of an answer. He said nothing, hating himself, hating Lord Lincoln, hating the man's cold, almost mocking stare that knew too much.

Lincoln waited for the silence to stretch, before smiling politely and detaching himself from the window. 'Mister Lyle, I do not believe I have ever seen you so animated. Do you have the Fuyun Plate?'

Silence.

'Mister Lyle?'

'No.'

'Do you think you are likely to find it shortly?'

Silence.

'Mister Lyle, I am not a patient man. I can easily find some-one else to investigate the matter.'

'Can you? Someone else who carries magnets in their pockets and understands the principles of forces and fields radiating out from a polarized centre? I saw their faces, I saw them recoil. *Can you?*'

Lincoln's face darkened. 'Do not overestimate your impor-tance, Mister Lyle. Are you likely to recover the Plate?'

'There's a chance.'

'What "chance"?'

'Before Bray died he said something that may lead to the Plate. I cannot say more.'

Lincoln studied Lyle's face for a long while, then sighed and half-turned away to look out at the street. Grey clouds were mustering overhead: more rain seemed to be in the offing, cold and dank. Watching the street Lincoln said in a dull, uninterested voice, 'The Tseiqin are very old and very powerful. I have reason to believe a number of them have infiltrated Her Majesty's Court, the civil service, the inner sanctums of power. They are a great threat to this nation and Her Majesty's Empire.'

'Are you going to tell me at any particular point about them not being human, or do I have to brood over the white blood for myself?'

'They are not human, Mister Lyle.'

'Thank you for telling me that. What are they?'

'They are . . . old. As I said.'

'That doesn't help me.'

Lincoln sighed, almost imperceptibly, like an impatient teacher. 'The Tseiqin come from the forests and the grasslands, live and thrive where nature does. Jungles and marshes are to them things of beauty. They hate us. Especially people like you and your father.'

'Why?'

'You deal in iron, Mister Lyle. You and your family have made a life out of clicking iron wheels. Being near iron upsets them.'

'Then how can they go near the cities?'

'I said it upset them, not that it harmed them. It . . . limits them. They want that limitation away.'

'The magnet seemed to harm them.'

Lincoln looked quickly up at Lyle's face. 'A magnet?'

'Yes.'

'Explain.'

'The magnet hurt them. He screamed when he touched it.'

'I see. I was aware that iron harmed them, limited them . . . maybe even caused them pain, turned them into weak beings, less even than the beggars on the street, fragile, their beauty gone. But *magnetic* iron – this is a new concept. Electricity is still very little understood, I gather. There is a link, is there not? Electricity and magnetism, one causes the other, electric induction by magnetic fields, magnetic induction by the passing of electricity? Is this not so? Perhaps one day you can explain it clearly.'

Lyle's voice was distant, his eyes focused somewhere else as his mind raced. 'Thomas screamed when he was shocked,' he murmured, almost inaudibly.

'How so?'

Lyle snapped back to reality. 'Pardon?'

'You spoke of someone being shocked.'

'Yes. Thomas. He came at me with a knife, screaming about eyes.'

Lincoln's only reaction was a single, brisk nod. 'The Tseiqin are said to be able to impose their wills on weaker minds. They are very beautiful, almost overpoweringly so. No one can disobey a Tseiqin's command, once under their spell.'

'Thank you for telling me this now,' muttered Lyle sourly. 'Your sense of timing is just impeccable.'

'I was not sure how far this would go.'

'It's already gone too far.'

'I am sorry you feel that way.'

'What's so important about the Plate?'

This time, Lincoln's sigh had more of regret about it than it had before. 'The Fuyun Plate is largely what legend claims it to be: an object of power. The Tseiqin, when they drink from the Plate, are changed. Iron will not stop them. Iron no longer harms them; that single element has been our greatest protection against the true strength of the Tseiqin for centuries, a strength you cannot begin to imagine. If they can overcome their *terror* of this element, the pain it causes them, I think it is no exaggeration to say that they can rule the world.'

'That must have Her Majesty's Empire upset,' sighed Lyle.

'It is not a laughing matter.'

'I know. Believe me. I know.' Lyle frowned, an idea slipping into his mind. 'The Bank of England has iron doors, doesn't it?'

'Indeed.'

'If only I'd been told about the occult, supernatural, semi-apocalyptic aspect of this investigation first, it would have saved me a lot of effort. Why didn't they just drink from the Plate before it ended up *behind* the doors, and save themselves the trouble?'

'It was damaged.'

'Damaged?'

'Many centuries ago, it was taken by priests who feared the Tseiqin, and locked in an iron box. The Tseiqin attacked the priests to reclaim the Plate. In the course of the attack, blood was spilt on it. There was a thunderstorm. Lighting hit the metal box in which the blood-soaked Plate lay. It was unscathed, but when the Tseiqin tried to touch it, it burnt their hands. The lightning strike had done something to the Plate.'

Lyle rubbed the bridge of his nose, and muttered distantly, 'Where was this?'

'Tibet.'

'Tibet?'

'Yes.'

'You heard of a man named Feng Darin?'

'Are you referring to one of the spies the Chinese doubtlessly have trailing you with orders to recover the Plate regardless of cost to human life?'

'Yes, that sounds about right.'

'Then yes, I have heard of Feng Darin. It is pleasing to have a name to put to the face. I presume you appreciate how willing he will be to kill you, to achieve his ends.'

'Yes, of course, I took that for granted. Why are the Tseiqin looking for the Plate now?'

'They believe they can repair it.'

'Why?'

'Perhaps because now we have machines which can simulate the lightning strike that first damaged the Plate?'

Lyle shook his head. 'This is immensely upsetting.'

'For a scientist?'

'Yes, for a scientist!'

'Do you think it is plausible, though?'

'People who have a fear of iron and magnets wanting to play around with something that got damaged in an iron box which itself was blasted with a huge, incredible electric charge like nothing we have the capacity to simulate? Well, I'll grant it has a certain poetic symmetry about it.'

Lincoln looked at him almost sadly, and said in a low, precise voice that gave nothing away, 'Mister Lyle, can you find the Plate?'

'I don't know.'

'If the Tseiqin find it, they will kill everything that has ever touched iron.'

'I'm almost on the verge of believing you. If you knew the Plate was so valuable, why didn't you destroy it?'

'Destroy something of that value? No. Besides, fire, flood and a very large drop and very short stop have so far failed even to chip it.'

'But being contained inside an iron box with a huge electric current running through it does damage it?'

'Mister Lyle, can you find the Plate?'

'I don't know. What do you know about Lord Moncorvo?'

'Moncorvo?'

'Yes. He's involved.'

'I know of him. He has a good deal of influence at the House of Lords. A prominent statesman.'

'I think he's . . .' Lyle seemed to flinch, and hastily said, 'one of them.'

'Tseiqin?'

'*Don't* push my credulity so far as to actually start talking about this in an easy, everyday voice, my lord.'

'Special Constable Lyle, *can you find the Plate?*'

Outside, in the grey dull street, rain started to fall, thick fat droplets bouncing up between the cobbles and pooling in the dirty gutters, washing down the soot-encrusted walls. Lyle stared at Lincoln with a slowly growing expression of understanding, and Lincoln stared back at Lyle defiantly.

Lyle said, 'If you knew the Tseiqin were after the Plate, why did you give it to the Elwick family to safeguard? Because you knew the Tseiqin would go after it? Because you wanted them to go after it? Why did you immediately come to me? Because you must have known the Tseiqin had tried to steal the Plate, that it was *them*. But you didn't know about Moncorvo. Why? Because you didn't know *who* the Tseiqin were, who the individuals were within your system, how deep they'd dug their claws into government, how many, how strong, how powerful, how ambitious – the strength of your enemy. You didn't know about Moncorvo. You *wanted* some-one to try and steal the Plate, so you could see who they were. You baited them, and hoped that I'd find out who they were. And now people are *dead* and I've nearly been killed, and the *children* have nearly been killed and have just seen things that

I wouldn't wish on a mad, opium-high, hashish-smoking, deranged axe murderer!'

Silence. Then, very quietly, 'Once again, Mister Lyle, you have shown yourself to be a wise choice of detective.'

Silence.

'Where is the Plate, Mister Lyle?'

Silence.

'Mister Lyle?'

'It's in the hands of justice, Lord Lincoln.'

Silence.

'I do not need to tell you more, Mister Lyle. You know enough. I know that you will do your duty. You may not believe what you are doing, but you are a rational man. You cannot explain away what you have seen by science, and therefore will take the only logical option available to you. I am sure I can count on your willing support.'

Silence.

'Good day, Mister Lyle. I look forward to hearing from you soon.'

Lyle didn't say a word as Lincoln turned and swept out.

CHAPTER 15

Justice

After lunch, the rain hammered down in dark sheets that poured angrily from the sky, as if in revenge for some forgotten sin. Tess sat by the fire, her feet up on a table, idly stroking Tate, who had learnt to recognize a soft touch when he saw one, and said, 'I ain't surprised. I thought it were magic all along.'

Upstairs, Thomas helped Milly wash out a dusty set of glass tubes and arrange them neatly on a table. 'Haven't you got a home to go to, dear?' she asked.

Thomas thought about this. 'No, ma'am. Not really.'

And by the light of a bright, burning lantern, Lyle leafed through page after page of an illustrated book entitled *Images in*

London, Heart of Empire, while on the table beside him the single vial of white blood from an alien heart lay waiting.

And as he worked, he thought, *The Tseiqin can't touch the Plate any more – they had to hire Carwell and his brother, the arrogant fool. And Carwell wanted more. He gives the Plate to Bray, Bray hides it. The Tseiqin find Bray, and we find the Tseiqin. The Plate is still somewhere out there, wherever Bray hid it. In the hands of justice, he said. It's in the hands of justice, but he wouldn't have given it to the police, he was talking about a different justice entirely.*

And Horatio Lyle thought: *I wonder if the Tseiqin are going to kill me after all? Murdered by a magical species that I don't believe can actually exist, for a plate that I don't honestly believe has any kind of special properties, by people who shout 'Don't look at the eyes' and run around with brass knives and scream at the touch of magnetic metal. Wouldn't that be ironic?*

Scream at the touch of magnets.

Or when the people who fear the green eyes, those incredible green eyes, start writhing and screaming at the discharging of a parallel-plate electric tube.

Like Thomas.

And Horatio Lyle thought: *Magnetism makes electricity, electricity makes magnetism – you can't have one without the other.*

And the passage of an electric current is magnetic, isn't it?

Even when it passes through an iron box during a thunderstorm.

Horatio Lyle looked down at the book open on the table in front of him, and frowned at a passage. He ran his finger along it, lips pursed, eyebrows knitted together. Then he looked at the picture of the statue next to it. And Horatio Lyle thought: *It's in the hands of justice.*

What can you do, Mister Lyle? What can you possibly threaten to do?

As the rain fell on the grimy streets of London and the factories belched and the iron cogs in the textile mills whirred and the iron wires in the Royal Institution hummed and the iron shovels dug down into the dirt and the iron pickaxes chipped away at the rock, Horatio Lyle started to smile.

'Children, get your shoes on!'

'Going, dear?'

'Yes, Ma. Thank you for looking after us.'

'Worked it out, have you, dear?'

'Yes, I think so.'

'So are you going to the old or the new?'

Lyle hesitated.

'Give your ma a hug, dear. And look after those children. And that dog of yours. I don't want to hear any bad report.'

'Yes, m'm.'

'And pay Teresa her sovereign.'

'Yes, m'm.'

'Have you got everything?'

'I think so . . .'

'Been to the privy?'

'Ma . . .'

'I have to ask, dear, it's a mother's prerogative. Have you got your dynamo?'

'Yes, m'm.'

'And you've had enough to eat?'

'Yes, m'm.'

'And you've got the spare bottle of magnesium sulphate?'

'Yes, m'm.'

'Right. Well, then. Off you go, dear. Don't do anything foolish.'

'No, Ma, I won't. I promise.'

She patted Lyle on the shoulder. 'Good lad.' Then she turned a stern look on Tess. 'I'm relying on you to make sure the lads don't do anything foolish.'

Thomas, Tate and Lyle all contrived to look sheepish. Tess put on a very serious expression. 'Yes, m'm. I'll keep 'em in order, m'm, don't you worry. But . . . m'm? If they don't come back with all the bits in the usual places, you ain't gonna blame me, are you?'

Milly examined Lyle and Thomas thoughtfully, then smiled a distinctly malign smile. 'No, dear. Not at all.'

They went back via Lyle's house, but Lyle didn't let the children leave the hansom cab. Followed by Tate, he darted towards the house.

When he put the key into the lock, it jammed and he had to struggle with it. After a few seconds it clicked, and he opened the door, slipping inside with a little frown on his face. It was cold in the house, feeling unlived in after only a day. He looked slowly around, frowning at the floor and at each door handle he passed. He took more time than he'd first meant to, drifting quietly and slowly downstairs to the kitchen, listening to the sound of the floorboards under his feet. He stopped on one, and swivelled his weight this way and that, listening to the creak. He sighed very faintly under his breath and pulled out from his pocket the long, slim clay tube with the wires at the end. Holding this like a knife, he wandered carefully into the kitchen. The wardrobe door was half-open. He kicked it gently back and looked into the second half-open panel behind it. A man was lying there, one leg trapped firmly in a metal vice. He whimpered as Lyle approached and squatted very quietly down in front of him.

'I dunno nothin'!' he whined.

'Of course you don't,' said Lyle politely. 'Believe me, I know exactly how you feel in that sense. Who sent you? Was it Moncorvo?'

'I dunno nothin'!'

'Do you know what gangrene is?' A flicker of doubt and fear passed across the man's face. Lyle grinned. 'See, that reaction was the reaction of a man who *does* know. I'm so glad to meet someone with an education at last. Do you know that when the books say *green*, they actually mean *green*?'

'He was . . . a chink.'

'Chinese?'

'That's right!'

'Crooked top hat, red scarf, taste for ginger biscuits, singular bulge in his left coat pocket where he's failed to hide the gun? That him?'

'Eh . . . yes, that's 'im!'

'What'd he ask you to find?'

'A plate, a stone plate!'

'And bring it to him?' Frantic nodding. Lyle sighed. 'All right. I'll send someone round to get you out, Mr . . . ?'

'Erm . . . Smith.'

'Mr Smith. Well, I suppose I can't complain. Thank you for your time, Mr Smith.'

Lyle slipped down into the basement, and by faint lamplight went round his shelves. He found a small bag of plain metal lumps and dragged them apart from each other with some difficulty, putting them carefully in separate pockets. Armed with the magnets, he also filled his pockets with a large handful of mixed test tubes, a few spheres of white, light glass, a spare box of matches and, after a little more consideration, a small handful of carefully capped needles in a brown paper bag. You never knew when you might need such things, he told himself. He filled Tate's water bowl, put out a fresh plate of food, pointed an accusing finger, said 'Stay' and was ignored as Tate lay down in his basket and rolled over. Lyle sighed, made a small bag of ham sandwiches in the kitchen, wrapped them in brown paper and went out to find answers.

Early evening in London, and though the rain still fell over the heart of the city, out to the west the black clouds had retreated to allow radiant pink and orange sunshine to burn through in a narrow thread across the horizon. In the east the tiny peep of light on the horizon was of a blackened blue variety, promising a colder, deeper night. The hansom cab rattled through the streets slowly, trapped in traffic. At Smithfield, the cab stopped entirely. There was the sound of bleating. Tess lowered the window and peered out. 'Sheep,' she said in a disinterested voice.

'Sheep?' Thomas craned to see. The street was boiling with trapped, terrified sheep, struggling to move.

Lyle hissed in frustration, leant out of the window of the cab, and called up at the cabby, 'It's all right, we can walk from here.'

The cabby looked surprised. 'You ain't goin' to get through those sheep!'

Lyle glanced inside the cab. 'Tess?'

'Yes?'

'See that lady selling the onions?'

She grinned. 'No problem, Mister Lyle.'

Ten minutes later, Inspector Vellum, Metropolitan Police, emerged from the large wooden doors of the Old Bailey, a building almost cathedral-like in Gothic extravagance, into a horde of panic-stricken sheep galloping through the cobbled streets, nearly mewing in distress, to the despair of their master. Some of them, Vellum noticed with interest, almost seemed to be crying. And there were bits of onion in some of their fleeces. He thought how remarkably chaotic the city was, and how good it was for the well-being of mankind that he was there to help remedy the defect. Feeling satisfied at this worthwhile conclusion, he turned, and looked straight into the humourless, smiling face of Horatio Lyle.

His joy faded. 'Constable Lyle,' he managed in a voice tinged with false politeness and bursting with undisguised contempt. 'I've been hearing all about your exploits. I hope you are satisfied?'

'Almost.'

'And why are you only "almost satisfied", Constable Lyle? It is not, I trust, because you have given credit to the scandalous rumours implying that your conduct has been a degradation to the honour of the police force – not that I would credit them for a moment, Constable Lyle?'

Lyle drew himself up a little straighter. Behind him, Tess muttered, 'Hit him!' Thomas chewed his lip uneasily.

'Well, Constable Lyle? You are not, I trust, being troubled by any premonitions of failure? I implore you, banish them to the back of your mind; a man in your position should not be concerned by the prospect of disgrace and dissolution.'

There was a long silence. 'Inspector Vellum,' said Lyle, his voice cautious and edgy, 'I assure you that I will take all your advice to heart and let no such disturbances trouble my sleep. I will endeavour – again, thanks to your kind advice – to consider what few achievements I already have at my back. Although rumours of my success in a matter that had baffled the Metropolitan Police are doubtlessly hugely exaggerated by my many supporters and spiritual acolytes, I will nevertheless attempt to dwell on what little credit there is in having essentially solved a case that baffled some of the most remarkable minds in this *majestic* city. I thank you for your kindness and support, and now if you'll excuse us, we have the Queen's business to attend to.'

Lyle pushed past Vellum without another word, keeping as straight a face as he could manage, and into the Old Bailey, followed by Thomas and lastly Tess, who bumped her shoulder against Vellum as she went. Vellum stood in the street for a while longer, seething with all the inner axe murderers he didn't have the self-perception to release, before mustering courage and spinning on his heel to follow Lyle, hoping to give him the punch he'd always wanted to.

He looked into a pair of intense green eyes, and smelt a wave of breath tainted with foreign fruits. The mouth that owned the breath smiled, revealing small, pointed teeth. Almost like fish. 'Inspector Vellum,' said a soft, cruel voice. 'I am Mr Dew.'

CHAPTER 16

Bailey

Tess was unhappy. The Old Bailey was full of bobbies, and even worse, full of people in cuffs who might recognize her and wonder why she wasn't among their number. She walked quickly, trying to hide between Lyle and Thomas, and hoped no one would notice her. The place had once been plush and grand, she decided, but now had a slightly run-down look. There were rumours that the Government was planning to demolish it and replace it with a more functional building, it being, after all, the *Central* Criminal Court, and thus something that ought to be *central* to justice, rather than a slightly wobbly limb. She thought that it would be a pity to get rid of all those dark wood banisters in the shape of pineapples, and those big padded leather chairs with the spring in them, and even the judges in their big wigs and long robes, which gave the place, to her mind, a more relaxed feeling – almost like the fairground.

'Teresa?' Lyle was walking fast and not looking at her, but she immediately knew what he was going to say.

'Yes, Mister Lyle?' she said, putting on her sweetest, most innocent face that prompted Thomas to shoot her a suspicious look.

'Teresa, I don't want you to think that I approve in any way . . .'

'Yes, Mister Lyle?'

'. . . and if you ever steal my fob watch, purse or monocle from out of my pocket, I will be very, very annoyed . . .'

'You don't have a monocle in your pocket, Mister Lyle. An' your purse ain't heavy enough to warrant the attention of a professional like myself.'

Silence. 'Teresa?'

'Yes?'

'*How do you know?*'

She coughed politely. 'You were sayin' something about not approvin'?'

Lyle fixed his eyes very firmly on the middle distance, and said in a slightly-too-confident voice, 'Yes. Erm . . . yes. I was going to say, that I would far rather you had waited until I could see Vellum's face when he found out.' He frowned slightly. 'Now I'm not so sure.'

'Mister Lyle?'

'Yes?'

'What the h . . . what are we doin' here?' Tess's voice was barely above a squeak. She affected innocence.

Thomas tried to look as if he knew the answer, while watching Lyle out of the corner of his eye. Lyle glanced up the stairs leading into the higher balconies of the Bailey, and muttered distantly, 'Looking for justice.'

When they were climbing the stairs, Thomas leant in close to him and murmured, 'Sir, you're not turning Miss Teresa in, are you?'

Lyle looked shocked. 'Me? I'm a copper! Of course not!'

Thomas felt relieved by this, but didn't know why. He smiled, nodded in what he hoped was a manly and mature manner, and tried to turn his resultant expression into one of determined profundity promising insight yet to come. Lyle saw it, and tried not to smile, as they shuffled upstairs.

It took them ten minutes to find the man Lyle was looking for, a man with ginger hair, freckles and a default expression of general goodwill towards humanity. He saw Lyle, unfolded himself from the plain chair at the far end of the corridor where he'd been lounging, and stood up with a slow nonchalance. 'Horatio,' he said in a distinct Welsh accent, shaking his hand, 'still not in an asylum?'

'You would not believe.'

'Never can anyway, Horatio. Who're the friends?'

'Thomas, Teresa, this is Charles.'

'Very pleased to meet you,' said Thomas stiffly, shaking his hand.

Charles waggled his eyebrows and said in almost perfect mimicry, 'And you, kind sir, and you.'

Tess glared at him. 'You're a *bobby*, ain't you?' The poison in her voice could have burnt through stones.

Charles put a hand melodramatically to his forehead. 'Only when I'm not on holiday, dearest.' He glanced at Lyle. 'Be careful of that one, Horatio. She'll have your purse before you can blink.'

'It's not worthy of the attention of a professional like herself,' sighed Lyle. 'Charles, I need your help.'

'Oh yes?' Suspicion fixed itself very firmly on Charles's face.

'I need to get on to the roof.'

'You what?'

'You *wha*?' echoed Tess.

'I beg your pardon?' hazarded Thomas, thinking that he should contribute somehow to the debate.

Lyle rolled his eyes. 'Ignore the ignorant. Can you get me on to the roof?'

'Will I get sacked for it?' asked Charles, a suggestion of concern creeping into his eyes.

'Why should you?'

''Cos last time you wanted to go up anywhere high it was to measure how hot a lightning strike could get a flagpole.'

Lyle started turning red. 'Well, yes . . . but no. This is far more restrained.'

'What you doin' up there, Mister Lyle?' demanded Tess.

'Can we help?' hazarded Thomas. 'I have a good head for heights.' He wasn't sure if this was true – he'd never had any real occasion to find out, but he felt he ought to offer anyway.

For a second Lyle looked tempted, then changed his mind. 'Thank you, no. I'd better go up there. Charles?'

Charles rolled his eyes. 'Jesus Christ. You people.'

The roof of the Old Bailey was a triangular slant, the tiles damp with the earlier drizzle and rain. There was still enough dusk light to see by, however, as Charles opened the attic hatch in the roof, peered up and said, 'Where'd I meet you, Horatio?'

'In a small pond, Charles.'

Charles's grin was a flash of whiteness in the dimming grey evening. 'Heh. That brings back memories.'

Lyle peered up the roof. Standing at the very end of it was a statue, looking down on the street far, far below, its back turned to him, arms held out as if crucified, bearing in one hand a large pair of scales, in the other a sword, a folded robe of stone drifting down to its ankles. He hesitated. The sounds of the city seemed a very long way off. A pigeon sat defiantly on the peak of the roof and glared at him first out of one eye, then out of the other, turning its head this way and that to see if either eye could muster a better opinion of him than the other. Clearly no eye liked him, because the pigeon started hopping back and forward agitatedly.

Slyly, behind him, Tess said, 'You ain't afraid of heights, are you, Mister Lyle?'

Immediately Thomas stepped forward. 'I will undertake to . . .'

'*No.*'

Thomas practically pouted, realized what he was doing and hoped that Tess hadn't seen his expression. Lyle took a handful of rope off Charles's hands, a hook tied at one end, and threw it towards the statue. On the fifth throw, Tess was trying hard not to laugh. On the sixth throw the hook landed over the out-stretched arm of the statue, clinking tight against stone. Lyle tugged until the rope went taut and gave Tess a dirty look.

'I didn't say nothin'!'

Lyle then glared at Charles. Charles raised his hands defen-sively. 'Hey, I'm more reverent than *she* is.'

Lyle scowled, tugged a few more times on the rope to make sure it was tight, and glanced down at the street a long way below. This proved to be a mistake. He felt his stomach churn. Behind him, Tess's intense silence was even worse than her laughter. He took a deep breath and started pulling himself up, hand over hand, feet braced against the slippery tiles. Down in the street people stopped to stare, peering at Lyle as he clambered slowly towards the statue. He felt a few spare droplets of driz-zle land on his hand, white where it clung to the rope, and glanced quickly at the sky. It was darkening from bruised grey to a deep blue-black. The wind rising from the river smelt of thick mud and decay, but carried a trace of a colder, cleaner air from the sea as well, tingling with salt. He kept climbing. On the other side of the road a small crowd was gathering to get a look.

Lyle reached the top of the roof, and balanced precariously on the peak, one foot on either side curled in like a gorilla's toes clinging to a tree. He leant on the statue for support, and in the fading light saw it more clearly now than he had when down below at the hatch on to the roof. It was a small statue of a woman, about two thirds of his height and made of stone and brass. The woman was turned towards the street, and stood on top of the Bailey like a patron saint on a cathedral, the god of all that went on inside the building. She wore a stone blindfold and her outstretched arms held, in one hand, a bronze sword, tarnished slightly by weather, and in the other, a pair of scales, also of bronze. Inside one metal scale the surface was dull. Lyle started to smile, as the drizzle increased. He looked at the roofs rising and falling unevenly around the Bailey, and tried to work out what route Bray must have taken. He looked at the statue of Justice, shiny with the rain, and down to one side of the scales. It was a good hiding place, he thought. He only wished he'd been able to tell Bray that.

From its resting place in the scales in the hands of Justice, he pulled out the Fuyun Plate.

It was indeed small and dull, cold in his hand. It looked as if it was made of plain grey limestone, but it was so smooth it was almost hard to carry, like a damp bar of soap. It was shallow and roughly the same size as his outstretched hand, too big for his coat pocket, but small enough to be easily missed. It seemed something of an anti-climax, he thought, to have gone to so much trouble to find the Fuyun Plate and finally, now, to have it. He turned it over, looking for any kind of distinctive marks, but there weren't any. It was just a plain, simple stone bowl. Something angry rose up inside Lyle as he thought about the blood that had covered his hands, for *this*, for a piece of stone and a collection of legends.

Thomas's voice drifted across the roof. 'Are you all right, sir?'

Lyle glanced towards Thomas and, for a second, thought he saw something in the street that drew his eyes back. He looked slowly round and swept the people again, trying to pick out once more that brief flash of green in all the dull greys and inconspicuous shadows of dusk. He thought he saw a gleam of bronze, and a second later felt a movement in the air. He ducked behind the statue, and the bronze crossbow bolt bounced lightly off the stone statue and away. For a second he looked down, and saw bright green eyes staring up at him. Then he heard the sound of clattering hooves.

It took the people in the street a good ten seconds to realize what was happening, and a woman took another five seconds before she saw the bent crossbow bolt lying in the dirt outside the court and started screaming. Then, as three black carriages came barrelling round the corner at high speed, the people of London did what sound instinct dictated was the best thing to do, and ran.

The shouts started far below. Tess, peering down into the street, was already yelling, 'Mister Lyle! We're goin' to have to run! *Again!*'

Lyle slipped gracelessly down from the roof, stuck the Plate crudely under one arm and handed Tess and Thomas a pair of magnets each. 'Put these in your pockets and don't take them out for moralizing or money! Tess, can you see a way off this roof that doesn't involve going *downward*?'

Tess looked around frantically, while Thomas stared at the Plate under Lyle's arm. 'Is that it? Is that the Fuyun Plate, sir?'

'Yes, Thomas, I think it is. Come on, Tess! Bray must have got up here somewhere, how do we get down?'

Charles was looking around, panic-struck. 'You're going to get me sacked, aren't you? You said you weren't and *now* look what's happening! Jesus, I knew I should've looked after the flocks and stayed in Abergavenny like my pa said!'

Tess suddenly stuck out a hand and pointed at a ledge on the other side of the roof. A pipe led past it. 'There, Mister Lyle.'

'Right.' Lyle was pulling off his jacket, wrapping the Plate in it tightly with string so that just the sleeves dangled. Using the sleeves as a form of strap, he tied one over a shoulder and the other under, so that the crumpled jacket turned into a bag. 'Tess, lead the way.' He glanced at Charles. 'You want to come?'

'Jesus Christ, no!' Charles disappeared into the gloom.

Tess led the way across the slippery roof, eyes screwed up in concentration. From the ledge, she looked down a long drop into a small, octagonal courtyard, overshadowed on all sides by buildings and their smooth walls. A black pipe led down from the ledge to a second, lower roof below the high one of the Bailey, just a few inches out of reach. She strained on her toes at the edge of the roof, and her fingers brushed the cold, rough iron. She closed her hand round it. Thomas stared at her, pale-faced. 'I . . . I don't know if . . .'

Tess hurled herself on to the pipe, catching it with her feet, and clinging with all her might. For a few seconds she slid, the world jerking violently, but finally caught herself and held on tightly, knuckles white. She looked back up at Lyle and Thomas. The pipe creaked under her. Below, far below, in the courtyard, two men appeared, with green eyes. Tess goggled as a bronze arrow bounced off the wall beside her and fell away. Lyle scowled and threw a small glass test tube down at them as hard as he could. It exploded into a cloud of purple-grey smoke, hissing unpleasantly. The two men staggered out of the smoke, rubbing their eyes, and Thomas threw a loose tile at them. It smashed on to the ground by their feet. Thomas dragged frantically at another tile. Lyle uncorked a bottle and poured a few careful drops into the cracks between the tile and the roof. The stuff hissed and smelt foul, and the tile came away. Thomas didn't even stop to grin, but threw the tile. This time it hit one of the men, who crumpled soundlessly.

As Thomas grabbed and threw more tiles, Tess wormed her way down the pipe, until her feet touched the lower roof, which was flat, with occasional holes revealing a dark, uneven floor below, as pot-holed as the roof itself. She looked up at Lyle and Thomas. 'Come on!'

Lyle glanced down at the drop between where he stood and the roof where Tess was cowering in the gloom. Thomas followed his gaze, looked at the gap and said, 'I can jump that, sir!'

He moved to take a run-up, but Lyle put a very firm hand on his shoulder. 'No you can't, lad.' He turned to the shadow that was Tess and shouted, 'Is there anything you can tie a rope to?'

Tess looked around, and her eyes settled on a pipe nearly on the other side of the roof. 'Yes, sir!'

'Right.' Lyle threw her the rope. She caught it clumsily, surprised at its weight, and ran for the other pipe. As she tied it round the pipe on the lower roof, Lyle fastened it to that on the other, and snapped at Thomas, 'You don't need your coat, do you?'

Thomas didn't hesitate, but started pulling it off. Lyle slung it over the rope, and tugged at it. It was taut. 'Right, lad, here's what you're going to do.'

Thomas stared at the coat. 'Erm . . .'

Another crossbow bolt bounced off the roof. 'Don't argue, lad, just don't let go either.'

Thomas found himself grabbing either side of the coat, and sidling to the edge of the roof. He took hold of a handful of coat on one side of the rope, and a handful on the other, wrapping it round his hand several times. He hesitated. Just as Lyle moved to push him, he jumped off the roof.

The drop down had seemed a very long way to look at it, but the coat slid along in a blur, and his legs flapped lazily behind him as he was dragged downwards along the rope. He saw the pale face of Tess ahead in the darkness, splitting into an expression of alarm as he careened towards her before she darted aside. 'Let go, you idiot!' she shouted just before he hit the pipe. He let go, dropping heavily on to his bottom on the cold rooftop with a thump. Behind him, Lyle had already slung his jacket over the rope and was looking down with a pale face, standing out in the gloom. He wondered how strong the Plate was. Enough, hopefully.

Down in the courtyard there were sounds of more shouting. 'Come on, Mister Lyle!'

Lyle grimaced, and didn't so much jump from the roof as stagger. He slid down the rope with his eyes firmly shut and his face screwed up into an expression of pain while the drizzle soaked through his shirt and made his hair hang dankly around his face, giving him the appearance of a tragic clown. Halfway down, as his feet just passed over the lower roof, the upper pipe creaked and bent, and the knot holding the rope taut gave way. It snapped like a whip, dropping Lyle the five feet remaining. He landed on the paper-thin roof with a thud, face green, and for a second sprawled motionless, waiting for something else bad to happen. Very slowly, it happened. The roof, barely a roof at all, creaked once, creaked twice and caved in. Lyle fell into darkness, still clinging on to his jacket.

'Mister Lyle!' Tess's shout bounced through the murk. She ran across the roof, Thomas in tow, knelt on the side of the roughly Lyle-shaped hole and peered down. 'Mister Lyle? You all right?'

In the darkness something hissed and started to burn. Bright white light rose up from the sphere in Lyle's hand, and slowly spread to cast a thin light across the floor. Lyle looked miserable, dirty and bruised, but called back in an unconvincing voice of bravery, 'I'm all right. Are you two all right?'

'Yes, Mister Lyle!'

'Yes, Mister Lyle.'

'Right. I think I can see a way out. I want you two to get out of here as fast as possible! If you don't find me, go to the Palace, go to Lord Lincoln, all right?'

'We aren't just leaving you, Mister Lyle . . .' began Thomas.

'We ain't?' asked Tess weakly.

'Well, you're not coming down here, if that's what you're thinking. Here, catch.' There was a clink in the shadows, and something rose out of the hole in the roof. Thomas caught it clumsily. It was the dynamo. 'Now get off the roof!'

Thomas hesitated, but Tess grabbed him by the collar and muttered, 'You heard the Mister, mister. Come on.'

She dragged him away into the gloom.

CHAPTER 17

Escape

Lyle picked his way slowly through the shadows of the abandoned building, listening to each creak of the floor and starting at loud noises. His imagination was playing tricks on him, so that he kept hearing the scuttling of rats, the chink of knives, the hiss of falling dust from undisturbed shelves. At least, he hoped his imagination was playing tricks on him. He could feel his heart pounding. The little ball of burning magnesium he held in his hand fizzed out and died. He sighed and tossed the sphere aside, digging into his pocket. Only a few more spheres left. There wasn't enough light in the day now to see by. Night was settling in to stay. He could hear a distant, gentle pattering of rain and, nearer, the louder dripping of little rivulets running down inside the building. He wished he'd brought more than one dynamo. He felt his way to a doorframe and clung to it, fingers dancing along the woodworm-plagued old, crumbling wood. Kneeling down he groped slowly through the darkness, mindful of concealed mice traps. His fingers touched a loose, splinter-full plank of wood, which he rested against the doorframe. He felt in his pocket for the matchbox, then with trembling fingers counted the matches. Four left. He struck one. It burnt for a few seconds and guttered. He struck another. It flared with a bright, smelly flame, which he touched to the dry, old wood. The flame caught some of the splinters near the top, which fizzled a dull orange, eaten away to little fiery worms. The third match caught the corner of the wood, and for a second he thought the thin flame was just going to burn and die. He blew very gently on it, and the flame guttered, then rose up again to gnaw a little more at the dry wood, until it burnt well enough to cast a strong orange light across the floor.

Holding the plank precariously at one end, feeling the rough splinters beneath his fingers, Lyle straightened up and looked round. He avoided the windows, and crept slowly through the house. He found a shattered flight of stairs, only the banisters and a few precarious planks remaining, hesitated, and tossed the plank down to the bottom of the stairs. Then, thinking that if Tess saw him she'd never stop laughing, he slunk to the banister and managed to throw one foot over it. He clung to the banister for dear life and let himself down a support at a time. Halfway down it creaked ominously, and he stopped clinging and slid the last of the way. The banister leaned just before the end, tossing him off like a rag doll, supports cracking and bending every which way they could. Lyle landed awkwardly almost in his own flaming torch, and felt pain blossom in his hand. He flinched and raised it to the dull light. A slim sliver of wood had embedded itself under the skin of his palm. He felt nauseous. Other people's blood he could deal with. He tried not to look at it, tried not to think about it, and stood up. Beside him, the flame from the old wooden plank gently went *whomph*, and was suddenly a good deal larger.

Lyle picked up the plank. Under it the old wooden floor, abused by too much neglect, was also burning in a square, soft flame of light. He backed away from it hastily, and nearly tripped over a two-legged table lying miserably on one side, half of it hacked away for some other purpose. He jumped away from this and saw a door. Scampering towards it as quickly as his fear of falling would let him, he eased it very gently open, peered out into the street beyond, and straight into the bright green eyes of Mr Dew.

A street away, there was a little thud, a whirring sound and light bloomed, revealing high alley walls and a small refuse pile next to an overflowing drain. The whirring sound died. The light went out. In the darkness, someone hissed, 'Keep turnin', bigwig!'

Light slowly bloomed again. Two small figures dropped down from a glassless window on to a pile of empty crates below. In the darkness, Tess said, 'They weren't *good* trousers, were they?'

Thomas didn't answer. Etiquette hadn't taught him how to

deal with this kind of situation. The alley they'd landed in smelt of old cats and tar. 'Where are we?'

'Don't ask things like that. Where we are now ain't as important as where we gotta be in a minute.'

'What *should* I ask?' he hissed, exasperation just starting to wear through his overwhelming sense of decorum.

'Is there anyone *else* here?'

Tess, he admitted grudgingly to himself, had a strong sense of priorities. She peered out round the corner. 'Can't see no one. They must've all run away. Come on.'

'What about Mister Lyle?'

'What about him?'

'We ought to go and help him! He might have been lying – he might be lying – with a broken leg in that house and . . . and bleeding and . . . and *shot* and . . .'

'You and me?'

'Yes!'

'All right,' said Tess, folding her arms. This unnerved Thomas, who stopped turning the handle of the dynamo. The light slowly went out, but he could still feel her venomous expression. 'You tell me just how you think you and me can help Mister Lyle deal with this whole bunch of evil faeries with an evil plan.'

He hesitated. 'Well . . . you could . . . or I could . . . but if we distract them . . . or perhaps if we could find a long enough bit of string . . .'

'We don't even know if Mister Lyle is there any more!'

'Well, yes, that's a thing, but I'm sure . . .'

'Thomas?' Tess's voice had a strained quality to it.

229

'No, don't say anything yet, I know we can think of something if we try . . .'

'*Thomas!*'

He realized Tess wasn't looking at him any more, but at a shadow standing behind him. He turned slowly, feeling dread in his stomach. The man standing above him smiled thinly. 'Well,' said Feng Darin politely, 'I have a few suggestions.'

Lyle looked into the bright eyes of Mr Dew, and instinct kicked in. He slammed the door, grabbed the half-sawn table and dragged it in front of the door in an instant. Outside, Mr Dew said, 'Mister Lyle, you have nowhere to go.'

Lyle glanced at the flame over his shoulder, slowly spreading up the flimsy wall as it made a bid for the wooden ceiling. The smoke was already rising in dirty, choking billows. He looked around for inspiration and tools. The door shook under the impact of a shoulder. His eyes fell on a wrought-iron kettle, lying on its side, without a lid. He looked around, and saw a pair of light metal kitchen ladles, lying neglected, and an iron fork. He thought about it, as fire lapped against the wall, brushed against a patch of mould that started hissing loudly, smelling of mouldy eggs and giving off a thick steam as the water dripping down through the leaking floors boiled. Steam and smoke blurred in a mixture of black and white that made Lyle's eyes water and choked him. He reached a decision, and reached for the kettle.

With a final scream, the door burst open, sending a small shower of wood in every direction. Mr Dew staggered through, murder in his eyes, a bronze knife in his hand. His green eyes that flashed like a cat's in the dark fell on Lyle, who was crouched in the flaring darkness of orange-black smoke and flame. Mr Dew grinned and moved after him, oblivious of the smoke. He got within a few feet of Lyle, and stopped, face frozen, eyes wide. Above Lyle's head, the kettle hung suspended from a rafter by a long piece of string. The iron fork was half-visible inside, its tines touching a band of velvet torn from Lyle's coat. The band itself was looped round the ladles, which spun and hissed with speed as they caught the steam billowing off the wall, pushing the contraption round like a windmill, and dragging the loop of velvet round faster and faster as the ladles spun, Lyle's magnet secured tightly inside their scoop, velvet scratching against the fork, humming inside the kettle. Lyle edged a little closer. A fat blue spark, brighter even than the fires around it, leapt with an angry pop from the surface of the kettle to a metal button on Lyle's sleeve, making him jump as it earthed into his skin. The entire thing looked like a clumsy accident at suppertime, but the pallor in Dew's face told a different story. Lyle watched him blurrily through the smoke-induced tears running from his eyes, saw him try to move a step closer, and flinch back again. Where the piece of wire in the kettle didn't quite touch the velvet, sparks flashed, big electric sparks.

'Is it the electric or the magnetic field that's causing you so much offence?' yelled Lyle over the roar of the flames and the scream of the steam. 'This is just an amateur static generator! What would you do if I had a decent steam engine and belt?'

Mr Dew's face was a mixture of pain and hatred. In the doorway, more green-eyed people were gathered, also looking pained. Lyle heard the spitting noise of more sparks dancing, then heard it again, from a direction he didn't expect. He felt something sharp and hot on his back, and reached behind himself for the bulk of the Fuyun Plate, swinging it round so he could see it more clearly. Inside the coat, in the presence of the magnetic field, the bowl was full of sparks, darting across it in thick blue waves, never quite managing to leave the surface. Lyle reached down and touched it. The sparks ran straight through his finger, cold to the touch, but underneath, the plate was warm. He heard a groan from the Tseiqin. Several had their hands over their ears, as if they couldn't bear the sound. Most were backing away, their faces masks of pain. Even Mr Dew was now at the door, retreating with an expression of pure hate. Lyle hesitated. He stared down at the plate, then at the makeshift static generator, then at the now-empty black doorway, then up at the ceiling. It was sagging, the fire crawling all over it. He looked down at the plate again. He thought, *Oh Jesus . . .*

The roof caved in, smashing down on the ladles, the kettle, and on the Lyle-shaped empty space.

Lyle's hand was bleeding. That was the first thing he thought. He coughed, tasting dry smoke in his mouth. He pulled himself up slowly, a little bit at a time, until he was on his knees, holding the Fuyun Plate close to his chest for protection. With the cave-in, his magnetic field had been destroyed, and now the Fuyun Plate felt as innocently cold as ever. He looked up slowly and saw a pair of black leather shoes. They didn't look as though they belonged to anyone he knew. His gaze wandered to a pair of black silk trousers, a black silk jacket and, finally, a pair of intense green eyes. The face had the finely cut features of Lord Moncorvo. And it was smiling.

His fingers tightened on the Plate. He thought, *Well, this is it, then. I made a small static electricity generator out of a kettle and a few kitchen utensils, and now I'm going to die. I wonder what Tate will do without me?*

'Mister Horatio Lyle,' said Moncorvo, smiling. 'You are full of surprises. But now . . .'

There was a noise at the end of the street. It was the sound of frantic horses neighing. A second later there was a clattering, and a carriage, driven by a wild-haired, wild-eyed Thomas, exploded round the corner, its wheels a blur as he slapped at the reins and shouted, 'Hey-ya!'

On the roof of the carriage, clinging on with just one hand, was a dark figure trailing a deep red scarf, and holding a gun. As the carriage roared down the street he fired, and with each deafening shot someone fell, the man's expression never once changing. The carriage neared Lyle, and Tess leant out of the wildly careening vehicle and kicked open the door. 'Come on, Mister Lyle, don't just sit there gawpin'!'

Lyle was on his feet. He shoved past Moncorvo and ran past him, towards the middle of the street. He threw the Plate into the open door of the carriage as it rushed past and grabbed at the side, fingers nearly slipping. He got one foot inside, pulled himself up, and Mr Dew grabbed his ankle. Lyle clung to the door of the carriage, while Mr Dew staggered, feet going out from under him. Lyle didn't let go.

'Mister Chink!' shouted Tess over the roar of the wheels. Feng Darin's face appeared above the side of the carriage. He took aim with the small iron revolver and pulled the trigger. There was a click on the empty barrel. Tess sighed. 'Bloody men!' she screamed. Leaning past Lyle, she started kicking at Mr Dew's fingers. Every other kick hit Lyle's ankle, but her grim expression of determination left no room for complaint. On the third kick, Dew's hold gave and he slipped back, falling into the road. Lyle toppled face first into the carriage while Tess dragged the door shut. As the carriage bounced away, rocking and screaming with the speed, Tess turned to the filthy Lyle, sprawled gracelessly across the floor, black with soot and dirt, and smiled her sweetest, most innocent smile.

'Miss us?' she asked.

CHAPTER 18

Magnet

Night settled over London. Horatio Lyle, as he climbed painfully out of the carriage, wondered if it was going to be the last night of his life. He hoped not. He never had had a chance to find out what happened if you mixed carbonated water with potassium.

Feng Darin hesitated on the doorstep of Lyle's house. He looked up at it with a long, deep frown. 'It would be more convenient, Mister Lyle, if you'd give me the Plate.'

'Don't take this wrong, but not a chance in heaven or hell, Sonny Jim.'

The lock clicked and the door swung open. There was a furious noise from behind it, as Tate bounced up, barking, imperiously summoning Lyle and the children inside. 'By the way,' muttered Lyle, as they slid into the gloom of the big, empty house, 'Mr Smith sends his regards.'

Still standing outside, Feng Darin frowned, thought about it, and the slow blossom of realization spread across his face. 'I will not apologize for my actions.'

'Hope is eternal.' Lyle turned and gave him a long, suspicious stare. Finally he said, 'Look, you can stand outside working out whether you're going to shoot me, or you can come in and have a cup of coffee.'

'Are the two mutually exclusive?'

'It would be *rude* to shoot me over a cup of coffee. And the mess would be dreadful.'

Feng looked up at the black sky and drew in a long, thoughtful breath. Then, without saying a word, he jogged up the steps two at a time and pushed his way past Lyle into the house, with the manner of a man who'd been planning on doing that all along, and you were a fool if you hadn't noticed. Lyle glanced up and down the length of the street behind Feng, quietly closed the door, turned every lock, and drew a bolt across the top, a chain across the middle and a small but distinctly heavy table across the bottom.

They went to Lyle's workroom in the basement, and Lyle lit the giant furnace. The huge magnet above it started to spin. Lyle put the Plate down on a table, resolutely not once looking at Feng, and threw several handfuls of water over his face. This didn't so much clean away the dirt, as spread it around more evenly.

Thomas said, 'What happens now?'

'What do you think, bigwig?' said Tess, rolling her eyes. 'They ain't gonna just let us *take* it.' She looked at Lyle. 'They ain't, are they?'

Feng answered before Lyle could. 'The Tseiqin have dedicated thousands of years towards acquiring this object, and repairing the damage caused to it while it was encaged in iron,' he said in a calm voice. 'They will not let anything stop them getting it now. Not even, I fear, your magnet, Mister Lyle.'

Lyle didn't answer. He was staring at the Plate.

'So what are we going to do with it?' said Thomas finally.

Silence. 'I say we sell it to Lord Lincoln. For a lot,' offered Tess.

'I am here to destroy it,' replied Feng quietly. Lyle smiled faintly, and looked down at the edge of the table, not moving.

Tess frowned. 'That ain't nice. We've gone to all this trouble to get it.' She brightened. 'If, on the other hand, you feel like *payin'* for the goods, on account of how it's technically *ours* 'cos we've gone to all this trouble of findin' it, then I'm here to offer a good deal.'

Lyle looked up slowly at her, eyebrows raised. Tess beamed. 'For sale, one mystic plate and . . . and token bigwig. Yours for . . . four hundred pound.'

'What?' said Thomas.

Tess patted him on the arm. 'You're worth at least a hundred pound.'

Feng smiled humourlessly at Tess, who shuffled uneasily away from the smile. 'Miss,' he said politely, 'I appreciate the gesture, but suspect that your employer Mister Lyle might have other intentions.'

All eyes turned to Lyle. He sighed. 'The Plate is a scientific phenomenon. An incredible phenomenon. And if I am slowly coming to accept that perhaps there is something a little irregular in the entire Tseiqin situation, then I don't honestly know if I can pass up the opportunity to learn about an object in whose acquisition they have invested so much energy.' Feng straightened up, his expression hardening. Lyle raised his hands in a conciliatory gesture. 'Not that I'm saying I'm going to give it to Lord Lincoln.'

Tess squeaked indignantly, 'But Mister *Lyle*! He'll *pay*! And it'd be safer with him than with us – he'd 'ave the army on his side!'

Thomas cleared his throat. 'Technically, sir, the Plate is under the care of the Elwick family . . .' Three pairs of unsympathetic eyes fixed on him. He coughed, and went on in the same level-headed voice, 'And as a representative of my family I, erm, give you full permission to dispose of it as you feel fit.'

'That's decent of you.'

He brightened. 'Yes. Yes, it is!'

Lyle slowly reached out and picked up the Plate by the very edges. Feng's fingers tightened ever so slightly on the edge of the table, though his expression remained fixed. Quietly, Lyle said, 'Teresa, Thomas? It might be a good idea if you check that the windows are locked and bolted. And draw the curtains.'

Thomas hesitated, but Tess immediately nodded, grabbed him by the sleeve and dragged him towards the door. The room seemed somehow larger and stiller without them. Lyle looked slowly up at Feng. 'If this object is so dangerous, it should be destroyed.'

'Yes.'

'But it should also be studied.'

Feng smiled thinly. 'You do not strike me as a man who leaves windows unlocked, Mister Lyle. Say what you want to say.'

Lyle sighed. 'Mr Feng, I can't do much outside building small electric generators in my kitchen, but I just want to clarify something. If you so much as *touch* the children, or threaten them in any way, I swear I'll do everything I possibly can to make your life . . .' he thought about it, '. . . horrid.' It seemed the only word really appropriate.

Feng thought about this. He looked up at the ceiling, and down at the floor, shoulders hunched up towards his ears, smile immovable behind his deep eyes. Lyle waited, clinging to the Plate tightly with his right hand, the bloody left hand still dangling at his side, fingers curled slightly in pain.

Very slowly, Feng raised his head, and stared straight at Lyle. 'No,' he said. 'The situation has advanced too far, Mister Lyle.'

'I thought you might say that.'

'Which is why you sent the children away?'

'Well, there was a chance I'd forgotten to lock something.'

Feng gradually started moving round the table, taking his time, swinging his arms loosely at his sides, threatening only in size, not speed. Even that was threatening enough. He didn't hold out his hand, didn't shout, didn't glare, but said politely, 'Please give me the Plate, Mister Lyle.'

'You can't just destroy something like this. It could have so many answers in it! And not just about where it came from and how it works, but *why* it works, why the Tseiqin want it, what makes it work, what makes *them* work, how they do what they do.'

'The Tseiqin will come here soon, Mister Lyle. They will take it before you can do anything,' he said quietly, advancing slowly towards Lyle.

Lyle backed away a little further, talking in a level but rapid voice. 'I saw it react when inside a magnetic field, sparking. Stone doesn't spark in a magnetic field; the idea is absurd. It wasn't even *cutting* the magnetic field, but it still reacted. The legend said that when the priests put it in an iron box, it was hit by lightning and that damaged the Plate. Electricity and magnetism are inseparable parts of the same force, magnetism changes the plate, magnetism changes the Tseiqin; *that* is why they do not like iron! *Listen to me!*'

Feng stopped a few steps from Lyle. Lyle's bloody left hand was clutching a very slim needle, the cap lying discarded on the floor. Feng frowned at it. 'What will you do with that, Mister Lyle?'

'Destroying this plate is like destroying the Rosetta Stone! You shut yourself out of a world, lose touch with something that we might never have a chance to understand ever again!'

'And if the Tseiqin take the Plate, Mister Lyle? If they take it and repair it, as they have waited so long to do, if they repair it and use it – what then? There won't be people like you left alive to learn its secrets any more, Mister Lyle. They are coming, Mister Lyle, and I doubt if they will be sympathetic to your sense of scientific curiosity.'

Lyle's fingers tightened on the needle, the point quavering towards Feng. Feng sighed, and his hand reached into his pocket. It came out holding the revolver. 'Mister Lyle, I respect you. But you and I really are from different worlds.'

He pulled the hammer back. Lyle swallowed. 'You know, I wasn't scared of death a few days ago?' Lyle's voice was very quiet. 'I thought that I knew what it would be like – nothing. Peaceful, empty, unaware nothing, a dreamless sleep. Now I'm not so sure. Uncertainty always brings a little fear. But I'm not afraid of you, Feng Darin. I don't think you'll shoot me. I'm almost certain of it. I have no proof, of course, but I'm willing to stake everything on the chance.'

Feng brought the gun up. 'Don't take the risk, Lyle.'

Lyle didn't move. 'You want the Plate?' He raised the needle, tiny between his hands. 'Come on. Take it.'

'Lyle! I will kill you!'

'If you were going to kill me you would have done it on the steps of my house.'

'Give me the Plate!'

'No.'

Feng hissed in frustration, his hand tightening over the butt of the gun. He moved a step towards Lyle, turning sideways and swinging the gun up to level directly at Lyle's impassive face. There was an explosion of noise beneath his outstretched arm, and the sound of ripping fabric. Tate dug his teeth deep into Feng's ankle, growling and snuffling through a mouthful of trouser and skin. Feng grunted, half-turning, trying to shake Tate off, but the dog wasn't budging. In the same second Lyle ran forward, reaching out with the tip of the needle to scratch at Feng's arm. Feng grabbed Lyle's wrist as he came, twisting it round sideways, suddenly oblivious of Tate's gnawing at his ankle, bending Lyle's arm back downwards until the bones creaked and Lyle's bloody hand spasmed instinctively with the grating nerves. The needle fell to the floor and Feng shoved Lyle to one side, grabbing the Plate out of Lyle's hand as he came. Lyle fell hard, head hitting the table. Feng kicked Tate off, scooped up the Plate, put it down firmly on the table, stood back, took aim and fired. It bounced on the table with the first bullet, which ricocheted away to bang against the wall, bounced again with the second, and the third, hopping along the table.

The Plate wasn't even chipped. Feng's eyes began to widen, fear starting to seep in. With a hiss of anger he turned the gun round and started smashing the butt against it with all his might. Not a chip, not a scratch. By the side of the table, Lyle half-stirred, blinking blearily. Blood was creeping through the hair behind his right ear. He tried to get up, his bloody hand shaking violently, and fell back.

Feng seized the Plate, looked around, and his eyes settled on the furnace. He walked towards it with a slow, stately purpose. As he drew near its metal bulk, the Fuyun Plate in his hands started to flash with fat blue sparks. So did the spinning magnet above the furnace itself. Feng grabbed a thick cloth off the desk by the furnace, and dragged open a small black iron door. Smelly orange flame lashed out of it angrily, clawing at the air beyond the furnace. Lyle staggered groggily to his feet. Feng, grinning, stood back and, as Lyle started to run towards him, tossed the Plate lightly on to the flames.

Lyle stopped dead. The furnace kept rumbling. On the floor, Tate whimpered. Lyle stared at the half-open furnace door. 'Jesus,' he whispered.

Feng was already dropping the gun back into his pocket,

smiling a thin, satisfied smile, shielding his eyes from the light and the heat as he tried to see into the flame. Lyle edged gradually towards him, drew level and looked.

There was a long silence. Feng's face slowly fell as he peered at the dark shape of the Plate, inside the flame. Fear was starting to creep in properly, slackening some muscles and tightening others, until his face was a battleground of contortion. Wordlessly, Lyle picked up a long hook from its stand by the furnace, and stuck it into the flames, until it caught the edge of the Plate. He pulled it out slowly, and let it drop to the floor. It wasn't even charred. Lyle gently pushed the furnace door shut, knelt down, ran his hand over the Plate, careful not to touch it, frowned slightly and, with the very end of his bloody left forefinger, felt it. It was cold to the touch. He looked up at Feng, whose face was a mask.

The magnet above the furnace, spinning in the fat coil of wire, suddenly accelerated, humming inside its bracket. Lyle looked down at the Plate. Where his bloody hand had touched the stone, red sparks were pooling, rushing back and forth across the Plate. Lyle stood up, holding the Plate. Sparks were flying off the metal furnace. And leaping out of Feng's pocket, where the gun sat. Feng took it out slowly, a look of surprise on his face, as red sparks also leapt off the metal of the gun. Lyle could feel the Plate pulling in his hand, tugging towards the large bulk of the furnace. He tightened his grip on it, and tried to drag it away from the iron. As it moved through the air in his grasp, it trailed more red sparks, which flew towards the furnace and bounced noisily off the iron, before sinking leisurely down to earth.

Around the room, cupboards were shaking, anything metal

was giving off red sparks, screws screaming as they tried to get out, the metallic compounds in their glass tubes bubbling and bouncing, the central table shaking from its internal iron rivets, the large wardrobe full of bits of scrap metal in one corner flying open and the metal crawling across the floor towards the Plate and Lyle. The metal trigger of Feng's gun, drawn towards the magnet, compressed and fired. The shot bounced away, but didn't reach the ceiling. Lyle threw the Plate to one side hastily and dived for cover under the table as the bullet headed straight for the Plate and clung to it like a flea to blood. Feng tossed the gun aside and ducked as a metal tripod flew across the room. Lyle grabbed the whimpering Tate and pulled him into safety under the table.

At the door to the room, Tess and Thomas appeared. Tess took one look at the whirlwind of metal and grabbed Thomas by the scruff of the neck, dragging him back behind the door and slamming it firmly shut. In the room, the giant electric bulbs guttered and exploded, showering glass and hot metal. The flames of the candles stretched, always bending the same way, always towards the Plate, then the metal candlesticks they sat on lifted up and joined the funnel of spiralling metal, spewing hot wax everywhere. Lights went out, except for the red sparks still flying around the Plate. Lyle felt the table above him wobbling, and clung to the table leg. Outside, there was a dull thud as something large slammed into the shut wooden door, which was straining on its hinges. The spinning magnet above the furnace was rocking back and forth, one side inexorably drawn towards the Plate, while the gears that drove it screamed in indignant pain. Lyle heard something go *thunk* and winced. The pipes in the ceiling strained and started to bend as they were drawn downwards, the furnace doors flew open, spewing out gushing flame, the wires screamed and . . .

It stopped. There was a clatter as bits of metal quickly fell to the ground and lay still. There was a slow whir as the magnet above the furnace started spinning again, slowly and stately, as if nothing had happened. The only light came from the flames still flickering out of the open furnace doors. At the end of the room, the other door opened. A frying pan had embedded itself in the wood. From under it, Tess peered, pale-faced. By the light of the furnace, she looked round the room, and finally saw Lyle, huddled with Tate in his arms, under the table. Somewhere, overhead and far outside the house, thunder rolled.

'Jesus,' she breathed. 'What the *hell* did you people do?'

CHAPTER 19

'This is going to sound unscientific . . .' began Lyle.

'But . . .' prompted Tess.

'Human blood.'

Thomas shut the furnace door while Lyle held his last match to a slightly bent-looking lantern, and set it on the table. Tate picked his way across a floor strewn with debris. Feng slowly and carefully reloaded his gun in the shadows just beyond the orange lantern light. The Fuyun Plate rested innocently on the table. Lyle kept his bloody left hand, the sliver of wood still lodged beneath the skin, as far from the Plate as he could. 'Perhaps it's something to do with the iron content in the blood?' he suggested hopefully. Feng sighed. Lyle started turning red. 'Or it might just be that it's human blood, the essence of our lives and souls and . . . other spiritual . . . matters . . .' he hazarded unevenly.

'You mean . . . you get blood on that, an' it goes mad?' suggested Tess cautiously.

'Yes.'

'You sure? You don't want to try and . . .'

'*No!*'

Thomas picked his way over to the desk, gathering up bits and pieces automatically as he went, and putting them on the side carefully, not sure what they did, but impressed anyway.

Lyle was watching Feng. He said in an almost fatherly voice, 'You don't know how to destroy it, do you?'

Feng stopped reloading his gun, glanced up once, saw Lyle's face, looked away again and went right on slotting bullets into the cylinder. Somewhere, thunder rumbled again, crawling up through the feet and down through the house. In the silence after it died away, Thomas said, 'I didn't know that there was going to be thunder tonight.'

Lyle looked up at the ceiling, as if he could see straight through it. 'There wasn't. The clouds weren't right, the pressure was too high.'

'Oh,' said Tess finally.

Thomas swallowed. 'Thunderstorms are magnetic, aren't they, Mister Lyle?'

Lyle nodded slowly, each nod turning his head until he looked at Feng again. He said quietly, 'The priests put it in an iron box. The iron box was hit by lightning, wasn't it? A thunderstorm.'

'That is so.'

'Is there any mention of *why* there's a thunderstorm?'

Silence. 'Thomas?'

'Yes, Mister Lyle?'

'There's a small box of magnets somewhere. Painted red at one end.'

Thomas nodded quickly and started scouring the floor. Lyle began opening drawers in the desk around one side of the wall, until he found something small and shiny that fitted easily into the palm of the hand. 'Teresa?'

Tess darted over. He handed it to her. She frowned at it. On the cover were the initials *HL*, engraved in flowery lettering. She opened it up. It was a compass, the internal dial swinging so that the North marker always pointed the same way no matter which way she spun it. She glanced up towards Lyle, eyebrows raised. He knelt down until his face was level with hers and said quietly, 'If it happens, *when* it happens, go to Lincoln. Tell him everything. If it happens, and it happens badly, follow the compass. It will be drawn towards the nearest strong magnetic pole. Follow it to the Plate. Don't try and help. You've got to get to Lincoln, you've got to tell him what's happening. Don't let Thomas do anything stupid.'

She nodded once, and slipped the compass into her pocket. 'I promise, Mister Lyle.'

He smiled, and briefly laid his hand on her shoulder, resting it there for just a second, before he stood up and without a word turned back to the table.

There was a knock on the door upstairs. Every pair of eyes immediately tried to read every other pair of eyes. Tate started to whimper. Lyle said quietly, 'That was quick.'

'Could we pretend we ain't here?'

There was another thunderous knocking, and a voice, very faint. 'Constable Lyle, I know you're in there!'

'Oh no,' whimpered Lyle, putting his head in his hands.

'You know this voice?' asked Feng sharply.

'Inspector Vellum,' muttered Thomas.

The knocking went on. Lyle sighed, straightened up, brushed himself down self-consciously to no effect, and said in a falsely determined voice, '*Right.*'

Upstairs, the more formal appearance of the house was made larger and darker by the dim lamplight. Lyle opened the door with the chain still on and frowned out at Vellum, standing in the street, swathed in a coat. 'Yes?' A cold wind was blowing from the black sky, smelling of thick static and heavy clouds.

'Constable Lyle,' said Vellum in a voice surprisingly neutral for his usual disposition. 'I have a warrant to search your house.' He held up a piece of paper.

Lyle stared at it in surprise. 'I beg your pardon?'

'Be so kind as to admit me, Constable Lyle.'

Lyle slid the chain off the door suspiciously, and immediately Vellum's foot stuck across the threshold. He pushed his way through the door and looked slowly round. 'The light of illumination,' he murmured, eyes falling on Tess, holding the lantern. '"What light through yonder window breaks?"' He blinked icily at Tess. 'Are you familiar with Shakespeare?'

Lyle glanced out of the door behind him, and frowned, slipping it shut and drawing the chain back across it. 'Inspector, where's your support?'

'Do we need support, Constable?' asked Vellum. Lyle took

another look at the warrant in his hand, and his frown deepened. He slowly scrutinized Vellum again.

'Inspector?'

'We might as well save ourselves difficulty, Constable Lyle,' continued Vellum, seemingly oblivious. 'Lord Lincoln has sent me to take the Plate back to him.'

Lyle blinked. 'Excuse *me?*' He felt cold. His stomach was turning. There was something almost obsidian in Vellum's unblinking stare.

'The Plate, Constable Lyle. For Lord Lincoln.'

Vellum's hand was resting lightly in his coat pocket. Lyle found his eyes drawn inexorably towards it. 'I'm sorry,' he said politely, his voice acquiring an edge. 'I destroyed it.'

Vellum's eyes flickered. 'I hardly see how, Constable Lyle.'

'Oh, it was really very easy, Inspector Vellum. Exposure to a massive magnetic field – *have you ever been in a large magnetic field, Inspector* – passage of an electric current, a little blood, a few sparks, a little lightning – *have you ever been hit by lightning, Inspector?* – nothing that someone who lives and *breathes* iron, *breathes* it, Inspector, can't do.'

Vellum's hand was halfway out of his pocket, the gun gleaming in it, when Feng rose up behind him, said, 'Excuse me, Inspector?' and swung a large, meaty fist into the Inspector's expression of grim hatred. Vellum crumpled with a little sigh, the gun falling from his hand. Feng kicked it casually to one side, and peered down at the unconscious form of the inspector.

'What is this?' he asked politely.

Lyle sighed. 'They found Vellum.' There was a thunderous

knocking at the door. 'Or possibly they just offered to read his poetry.'

The knocking suddenly stopped. A soft, female voice drifted through, like silk. 'Horatio?' Lyle glanced at Feng. No one moved. 'Horatio, where will you go? Who can help you? All you need to do is give us the Plate, and we'll leave. We'll let you go, Horatio. If you give it to us now, we may even let you survive the storm, our coming storm, let you share in the wonder of the new world. You and your friends. Think of the children, Horatio. Think of the screams of your friends.'

Feng thoughtfully picked up Vellum's fallen gun, and slipped it into his pocket. Lyle said, 'Help me carry Vellum downstairs.'

'Are you sure?'

'He'll be killed if we leave him up here. Come on.'

'Horatio?' Lady Lacebark's voice drifted down the stairs after them, like a living thing seeking them out. 'We can bring you happiness. A new, clear world, free from the black smoke of choking machines. A cleaner, purer world, Horatio. *Just give us the Plate.*'

Lyle and Feng laid the unconscious Vellum in the corner of the furnace room. Thomas was holding a small box of magnets. Lyle took it quickly from him, laying it down on the table, next to the Plate. Feng's eyes were fixed icily on the Plate, his expression grim.

'Thomas, help Feng move furniture across the door here.'

Thomas nodded quickly, hesitated in front of the frozen Feng, glanced at Tess, then grabbed Feng's sleeve, pulled on it sharply and said, 'Come on!' Feng snapped back to awareness, glanced at Thomas, seemed to see him for the first time, then nodded. The two disappeared into the corridor outside the furnace room.

Lyle was frantically tipping magnets on to the table. He grabbed one and held it up next to the Plate. It trembled in his fingers. He let it go. It stuck to the Plate. He pulled out another and held it on the other side of the Plate. It also stuck. Lyle grimaced. 'What's it mean?' asked Tess, her hand white where she clung to the compass.

'It means that this plate is polarized. Pass me that wire, will you?'

She passed it. Lyle dropped two ends of the wire into the bowl, placing the other two ends in a large glass beaker, selected a bottle from a shelf and poured the contents into the beaker. It hissed, like acid, as it sloshed into the glass. Sparks flashed up from the Plate where the wires touched. And the plain grey stone started, very faintly, to whiten. Lyle grinned.

Upstairs, the door thundered under a sudden shocked impact. Tess watched as the faint pinpricks of whiteness spread through the stone.

'What's it mean?'

'I'm beginning to understand, Tess.' Lyle tossed the wires to one side, and looked up sharply as, somewhere, a bell rang.

'What's *that* mean?'

'Someone's just smashed a window.' He handed her a magnet. 'Don't let go of this for anything.' He opened a cupboard full of test tubes, chose three and passed them to her. 'Don't mix the red and the blue unless you're standing at least five feet away,' he said quickly. 'The grey will smoke and spark, but it won't hurt you. Use them in an emergency.'

She nodded, swallowing down her fear. Upstairs, there was a short, sharp scream. She flinched. 'What's that?' Her voice was barely above a whisper.

'Someone's just tried to force a lock.'

'And?'

'Don't ask.'

Feng and Thomas reappeared in the corridor. Thomas was carrying an iron poker in one hand. Lyle pushed magnets at both of them, without a word. Upstairs, the floor sang as someone walked across it. Lyle ran to the furnace, and started turning dials. The magnet spinning in its coil started to scream, spinning round in a blur. 'Thomas, get that wire!' he snapped, pointing at a fat coil. 'Tess, the steps.'

Tess dragged a short set of wooden steps over to the side of the furnace. Lyle grabbed the thick industrial wire, climbed up the steps and started wrapping the wire round metal nodes sticking out of the generator. When he was happy with this, he dragged a heavy brass lever down, and for a second the magnet stopped spinning. Then something clicked. The magnet started spinning again, blurring with speed. Lyle jumped down from the steps as another bell started ringing in the corridor.

'They're on the stairs.'

They peered out into the dark corridor beyond the furnace room at the dresser Thomas and Feng had dragged across the door. It started to shake as a new, nearer knocking began. Lyle put his hand on Thomas's shoulder. 'Lad? You know about the principle of a Faraday wheel?'

'I think so. Induction by an alternating current . . .'

'That dresser has a steel frame inside it.'

Thomas glanced from Lyle's face to the thick coil of wire running down uselessly from the furnace, then back again. He nodded. 'Yes, sir!'

Lyle glanced at Feng. He had his gun out, and was poised like a tiger. 'Come on, you.'

The door thundered once again.

CHAPTER 20

Lyle led Feng to the far end of the corridor, and stopped in front of a plain bit of wall. He kicked it on a scuffed area of wallpaper, and the whole end of the corridor swung out. Beyond it was a ladder, steep and in darkness. They started climbing up the passage full of warm, stagnant air, while somewhere above the house, thunder rumbled again, the sound bouncing down the passageway. Behind them, the section of opening wall slid shut, plunging the ladder into darkness. They kept climbing, feeling their way up the tight corridor, until the ladder abruptly stopped. There was a dull *thunk* as Lyle drove his elbow into a loose wood panel to one side. It gave way stiffly, falling away to let in the pale grey light of evening. Lyle crawled through it on hands and knees. Feng followed.

They were in an attic, heavy rain hammering down on the sloped, low triangular roof, which was too shallow to let anyone stand. A dim light seeped through a window at the far end. Lyle crawled through a maze of trunks and bags, dusty with age and neglect, until he reached a trapdoor. He opened it very carefully and peered down at the corridor below. It was empty. Voices drifted up the stairs, shouting orders. Feng quietly cocked his pistol. Lyle swung round so that he was half-sitting on the edge of the trapdoor, then dropped down heavily on to the corridor below. Feng followed, landing in cat-like silence. Lyle crept to the edge of the corridor, motioning at Feng to avoid certain floorboards, and peered down at the stairs below.

In the darkness, he could hear Feng's low breathing, and feel him as a hot presence to his side. He whispered, 'We've got to draw them away.'

Feng nodded wordlessly. Lyle reached into his tattered pockets and pulled out the small bundle of needles. Unwrapping them, he tossed the whole lot down on to the stairs below the landing where they stood, hearing them clatter faintly as they fell. It was going to be difficult to clear up, he reasoned, but it had to be done. He then pulled out one last test tube. It was larger than the others, and full to the brim of a compacted yellow powder.

'When this is exposed to air,' said Lyle quietly, 'it will smoke and burn. Whatever you do, *don't breathe the fumes.*'

Feng nodded soundlessly. Lyle took a deep breath and

shouted, 'Coo-eeee!' There was a sudden silence from a long way below. 'Erm . . . yes . . .' mumbled Lyle, then, 'Hello! Can we talk about this at all? I mean, insurance alone is . . .'

A brass crossbow bolt slammed into the wall by Lyle's right ear. Lyle yelped and scrambled back. Silence a second longer below, then a renewed, louder shouting and the sound of people on the stairs, running up, getting nearer in a thunder louder than the belting rain.

He knew when they ran into the fallen needles, because that was when the screaming started.

The door in the basement had stopped thundering. The silence was, if anything, worse than the noise. Tess held a fat coil of wire and said in a hushed voice, 'What's goin' on?'

Thomas stared up at the door. 'We should help them.'

'No! Let's finish what Mister Lyle said we should do!'

Thomas swallowed and nodded. 'Wrap the wire around that beam.'

'Why?'

'It's a Faraday wheel. It creates a magnetic field between two bits of wire by using the electricity from the furnace. We can make a magnetic field across the door.'

She nodded, thinking about this, then started wrapping the wire round the metal frame of the dresser. Upstairs, she heard a sudden sound of screaming, and hoped it wasn't Lyle.

Feng saw the first climber before Lyle, and fired, the flash from the muzzle of the gun blinding in the darkness. The figure fell back, but another pushed into his place, green eyes flashing cat-like, fixing on Feng and Lyle. A second bronze crossbow bolt thudded into the wall by Lyle, who ducked even after it had finished quivering. Another shot from Feng; another body fell back. And another shot. Feng finished his round and, sensing that he needed time to reload, the Tseiqin rushed forward, charging up the stairs in a pile. Lyle pulled out the test tube, held it over the edge of the landing, took a deep breath, and let it go. It fell into darkness. A few seconds later, there was the faint sound of shattering glass, a clink and a *whumph*. Lyle covered his head with his arms as shattered wood was thrown up the stairs, jagged shards embedding themselves into the ceiling. Shouts and screams drifted upstairs, carried with a thick yellow smoke. Lyle grabbed Feng by the shoulder as the other man slipped the last bullet into the gun and started firing again, dragging him into another room containing a metal bathtub, a washing bowl, a mirror and a small window. Lyle tore a strip off his filthy shirtsleeve, dipped it in the cold water in the bowl and tied it across his nose and mouth. Outside, people were coughing and choking. Yellow smoke lapped at the gap under the door. Lyle thrust a damp cloth at Feng, who hastily tied it around his face as well. Lyle pushed the window open and peered out. Down below, the street was thronged with black-clad, green-eyed Tseiqin. There was a shout, and the crossbow bolt shattered the glass of the window as Lyle dived for cover. Feng shouted over the din of cracking wood and shouting attackers, 'What now?'

Wordlessly, Lyle pointed at the ceiling of the small room. There was a hatch in it.

The door to the room shook under a sudden impact. Feng

fired through it. The shaking stopped. Then started again, harder, with renewed vigour. Feng turned to Lyle. 'Put your foot in my hand.'

Lyle stepped into Feng's cupped hand and was pushed up towards the ceiling. He slammed his bloody fist against the hatch, which popped back, and wormed through, pulling himself up over the edge. The door shook again. Feng fired into it, but the shaking kept up regardless. Lyle reached down with one hand. 'Come on! Take my hand!'

Feng glanced at Lyle in the darkness, and behind his mask, smiled. He reached into the recesses of his coat, and pulled out a long, slim steel blade. Lyle shook his head. 'Don't be bloody stupid! There's *hundreds* of them!'

Feng grinned, a flash of white in the gloom, turned to the door, fired three times through the worn wood, and ran at it, exploding through the wood into darkness.

Lyle cursed, kicking the hatch shut in the ceiling, and crawled through the darkness for the ladder leading down.

Thomas ran through the basement as the hammering against the door started again, shaking the dresser that blocked it. He thought he could hear the crunching sound of an axe, but it was hard to tell through the din. The dresser was now wide open, the internal steel frame covered with wire. He found Tess twiddling the last coil of wire into a node on the furnace. Looking along the trails of wire running out of the door, suspended a foot or so above the ground by the tension, he felt a moment's satisfaction. He wiped the sweat from his forehead and nodded briskly at Tess. 'All right, now . . .'

Lyle exploded into the room, dragging off the mask around his nose and mouth. 'Is it ready?'

They nodded.

'Right. Go on, Thomas.'

Thomas pulled a lever. Electricity raced along the wires, and the hammering at the door suddenly stopped. Lyle rushed to the corridor and peered down towards the door into the basement. The wires almost hummed with electricity.

Silence settled, and in it the sounds that had been previously obliterated slunk back in. They listened to the humming of the spinning magnet above the furnace, to the distant thrumming of the rain, to the rolling of the thunder far off, to each other's breathing, to footsteps squeaking on floors high above. Thick, noisy silence.

'Mister Lyle?' Tess's voice was shaking.

'Yes?'

'Where's Mr Feng?'

Lyle didn't answer. They listened to the furnace ticking busily, to Tate snuffling, to horses' hooves stamping in the street, to the hiss-crack of a lightning strike fizzling somewhere in the distance, to the drumming of the rain, to a bell, somewhere, striking the hour. Lyle counted the strokes.

'It's midnight, ain't it?' said Tess quietly.

'Yes.'

'Mister Lyle? It is goin' to be all right, ain't it?'

Somewhere else, a different clock was striking, as slowly the city reached a uniform decision about the hour. Lyle didn't answer.

'Mister Lyle?'

'It'll be all right, Tess.'

There was the faintest sound in the furnace room. It was the sound of someone groaning. They slipped inside. The single lantern still burnt dimly on the table, dull orange light falling on to the Fuyun Plate.

Tess walked slowly over to it, and touched its cool surface, rubbing the thin white spots on the Plate. 'Mister Lyle?'

'I think I know how to destroy the Plate, Tess.'

She looked up sharply. 'How?' asked Thomas.

'Electricity. Not around it – when the lightning struck the box the Plate was in, it must have changed the polarity, rendering the Plate useless to the Tseiqin. But the Plate didn't have a current through it, just around it. When I passed a small current through it, though, it reacted.'

There was the faintest sound of a moan again. Lyle looked towards the shape of Vellum, hunched in the darkness. The man was halfway on to his feet. He blinked. 'Lyle?' he whispered. Then he looked around and slowly realized where he was. 'This is an interesting shift in events, wouldn't you agree?' he muttered. He straightened up, cleared his throat. 'Perhaps you can explain what you're doing here.'

'What *I'm* doing here?'

'Yes, Constable.'

'This is *my* house.'

'But Constable . . . why would I be in your house?' Upstairs, there was a sudden scream. Vellum's eyes snapped upwards. 'Good God, what was that?'

'The ill-advised consequence of rash experimentation with phosphorus and acid?' suggested Lyle wanly.

'Well, we must go and find out!'

'No, sir, that really wouldn't be wise. How much do you remember?'

'Goddammit, Constable, I am the senior officer here! You, girl, what do you think you're doing?'

'Erm . . . eyeballin', sir.'

'Do you think you're being *amusing*, child?'

Tess looked helplessly to Lyle for advice. Lyle sighed and walked towards Vellum in a businesslike manner. 'Inspector, please don't be offended by this, it's really for your own good, in every possible sense, but . . .' He bunched up his fingers, bent his elbow and swung a punch for all he was worth. Vellum collapsed back on to the floor. Lyle cradled his fist and hopped from foot to foot muttering, 'Ouch ow ouch *ow*!'

Tess rolled her eyes. 'Don't be a baby, sir.'

There was a sudden click from the corridor outside. Lyle turned white. 'Feng?' he whispered.

There was a low thud, and silence. The deepest silence of them all. Lyle grabbed Tate, put him into Thomas's surprised arms, took Tess and Thomas by a shoulder each and started dragging them towards the wardrobe full of scrap metal. 'In here, *now*.'

'But Mister Lyle . . .!'

'No arguments!' He kicked the scrap metal aside and slammed a foot into the back of the wardrobe. It swung open. Beyond it, the dim light fell on sheaves of paper, scrawled with a thousand diagrams. Thomas's eye fell on one. The pencil diagram on it resembled a form of bird, made entirely of wood and cloth. He felt his heart race, and as Lyle pushed him, Tess and Tate inside, he turned to Lyle, mouth open. Lyle shook his head. 'Not now, lad.'

'Mister Lyle . . .' began Tess, wheedling.

'Tess!' Lyle's face was white, his voice on edge. 'Whatever happens, whatever you hear, whatever you think might be happening, you don't leave this wardrobe until it's over, you understand? Swear it!' They didn't move. '*Swear it!*'

'I promise,' murmured Tess.

'Thomas!'

'I promise.'

Lyle swallowed, and nodded. 'All right. Teresa?'

'Yes, Mister Lyle?'

'You've still got the compass?'

'Yes, Mister Lyle.'

'Good. It will tell you when it happens.' He hesitated, wanting to say something else, but not sure what else it could be. So he smiled, a long, tired smile, and nodded once, and closed the door to the wardrobe, plunging Tess and Thomas into darkness.

Outside, the wall at the end of the corridor swung open, and a bloody, dishevelled Feng dropped down from the ladder.

Behind him, unfolding from the darkness, stepped Lady Lacebark.

CHAPTER 21

Hand

The Tseiqin carried torches, simple sticks of wood wrapped with soaked cloths at the top, that gave off a smelly bright light. They descended from the attic ladder behind the glassy-eyed Feng, and filled the doorway, flinching from the wire. Lyle cradled the Plate close to himself and backed away towards the furnace and the spinning magnet, sheltering in its invisible field, pressing his back against the warm metal.

The Tseiqin came no further than the doorway. Lady Lacebark pushed her way to the front, and smiled at him. Behind her came Moncorvo and Mr Dew. 'Horatio,' she said, in a mild, reproving voice. 'Was it really all worth this?'

Lyle's fingers tightened over the Plate. 'You can't touch me,' he muttered. 'You can't come into the magnetic field.'

'You could give us the Plate, Horatio. We're going to take it anyway.'

Lyle swallowed and edged closer to the coil of wire running from the furnace. 'Keep back!'

Lacebark put on a crooked half-shrug of an expression, lips bending up and down all at once, and made a little 'hum' sound. 'Well, if you're going to be like that.' She made a gesture. Moncorvo, Lyle noticed, was grinning. Behind him, Mr Dew levelled a bronze crossbow, taking aim at Lyle with malicious slowness.

Lyle thrust his hand out, holding the Plate over the wire. 'Shoot me, and I'll drop it on to the wire. There's a *very* large current going through it. I don't know if it's enough to destroy the Plate, but I'm prepared to find out.'

Moncorvo immediately laid a hand on Dew's arm. Lacebark glared at Moncorvo, who hung his head, then turned back to Lyle, presenting a dazzling smile, only slightly edged with pain to be so close to the magnetic field.

'Why do you think that will intimidate us, Horatio? Do you honestly think you can destroy the Plate?'

'Shoot me and find out.'

Lacebark sighed. 'You and your family are all the same, Horatio. Iron in the blood. Do you really think that humanity will be made happier by your twisting of the nature that spawned your kind into straight grey lines?'

'I don't know,' he replied simply. 'But that's half the adventure, isn't it?'

'This is your last chance, Horatio. Give us the Plate.'

'*No.*'

She sighed fractionally, and moved to one side. Feng stepped forward, glassy-eyed. From behind him, sleepwalker style, emerged the nightrobe-clad shape of Miss Mercy Chaste. Lyle started to see her there, heart sinking. Feng, gaze fixed sightlessly on Lyle, pulled out a gun and pointed it calmly, levelly, at Mercy's left temple.

Lacebark said quietly, 'And now, Mister Lyle?'

He stared into Mercy's empty eyes, and, hating himself and the churning in his stomach, said, 'You've been watching me. You know she means nothing to me. An inconvenience. Nothing more.'

'Is your heart of iron too?' asked Lacebark quietly.

And, in a low, level voice, Feng said, jaw moving as if it was being controlled by a puppeteer, 'Lyle is bluffing.'

'I don't have the *talent* to bluff,' snapped Lyle.

'But we don't bluff,' snapped Moncorvo. 'Pull the trigger!'

Feng pulled the hammer back from the gun, moving quickly, and Lyle knew he was going to do it, and knew he couldn't let him. 'Wait!' He'd spoken even before his thoughts had finished racing. 'Wait.' Voice quieter. The fear filled him from top to toe. '*Wait.*'

Lacebark was smiling at him. Dew was grinning. Mercy's face was expressionless, her arms limp at her sides.

'Give us the Plate, Horatio.'

Lyle looked from Feng to Mercy to Lacebark, then to the Plate. He slowly moved it from where it hung over the wire, and held it up ponderously, staring at the plain stone surface. He looked up, and stared straight into Mercy's vacant eyes. 'I'm sorry,' he whispered, and closed his bloody left hand over the Plate, pressing the skewer of wood deep into his palm. Lacebark started forward, shouting, 'Shoot him!' – too late. Blood flowed from his hand, slipping into the Plate, turning the stone deep black-red.

The stone erupted in red sparks, leaping up from the blood-soaked plate and around the room. The magnet on the furnace screamed. Lyle couldn't hold on to the Plate as it leapt from his fingers, trailing blood and blood-red sparks. Metal shattered, bent, flew across the room towards the Plate, which spun wildly as a whirlwind of metal formed a thick, deadly tornado in the centre of the room, focused on the Plate. The Tseiqin were screaming, clutching at their ears. Some were bleeding, white blood running down from their noses and ears, the metal slicing through the air with a scream. The fat coils of wire leapt up, dragging anything they were attached to with them, and snaked in the air like a waking dragon. Lyle heard the creak of the metal furnace behind him and half-turned. The furnace doors burst open, spurting fire, the wire around the magnet contorted and lashed, breaking into pieces and flying towards the centre of the room, the magnet buckling and twisting, the furnace warping and bending. Lyle ran for a corner, diving for cover as, with a twisted scream, the furnace ruptured, spewing hot fire across the room. He hit the floor and curled up, hands over his head, knees tucked in. With a final groan, the giant metal furnace exploded, tortured beyond all extremes by forces pushing every which way, red sparks pouring off it in a bloody flood.

*

Tess felt the explosion rise up through her feet all the way to the tips of her hair, and thought that perhaps the world had ended. The noise went on so long that she began to think it wasn't noise at all, but perfect silence, and she was deaf. The shock wave pushed her and made bile rise in her throat, made Tate curl up at her foot and whimper. When it was over, she wasn't even sure it was over, because the after-ring in her mind went on and on, a deafening roar of shattered worlds. Over the burning sound left in her ears, she heard the clink of falling masonry, the hiss of dying flames, the clicking of cooling tortured metal, the thud of debris falling to the earth, and ultimately, a very final silence.

She crouched on her hands and knees and peered out through the narrow gap under the wardrobe. A hand was right in front of her, bloody and still, the fingers bent loosely in the middle to form a shallow arch, the blood pooling gently around it. She saw a torn sleeve attached to an arm and, just behind it, the top of a head of sandy hair, turned away from her, so that all she could make out was a small halo of hair beyond the arm, utterly motionless. She held her breath and kept as still as a stone while the silence dragged. Finally there was a voice, so faint and far off, she could barely hear it. Then footsteps. Then a voice.

'Mr Dew's assistant is dead,' said a voice like black leather.

'Unfortunate,' said a silken voice, slightly shaken. 'Feng? Take the Plate.'

There was a click. A foot appeared in front of the bloody hand, shod in black leather. The point of a crossbow appeared in Tess's line of view. Thomas's breathing behind her was deafeningly loud. A voice said, 'Wait.' A different shoe appeared, a woman's. 'He can still be of use to us.'

The crossbow tip wavered. The tip of the shoe prodded the limp arm. Tess heard the click of metal cooling, like the heartbeat of time. A black-leather-gloved hand reached down and picked up the arm, dragging the head with it. As it went up, Tess saw that blood was trickling with slow thickness down one side of Lyle's still face, and that his eyes were closed, his face relaxed, like one in sleep. Then it disappeared out of her line of sight. Behind her, she could hear Thomas's frantically fast breathing, and thought, *Don't give us away. Oh God I don't want to die, please, please don't hear . . .*

She heard footsteps across the floor, and a slow dragging sound behind them. Somewhere, thunder was rolling, rain falling. The little sounds behind the silence started to slip back in. She held her breath, and kept on holding. Hot metal cooled.

Tick tick tick . . .

She tried to count seconds in her mind, but couldn't tell whether they were heartbeats, seconds or the *tick tick tick* of the metal.

Thomas's hand rested on the wood of the door in front of her, ready to push. She grabbed it. His pulse underneath the shirt was racing desperately fast. She swallowed.

Tick tick tick . . .

She counted a hundred ticks, never once letting go of Thomas's sleeve, and gently pushed open the door. The room beyond was black apart from the red-hot slivers of shattered metal and a few, feeble fires still clinging to the contorted skeleton of the furnace, most of which was now embedded in various parts of the wall. The floor was littered with twisted metal and wood. There were dead Tseiqin lying still, some trapped under the debris of the explosion, some just lying with their eyes open in shock. Tess's hands and knees shook as she picked her way across the floor. Near the wardrobe there was a bloodstain that was human, deep red. And there was a lot of it. Tate started barking, and suddenly ran ahead, bounding into the corridor. Tess and Thomas followed as fast as their shaking legs allowed them.

Mercy Chaste was curled up, knees to her chin, in the corridor, quaking in wordless terror. Thomas knelt down next to her. 'Miss?' he murmured.

'Mnnmnn!' she chattered, trying to eat her fingers.

'Miss, are you all right?'

'*Mnnnmnnn!*'

Tess put a hand on Thomas's shoulder. 'We've got to get to Lord Lincoln. Thomas!'

He looked up weakly at her. 'Tess?'

'We've got to get to the Palace. Come *on*! It's still not finished!'

She dragged him away.

CHAPTER 22

Cathedral

Lyle thought he heard a carriage, felt it bumping over stones. *Odd. I wonder if I'm dead?* He pondered this. *Well, I'm breathing, and I think that's a pulse going on somewhere down there, which is always a good sign.*

And as awareness slowly came back, it brought with it memory and pain.

He opened his eyes. Mr Dew stared at him and grinned. He gently patted Lyle on the cheek, before leaning against the back of the carriage, smile still fixed.

'Damn,' muttered Lyle, then turned his face away and closed his eyes again. There were some things he just didn't want to see.

*

'Come on!'

'I'm coming!'

'Come *on*!'

'I'm *coming*! Cabby! Cabby!'

'What in Gawd's name are you?'

'This is Lady Teresa de le Hatch. I am the Honourable Thomas Edward Elwick. Take us to the Palace!'

'You tryin' to be funny, laddie?'

'Oi! Don't talk to him like that. My uncle's king of . . . China . . . you know?!'

'Children, get to bed. Go on, be off with you.'

'You don't understand! It's *urgent*! The fate of the Empire depends on it!'

'Be off with you.' A clattering sound. 'Oi, what the hell do you think you're doing?'

'Bigwig, what *are* you doing?'

'If you won't drive us, I'll take us there *myself*!'

'You what?'

'You *what*?'

'Get in, Teresa!'

'Lad, a joke is a joke, but this is . . .'

In the sound there was a dull *thwack*, followed by a reverential silence. Finally, 'Christ.'

'Come on, Teresa.'

'Can you drive this thing?'

'I am familiar with all arts of horsemanship, including the long rein . . .'

'That means you can drive it, or not?'

'I'm sure I can.'

'But you just *hit* . . .'

'No time to think about that now! *Come on!*'

'*All right!*'

And across London the church bells are proclaiming the hour anew, and the clouds are gathering and the pigeons are cooing in the gutters of old roofs and the drains are burbling with the rivers of rainwater that run down Ludgate Hill and slosh over the sides of Blackfriars Bridge into the sluggish river, which rises higher against the stone of the banks as the tide changes. And the factories yawn and the rigging creaks and the fires burn and the rain falls, always the rain falls, cutting through the night and making the streets shine silver. And the rain falls on Horatio Lyle as he is dragged out of a carriage that is just one in a convoy of carriages, and looks up slowly at the towering round dome of St Paul's Cathedral, half-covered in scaffold that runs right up one side of the dome. And overhead, lighting stabs the sky, and thunder trails after it, a loyal shadow in the broken night.

Horatio Lyle, filthy, bloody Horatio Lyle, shirt torn and blackened, wrapping his bloody arms around himself as the rain falls, watches while the sleepwalking Feng climbs out of another carriage, carrying reverentially in both hands the Fuyun Plate.

A fist grabs Lyle by the hair and pulls his head back until he can see the golden cross on the top of the cathedral, half-lost behind the rain that stings his eyes. In his ear Mr Dew whispers, 'You make gods of gold and iron, Mister Lyle. But we are the lords of flesh and blood.'

And Moncorvo is hammering on the iron doors of the

cathedral, and while Lyle thinks *No!* the door is opened by a priest who peers out from the candlelit interior and says, 'Yes?'

The priest is now crumpled in a corner as Lyle is dragged up the central aisle of the cathedral, across the marble floor, towards the altar beneath the towering dome. Shaking with cold, he looks up at the lightning flashing behind the windows in the nave. Moncorvo walks unhurriedly up to him.

'Why aren't I dead or sleepwalking?' snaps Lyle, fear giving him confidence. He meets Moncorvo's green eyes without flinching.

Moncorvo doesn't answer. His eyes move past Lyle to a pair of struggling, sweating Tseiqin. Lyle turns slowly and stares. The two drag large sacks behind them. They drop them on to the ground. Moncorvo nods briskly at Lyle. 'Open it.' His voice leaves no room for disagreement. Lyle kneels and, thinking of snakes and venom, reaches into the bag. His fingers close around something cold. He pulls it out. It is a cable of thick copper wire, almost as fat as his arm. He looks back up at Moncorvo, who wordlessly tosses something down on to the floor by Lyle. He picks it up uncertainly. It is a diagram, neatly drawn on a piece of battered paper. He looks back up at Moncorvo. 'A Faraday wheel?'

Wordlessly, Moncorvo points up into the dome. Lyle looks, and sees, running round the inside of the dome, a long, long way up, the iron railing of the Whispering Gallery. Lightning flashes again in the windows. He glances down at the diagram and thinks, *Lightning strikes the highest point it can find, taking the path of least resistance. St Paul's is the tallest building in London . . . run the wire from the cross to the Whispering Gallery, wrap it round the*

railing as a core, run the secondary coil down to earth, wait for light-
ning to strike . . .

. . . locked in an iron box . . .

. . . Thunderstorms . . . are . . . magnetic, aren't they, Mister
Lyle?

Oh Jesus. The magnetic field will be big enough to repolarize.
They weren't waiting thousands of years to take the Plate back
because of any mystic sensibilities – they were waiting for the tech-
nology to develop, for someone to understand the principles of
magnetism, for the knowledge needed to repair the Plate, to put it
into a large enough magnetic field and . . .

He studies Moncorvo's expression. In one corner, Feng stands
utterly motionless, head bowed, holding the Plate. In another,
the priest is slumped. The endless candles dazzle Lyle's tired
eyes.

Moncorvo points imperiously at the diagram. '*Make it work.*'

And Lyle thinks, *They need me aware, because they don't want*
to handle all that magnetic material . . . they need my knowledge of
science . . . they want me to make them immune to the iron, to its
power, so they can destroy everything I've ever believed in, everything
I've ever done . . .

And Lyle knows that if he says no, they'll kill him, and find
someone else.

Lyle stands up. He thinks, *This is still magnetic. The Plate is*
still magnetic. I'm not affected by it. They are. There may still be a
chance.

He swallows. 'I need to go to the Whispering Gallery.'

Moncorvo starts to smile.

*

And the dogs bark in Piccadilly, and the cats mew in Chancery Lane, and the lawyers snore in Lincoln's Inn, and the politicians slumber in Westminster, and the guards shiver in the Tower, and the bobbies shuffle in Aldgate, and a carriage races through the streets of London, from which voices can be faintly heard.

'I thought you knew where we were going?!'

'I do!'

'It's left! Left *there*!'

'How many times have you been to the Palace?'

'Once!'

'Oh. Really?'

'Turn there!'

'I'm driving!'

And a little, quiet hiss. '*Badly.*'

And in the high Whispering Gallery of St Paul's Cathedral, watched over by the saints, Lyle passes his hand along the smooth stone of the dome, and looks at the iron railing running around its interior. He felt along the cold black iron, feeling the green-eyed stares of Tseiqin above and below fixed on him. He takes the end of a long piece of heavy copper cable, draws a long, deep breath, and slowly starts to wrap it round and round the iron rail.

Outside the Palace, a frantically weaving carriage skids to a halt and a pair of dishevelled figures and their dog leap down, running through the rain, hammering at a side gate. 'Let us in!'

A hatch opens. 'Who are you? *What* are you?'

'You'vegottoletusinit'surgentwhere'sLordLincolnthey'vegot
MisterLyle . . .'

'Do you know what time it is?'

'We've got to see Lord Lincoln!'

'His lordship doesn't just see anyone! Go and find your . . .'

*'Do you know who I am, you peasant? It is no ordinary person to
whom you address yourself! I am the Honourable Thomas Edward
Elwick, son and heir to Thomas Henry Elwick, Baron of that name,
Order of the Magpie, Cross of the Sallow Oak, Knight of the
Daffodil, and I am here on the business of Her Most Royal Majesty
Queen Victoria, by the grace of God Regina Britannicae and
Defender of the Faith, Empress of the Seven Seas, Lady of the Red
Rose of a Thousand Years, Dame of the Yellow Garter, and I
demand by the terms of my service and my duty to be admitted to
the presence of Lord Lincoln immediately!'*

'Oh. Well, when you put it like that . . . I'll see if he's receiving, shall I?'

'Thank you.'

'It's no trouble. Don't go anywhere, erm . . . sir.'

'We won't.'

And in the scaffold that clings to half of the dome of St Paul's,
there is a small, wet, cold figure climbing, a mass of copper wire
slung over one shoulder, pulling himself up wobbly ladders as
the rain lashes and thunder rumbles overhead, until finally he is
at the top of the dome. Horatio Lyle balances precariously on the
edge of the scaffold, and reaches out towards the golden cross
raised majestically above it all. For a second he is alone, looking
down on a slumbering, dark city stretching all the way to the

darker fields beyond, the lightning flashing off the river far below. He feels the cold wind tearing through his fingers, feels the excitement and the lurch of the drop far below, and thinks, for just a second, that what he's looking at, that filthy, dark compression of squashed, crawling life, is really very beautiful indeed. He can feel dry blood caking the back of his head and hand, but the cold wind coming down from the storm is soothing the pain, driving it back into a numb, colder place. For a second, he almost smiles.

'Whenever you are ready, Mister Lyle.'

The voice, that alien, inhuman voice, brings him back to reality. He swallows, and starts looping the copper wire over the gold cross. Somewhere in the distance, a stab of lightning digs into the darkness. Lyle hesitates, counting under his breath. Fifteen seconds later, the thunder breaks slowly across the city, rolling like a wave from the sea. Lyle waits for it to pass, and keeps wrapping wire. He hesitates briefly at the next stroke of lightning, and counts. Ten seconds later, the thunder strikes. The storm is getting closer.

And in the depths of the Palace, Lord Lincoln pushes open a door. He is wearing a burgundy dressing gown and thick tartan slippers. He is also wearing a nightcap. Tess tries not to snigger.

Lord Lincoln stares icily at them, and snaps, 'Where is Horatio Lyle?'

'They've got him, sir,' said Thomas quietly. 'And the Plate.'

Lincoln doesn't blink, but Tess sees his lips grow white. She feels in her pocket, and her hand closes round something small, circular and metal. She pulls it out. It gleams in the candlelight.

'Where did they take it?'

'We don't know, sir. He was hurt.'

'Was this Moncorvo?'

'Yes, sir. Moncorvo and Lady Lacebark, sir.'

Lincoln briefly scowls, eyes darkening. 'Did he say anything? Do you have any idea where they have taken the Plate?'

'No, sir, perhaps the Norfolk Club or . . .'

Very quietly, Tess looks up and says, 'I know where they've gone, sir.'

Two pairs of surprised eyes turn on her. Tess holds the open compass in her hand. She points at the door. 'That way's north, isn't it, sir?'

'Is this relevant?'

She holds up the compass. Slowly, without her moving, the needle is starting to spin.

CHAPTER 23

Storm

Lyle dropped the last coil of wire. It fell to the floor, spinning as it dropped, from where he'd wrapped it round the rail of the Whispering Gallery inside the cathedral, and hung like a creeper just next to the altar. He looked slowly up into Moncorvo's impassive face. 'That's it,' he said quietly.

Moncorvo glanced thoughtfully around at the dome. Wire was coiled everywhere, running along the iron railing and up the stairs out of the gallery towards the roof. The dull slap of the wire against the dome as the wind buffeted it made Lyle flinch with each bang. The Tseiqin were assembled all round the edge of the gallery. Those who couldn't fit into the gallery were crowded around the altar down below, staring upwards. Feng appeared from the dark, narrow doorway at ground level and solemnly raised the Plate. Lyle looked round the gallery by the dull flickering candlelight, and saw how drawn the shadows were on the faces of all the saints. He thought, *Dear God, I don't believe in you, I never have, but if you can give a miracle now, please, please do.*

He felt an icy hand brush his cheek. He flinched, and Lacebark smiled. 'If this doesn't work, Horatio,' she whispered, leaning in so her face was right next to his, 'you, and every man, woman and child who lives within a mile of this place, will die.' Lyle flinched as she very gently kissed his cheek and, smiling, drifted on to stand next to Mr Dew and Feng at one end of the dome, looking down on the altar, far below. Moncorvo walked slowly towards Lyle, careful not to touch the iron railing.

'Horatio Lyle,' he said in a drawn-out, almost sad voice, 'you and your kind are not as old as we are, but you have spread. Like flies to a corpse. I have seen your cities and your towns grow, watched you squeeze into smaller spaces like maggots. Everything your kind touches is contaminated. You bring burnt darkness and smoking fires wherever you go. I have seen whole forests wither and die, the deserts grow and the mountains crack. I have seen blood dye the rivers, the fish choking on your life and your death, flapping breathlessly on dirty banks where the soil has been scraped clean of its goodness to feed fat bellies that feast on the flesh of creatures that have lived fifty years or more, kings of their own worlds. You don't just break a world, you break all worlds. You destroy the worlds of every other creature that has to live on the same Earth as you. It is fitting that your people should have learnt so early to kill each other with iron.

Your life depends on it, on blasted craters in still-growing mountains, you live and breathe it. It eats your hearts. Your life will be
your death, Mister Lyle. And the only good you will ever do in
your life is to die, decay and return to the soil all that your life
has stolen from it.' Feng stepped forward, offering the Plate.
Moncorvo smiled. 'Hold out your hand.'

Lyle couldn't stop himself. He tried to fight it, but there was
nothing there to fight with. He held out his hand. Moncorvo
slipped a bronze knife into it. Lyle tried to stab at him, tried to
move. He couldn't. Moncorvo's smile widened. Lyle saw himself
turn the knife round, rest the blade on the palm of his own hand
and pull it back slowly. He did feel the pain, and every nerve
jerked and cried out for him to stop. He couldn't. He watched the
blood well up in his palm. Feng offered the Plate. Lyle shook as
he tried to resist, tried with every ounce of strength he had to
will his own hand not to move. His arm ached. He felt the knife
fall from his other fist as his whole body shook with the effort of
not moving. The shaking sent little waves through the blood
cupped in his palm. A drop fell. It hissed as it struck the Fuyun
Plate. Lyle's control snapped, and his hand jerked, the blood
falling directly into the Plate.

Overhead, thunder roared.

Later, the 1864 Storm would be put down as something of a cli-
matic phenomenon. Scientists would say that the way every
clock that had an ounce of metal suddenly stopped, every gear
straining towards the eye of the storm, and the way every screw
shook, the way all the birds suddenly started screaming, the way
the ravens in the Tower were seen to cry, the way the tide in the

river suddenly and unexpectedly changed, was all to do with *ether*. The storm, they said, was clearly affecting the way everything interacted. The ether was being shaken up by all the air moving around. As it stirred, it rubbed against air travelling in other directions, and that stirred up the ether, which also moved around, being pushed outwards, creating an ether vacuum around the storm, and then falling inwards. When it fell inwards, it dragged lots of things with it. Metal things.

It would take another twenty or more years for someone to prove that this hypothesis was very, very wrong. By that time, no one really cared any more.

Carriages raced through the streets of London. Tess stood on the driver's seat of one, holding the compass in the palm of her hand. The needle was pointing unwaveringly towards the east. 'That way!' she shouted triumphantly, stabbing a finger after the needle.

Thomas leant out of one of the windows and peered up at the sky. Ahead, getting closer as the carriages hurtled towards it, the sky was spiralling angrily, the centre hanging directly above the bulging dome of St Paul's Cathedral. He glanced across at Lord Lincoln, still in his dressing gown, squashed between a pair of guardsmen, rifles ready at their sides. Lincoln glanced out of the window and saw the spiralling clouds, angry black, illuminated by lightning flashing behind them, the epicentre of the spinning storm focused above the cathedral. He glanced at Thomas, then leant out and shouted at the driver, 'St Paul's Cathedral! Faster!'

And still the compass needle pointed unerringly towards the dome.

*

As the Plate filled with blood, the Tseiqin started screaming. Red sparks exploded out of the bowl, and Lyle suddenly had control of his hands once more. He leapt back, pushing past the curled-over Moncorvo. Feng, his expression one of surprise, blinked, realized he was holding the Plate and dropped it. It bounced on the stones below the railing. Sparks flashed from the railing and the wire, from the frames of the windows, from the candlesticks, from the cross on the altar, rose up and filled the cathedral so that every inch was dancing with red fireflies leaping this way and that. Lyle reached out for the Plate as the noise rose, and as his fingers touched the warm stone, the lightning struck.

It struck the golden cross on the dome of St Paul's Cathedral, melting it instantaneously, ran down the copper coil of cable, boiling the roof below it as it went, danced across the floor along the wire, spitting angry white fire as it went, followed the cable down into the cathedral, crawled up and erupted along the iron railing of the Whispering Gallery.

Answering white fire immediately exploded in the second coil of copper cable wrapped round the other side of the railing, crawling down the wire and dancing off everything it could touch, searing the wall as it bounced this way and that through metal and through the air, crawling down the cable in a snake of fire, until it slammed into the altar and wormed away. The dome was filled with burning bright whiteness, impossible to see through, and the smell of smoke.

Then the thunder rolled. It went on for a very, very long time, shook the windows, shook the stones, bounced off the walls and echoed through the floor, while the melted copper cable slowly dripped and pooled on to the ground far below.

Still the iron railing burnt, hissing, fat iron blobs falling away, and the Tseiqin held their hands to their ears and screamed, screamed with one breath, one force. Lyle's fingers closed over the Plate. The shock that ran through his arm lifted him off his feet and threw him back against the wall of the Whispering Gallery, where his head knocked against the stone and he heard the echoes bounce round and round. Blearily, he saw the Plate half-rise off the ground, on one edge, and the cascade of red sparks began to change colour, turning from red to white as still the lightning danced through the iron railing.

In the centre of the dome, drawn by the brief magnetic field, bits of molten iron and copper started spiralling, trapped within the field created inside the ring of the iron balcony. Shards of shattered iron framework from the windows rose as well, joining in a whirlwind of screaming metal that sliced the air into thin parts, dragging with it the now-white sparks pouring from the Plate. Lyle saw the Plate wobble precariously, flashing white, and then came the counter-strike. The lightning leapt up from the bowl of the Plate, lanced through the dome and spread out through it, too bright and too white to look at, so hot he could feel it where he sat. He could feel his hair standing on end, and when he moved, his hand trailed white sparks. He pulled himself away from the wall with inexorable slowness, feeling the stone trying to stick with static to his clothes, feeling the floor trying to stick to him, each movement sending a thousand little shocks tickling down his nerves. He reached out one last time and finally caught the Plate and held on to it.

He swept it into his arms as the outpouring of white sparks

began to fade, cradling it close, but still the whirlwind of metal went on. He dragged himself on his hands and knees towards the door, and each step was agony, each lurch as clumsy and weak as a child's first. A hand fell on his collar and dragged him upwards. He saw the grinning face of Mr Dew, then he saw the ceiling, and felt Dew's boot drawing back for a kick as he curled in on his side, trying to blank the pain, clinging to the Plate for all he was worth, while the storm raged.

Tess saw the lightning strike St Paul's Cathedral, a white bolt that fell straight down with unerring aim. She saw it creep along the outside of the dome as if it was being drawn by cables, and a few seconds later she saw the counter-strike lance out of the inside of the dome itself, crawling through the roof and upwards, as though pressed out from a sponge. As the carriages swung to a halt below the steps of the cathedral, she jumped down, the compass almost leaping out of her hand, and said, 'Come *on*!'

Soldiers were piling out of the carriages, Her Majesty's personal guard. They were having problems, though. Swords were shaking in their sheaths, and riflemen were having difficulty aiming their muzzles anywhere but directly towards the door. Tate leapt up and bounded towards the iron doors, which were creaking on their hinges and trying to wrench themselves free. He howled at the doors, and as Tess watched, they gave way with a final roar and flew backwards, into the cathedral. Tate bounded inside and she rushed forward.

The inside of the cathedral was in chaos. Anything that contained even a trace of metal was spinning round the centre of the dome like tea leaves in a stormy cup. Sparks were flying from everything, including the swords of the soldiers and their guns. Several troops fired, the bullets streaming towards the altar to join the spinning tornado of metal. She saw people turning, green eyes fixing on the doors. A soldier took aim with great difficulty and fired. A Tseiqin fell. A shout went up, spread. She looked above to the balcony of the Whispering Gallery, and saw a familiar figure lying curled up in a ball, cradling something that burnt with impossible whiteness and sparked a river of light. She called out a warning, and pointed. A soldier fired. The man standing over the fallen figure ducked as the bullet whistled overhead, and turned with a look of intense malice, to stare straight at Tess.

Down below, she heard the hiss of swords being drawn. Thomas grabbed a simple wooden cross from the door, taking it in both hands, and shouted what could have been anything, but was probably meant as a battle cry. Tess felt in her pockets. Her hands closed over the test tubes Lyle had given her. She grinned.

As one, the Tseiqin charged, and Her Majesty's Guard ran to meet them.

CHAPTER 24

As chaos exploded in the nave of the church, Moncorvo drew a slim bronze blade and turned to Lacebark. She was shouting orders, moving almost too fast to see. A bullet bounced into the stone above his head. He ducked, his hand accidentally brushing the iron railing. It burnt his skin. Overhead, the thunder rolled again. Water was seeping through the roof where the counter-strike of lightning had dug its way out, dripping down on to the altar below. Around him Tseiqin took aim with crossbows and let fire, to receive an answering hail of gunfire. He saw two more Tseiqin fall, and looking down saw the first rank of Tseiqin on the ground charge, furiously, into the swords of the waiting guardsmen, running down the aisles and climbing over the benches to try and get to the fray. In the centre of the dome, the whirlwind was gently falling, but still the smaller bits of metal spun, a shower of hot metal flying down towards the ground while the rest still screamed through the air.

At his side, Lacebark screeched over the din, 'The Plate!'

Moncorvo looked round, just in time to see Lyle disappear up a staircase, clutching the Plate to himself. He growled and leapt after him, but was pushed aside.

Feng Darin rose up in front of him, his face a mask of vengeance, holding a bronze blade in either hand. Moncorvo hesitated, feeling the burning of the magnetic field still buzzing in his mind. He switched the knife to his other fist, and lunged at Feng.

Feng parried easily, lunging up with a slash for his belly that Moncorvo only just avoided. He staggered back clumsily, shocked. Lacebark pushed past him, her face set, blade gleaming in her hand. 'Let me,' she snarled. 'You get down there!'

Moncorvo didn't argue. He turned and ran for the staircase.

As the magnetic field faded inside the dome, Lyle ran, skidding and sliding on the stone staircase, pushing his way through dark stone corridors so narrow he had to turn sideways to move through them, scrambling for the upper level. He heard footsteps on the stone behind him and ran faster, as fast as every ache and every bone could allow, bumping and sliding against the walls. He reached a staircase and dragged himself up it, slipping and crawling on hands and feet, then mustering the strength to push himself on to his feet again and taking the steps two at a time, bounding up with the Plate burning under his fingers, the light it gave out now fading. He heard a shout behind him and felt the crossbow bolt whiz through the air, slamming into the wall an inch from his ear, then the chink of the bow itself being discarded, tossed to one side. Lyle saw a door ahead and crashed into it, sending it bursting open. He stepped out into a storm, the wind lashing at his face, stinging his eyes, the rain tearing through everything it could touch, the air heavy. He heaved his shoulder against the door, pushing it shut. The lock went *click*, and he turned and ran.

Tess found herself on one of the side aisles, pushed behind a line of guardsmen as steel flashed and sang. She looked around and saw a flight of steps spiralling upwards. She darted towards it, diving under the arms of the fighters, racing through a wall of steel and into the darkness of the staircase. Way up she heard the sound of footsteps and froze. Moncorvo appeared around the turn, eyes flashing in the dark. He saw her and scowled. Reaching out for her hair, he ran at her, and she ducked under, turning and running back down the way she'd come, clinging to the side of the wall, feet skipping on the narrowest part of the stair, just next to the centre of the spiral. As she ran, she fumbled with the test tubes, trying to work out which was which. She found one, and tossed it on to the stones ahead of her. It didn't smoke, and it didn't spark, but smelt of ammonia, a thick, retch-inducing taste in her mouth. She hopped over it, slipping on the edge of the spill and sliding down, banging hard against the bottom of the staircase. She half-turned to look up, fumbling with the other tube. Moncorvo appeared behind her, smelt the ammonia and hesitated. She grinned and raised the second test tube. As Moncorvo's eyes widened, she hurled it at the pool of shattered glass and ammonia, and dived for cover.

There was a hiss, and a roar that she could feel in her stomach. Dust and smoke exploded out of the doorway behind her, spitting across the floor. She leapt to her feet, high on adrenaline, and practically danced on the spot. Then a hand closed on the back of her head.

Thomas saw the Tseiqin grab Tess, and didn't think twice. He ran towards the man, wildly swinging the wooden cross. But Tate got there first, leaping up to snap at the creature, death in his generally lethargic eyes, ears flapping. The Tseiqin howled as Tate's teeth closed, and Tess wormed out from under his grip. Thomas swung the cross once, swung it again, saw the man stagger back, surprise in his eyes, and then Tess grabbed hold of Thomas and pulled him down, as a sword sailed through the place where, a second before, his head had been. She dragged him towards a dark stairway leading downwards and hissed, 'Come *on*!'

They barrelled down the stairs into the gloom and relative quietness of the crypt, dully lit by candles. Tess collapsed behind a giant tomb and stared silently at nothing.

Thomas slumped down next to her, cross falling from his hand. In the silence, they could hear the sounds of fighting and the screams of the injured above. Finally Thomas said, 'Tess?'

'Yes?'

'Your hands are shaking.'

'So are yours.'

'I've never been . . . I mean, I've never . . .'

'Me neither.' Tess frowned. 'Mister Lyle.'

'What?'

She stood up slowly, unevenly, leaning against the side of the stone. She looked at the one test tube in her hand. 'We ought to see if Mister Lyle's all right.'

Thomas swallowed, but nodded quickly. 'Right. Let's . . .' He hesitated.

'Give 'em hell?' hazarded Tess.

He thought about it. 'Yes. Yes! That sounds about right!'

She tightened her grip on the test tube. He seized the wooden cross again. They took deep breaths, and charged back up the stairs.

And Lyle reached the foot of the scaffolding, slipping the Plate into his jacket pocket, and looked up towards the towering shape of the dome. He thought, *Well, this is it. I wish I wasn't scared of heights.*

He reached out for the nearest ladder. A hand closed on his hair and dragged him back. He stared into the grinning face of Mr Dew, who hissed, 'Horatio Lyle.'

Instinct took over. He kicked backwards, hitting Dew in the shin, while grabbing the wrist behind his head and turning, dragging Dew towards him as he went. Dew staggered a little, his grip slackening, and Lyle darted away, swinging himself on to the ladder and hauling himself up. Dew grabbed at his ankle, but he kicked free and swung up on to the first level of scaffolding.

Dew was already on the ladder. Lyle aimed a kick at it, sending it spinning backwards, but it caught the frame of the scaffolding and didn't fall. Dew climbed it, though it leant out backwards above a drop, swinging himself over one of the poles of the scaffolding, and up.

Lyle was already running for the next ladder, the planks thundering underfoot. He grabbed the second ladder, and was halfway up as Dew pulled at it from beneath. The ladder lurched, nearly throwing him off. He swung round precariously, until he was hanging by a hand and a foot off the wrong side of the ladder, and saw Dew just below. His grip weakened and he fell. Out near the Palace of Westminster, lightning tore through the heavens and struck; thunder shook the planks so that they hummed.

Lyle's fall took him straight past the planks below, and he caught by sheer chance one of the supporting poles, dangling with his feet a few inches above the first layer. Dew appeared overhead and, as he knelt to reach for the Plate slipping out of Lyle's pocket, Lyle let go of the scaffolding and dropped the last few feet back down to the first level. He landed heavily, picked himself up and turned to flee. He could hear Dew running above him, could see the planks shake. He reached a ladder and looked up into Dew's grinning face, dragged at the ladder, making it lash back towards Dew, who sprang away from it almost too fast to see. Lyle turned and ran the other way, saw a bundle of sandbags lying attached to a rope pulley, heavy with water as well as sand. He hesitated, then ducked as one of the planks shattered above him, Dew's foot sticking through it, sending slivers and shards crashing down. Dew's face appeared again in the hole, grimacing at him. 'Where are you going, Mister Lyle?'

Lyle grabbed one end of the rope and kicked the sandbags off. They plummeted away towards the ground far below, pulling the rope down after them. As the rope raced through the pulley, Lyle shot upwards, arms screaming indignantly, hands slipping and burning on the raw, wet rope, banging his legs against the side of the scaffold as he rose. For a brief second he saw the surprised face of Dew and then he was rising up past him, trying not to look down. The rope swung wildly and knocked him towards the dome.

Lyle landed on the third level of scaffolding, banging against the wet, smooth metal of the dome, rolling away and nearly falling. One hand slipped off the edge of the scaffold. He looked down, and thought he was going to be sick, heard the sound of running feet below him. He ran for the next ladder, while overhead sheet lightning rippled across the sky and the wind whirled round the white eye of the storm that still hung directly over the cathedral. Lyle heard gunfire a long way below, but couldn't make himself care, not with the water in his eyes and the aching in his legs. He started climbing again, and heard the thunderous sound of Dew scrambling up the next ladder along, his head appearing less than thirty yards away just above the planks at its top as Lyle reached the fourth level of scaffolding.

The scaffolding was narrowing, getting smaller by degrees as it crawled up the side of the dome towards the peak – Dew was only fifteen yards away. Lyle crawled up to the next level, and saw that there was just one ladder, surrounded by sandbags and damp rope. He ran towards it and, as he did so, Dew appeared over the ladder at the opposite end of the walkway. At the moment that Lyle put his foot on the ladder up to the top of the dome, Dew's hand closed around his ankle, and the Plate slipped from Lyle's pocket.

Smoke and sparks exploded around the altar of the church as Tess hurled down the last test tube and ran towards the guardsmen. There were fewer of them than there had been, and those that were left were confused. But there were also fewer Tseiqin. As she ran for cover behind a pillar, she saw Thomas cowering with a group of guardsmen reloading their rifles behind a long wooden pew. A volley of crossbow bolts slammed into the bench, the tips peeking through the other side. She ducked down at the base of the pillar and saw that one of the tables of candles for commemorating the deceased had been knocked over. Saying a quick apology to the God she hoped wasn't up there, she grabbed the nearest still-flickering candle and lobbed it towards the altar. It trailed hot wax as it flew, and bounced off the stones of a pillar behind which a Tseiqin was hiding. She grabbed another missile and threw it, sending Tseiqin scampering for cover. From behind the bench, guardsmen rose up, fired and instantly ducked for cover again. The sound of gunfire echoed round the cathedral. Tess risked a glance out from around the pillar, and a crossbow bolt nearly took her ear off. The Tseiqin were half-indistinct shapes behind the smoke, but so were the guardsmen.

She heard a clattering outside. Men exploded through the doors. Tess saw dark blue uniforms, and recognized their wearers as policemen. One man stepped forward. It was Charles. A cross-bow bolt bounced off the stone beside him; he frowned but didn't flinch. Seeing Tess he said briskly, 'You? Is that Horatio who's causing all of this?'

'Have you seen Mister Lyle?'

'Not lately. You?'

She shook her head. Charles sighed. 'Right, well, I suppose we ought to restore a little order here.'

Lyle fell, the Plate bouncing away from his stretched fingertips. Dew crawled past and *over* him, digging an elbow into the small of Lyle's back as he went, stretching for the Plate. Lyle felt anger rise up inside him, and rolled savagely to one side, knocking Dew off. Dew slammed against the scaffold, his back precariously close to the edge, knees bent, arms trying to catch a pole to hold him in. Lyle ran for the Plate again, the wind pushing against him, then he bent down, curled his fingers round it, and heard a cracking sound behind him. Dew was on his feet, and he had a loose section of pole in his hands. Lyle paled and backed away as Dew swung it loosely, enjoying the feeling of weight at the end of his arms. Lyle ducked to avoid the first swipe, which bounced off the dome.

Far below, Tess heard the echoes of the strike, and felt her stomach turn.

As Dew swung again, lazily, Lyle raised the Plate, and the pole bounced off it without a scratch. Lyle dropped to the floor, slid his knees out over the edge of the planks, grabbed hold of a pole with his spare hand and swung himself off, sliding down until he landed hard on the next layer of planks. Beside a pile of sandbags he saw a loose pole, shorter and slimmer than the monstrous weapon Dew wielded like a feather. He grabbed it in one hand just as Dew dropped lightly down from the layer above, streaming with water from the rain and still clasping the pole. He advanced towards Lyle, who fought the instinct to run.

Lyle brought the pole up clumsily in one hand, feeling it slip through his bloody fingers. Dew just grinned, swiping easily at it like a cat playing with string. The blow almost knocked the pole from Lyle's hand. Lyle hesitated, then tossed the Plate down at Dew's feet. Dew frowned, then in a single movement reached forward to grab it. Lyle ran at him, both hands on the pole, bringing it up towards Dew. It struck somewhere soft, and Dew bent over with a little *umph*. In the same movement Lyle bent, grabbed the Plate, kicked Dew very firmly in the kneecap, tossed the pole aside and swung on to the ladder. He crawled up, and up again, until he stood on the very top of the scaffold, staring at the golden cross that crowned the cathedral. It was half-melted from the lightning strike, the thick cable trailing limply around it. Lyle sidled towards it, clenching his bloody fingers tighter on to the Plate, heart pounding. He looked at the sky above, at the clouds spiralling, at the night. He looked at the city, spread out before him like a carpet.

He heard the sound of his own breathing. He heard carts rattling far away, the rigging by the Thames, the tide changing, the dogs barking, the cats fighting, the inn doors banging, the windows creaking, the rain falling. He saw the messy, higgledy-piggledy streets stretching away, pinpricked with light. He saw the rain shining on the cobbles. He tasted the cold wind and the dirty rain, smelling of a million lives scratching across the old stones day after day, of tar and orange peel, of salt and dried fish, of iron and coal. He thought about it, smiled, looked at the storm and held up the Plate.

Mr Dew, bloody and dishevelled, hit him over the back of the head with a pole.

CHAPTER 25

The Tseiqin fell back under a rush of police and guardsmen, slowly pressed into the far end of the church, beyond the altar. They fought furiously, but the soldiers were angry now at the loss of their comrades, and with the extra police swinging truncheons and the weapons of the fallen, fought with more confidence. As they advanced, the pathway to the stairs cleared. Tess grabbed Charles by the sleeve, and she, Thomas and the bemused copper followed Tate as he bounded, yapping furiously, up the steps, smelling his master at hand. The stairs seemed to go on for ever, endless spirals and corridors, working through the intestines of the cathedral. Tess could hardly breathe, and her legs screamed at her to stop, but still Tate was barking ahead, galloping up the stairs as fast as his paws would allow him. They reached a shattered door out into the storm and piled past it. From there they looked at a dark scaffold above, and then beyond, towards the gleam of the cross. Tate started howling at the sky, water streaming off his fur. Thomas said, 'There are people up there!' Tess said nothing. She felt the compass, still in her pocket. As Thomas rushed for the ladder, Charles in tow, she stood still, and looked at the compass. The North-aligned needle was pointing directly towards the top of the dome. Even though that wasn't where North lay.

Pain was happening. Lyle knew that much. He tried to get up, and a boot connected with his side. He collapsed, tasting blood in his mouth. His bloody fingers danced blindly across the planks, and touched the very edge of the warm stone Plate, which was still giving off white sparks. A boot landed on his fingers and pressed down. Dew's face swam into focus.

'Mister Horatio Lyle,' he whispered. 'This is a pleasure.'

Lyle tried to speak, but could only cough blood. Dew reached past him and picked up the Plate. Smiling, he held it to the sky, letting the water fill its bowl while Lyle lay helpless and watched. The water blended with Lyle's blood. Dew slowly turned, so that Lyle could see everything in perfect detail.

'I pity your kind,' said Dew softly. 'Animals grown too intelligent for their own petty needs. I pity your death. It is trivial. Your kind will come and go like the tide. Nothing you do will ever change Earth. It will endure with or without you. You cannot make or create. You can only change what is there, and eventually, it will change back. What a futile life; what a futile death.'

Lyle crawled on to his knees, curled in over the pain that seemed to want to slither out of his skin. He looked into the face of Dew as, grinning like a shark, Dew tipped back the Plate and drank the bloody water trapped in its bowl. Lyle didn't move. Dew lowered the Plate again, eyes shut as if to savour the taste, water trickling down either side of his mouth. He let out a long, relaxed breath, and opened his eyes. They were pure white. He turned over his hand. Where it had held the pole, the skin was burnt. But even as Lyle watched, it started to heal.

'Do you see your own end, Mister Lyle?' asked Dew quietly.

Lyle licked the rainwater around his lips, swallowed as much as he could, and felt the croak of words come to him. He tried to speak. The words were faint and hoarse, but came nonetheless. 'You bloody fool,' he muttered. 'Didn't your mother tell you not to stand in high places during thunderstorms?'

As the look of fear flashed across Dew's face, Lyle staggered on to his feet and grabbed Dew's hands. They burnt his fingers to touch; they seemed to crackle with electricity. He dragged them up, pulling the Plate still clenched in Dew's fingers with him, until the Plate was high above them both and his face was an inch from Dew's. Lyle screamed with the wind and the rain, '*This thing is still magne—*'

Lightning struck.

Later, Tess thought that perhaps the lightning hadn't fallen from the sky to the ground, but perhaps the ground had gone up to the sky, all corners of the earth folding in on each other towards that one point of blinding light. The sky cracked in two, the dome of the cathedral ran with white fire, and the Plate, held up as an offering, the highest point in all of London, turned white and exploded.

Shards of white stone bounced down the side of the dome, rolled along the stone of the walkway, slid through the gaps between the balcony, and fell away to earth. Tess heard them hit a long way down, little thuds in the night, like heavy balls bouncing against hard wood floors. A piece rolled near her foot, ricocheted off it, and lay in the pooling water, steaming. She looked at the compass in her hand. The needle was slowly turning, to spin towards true magnetic North. The rain was slackening. The wind was dying down. As it blew this way and that, it brought with it Tate's intermittent howl.

The thunder rolled, one last time. It poured through the narrow, dirty black streets, slid into the gaps between cobbles, rippled across the water of the river, made the still bells hum, and passed on, spreading out into the countryside beyond, where it bent the grass, whispered in the trees and eventually died away.

Clouds raced along like frightened fish, trying to pretend they hadn't been there, spreading out in wisps that faded into the night. Behind them, the stars were wetly visible, made larger and more twinkling by the water still hanging heavy in the air. The moon was huge on the horizon, silver light slowly spreading and catching the rain as the clouds retreated.

A black shape slid off the dome, rolling down the damp metal like a barrel down a hill, smoke rising from its feet, falling in total silence; it hit the base of the dome with a little splash, tumbled until it bounced against the stone balcony, then didn't move. The rain slowly pooled around it, sliding off it in trickles, mingling with the blood on its fingers. The figure blended with the night, just another statue in a cathedral of stone shapes, and, as the lights of distant lamps multiplied, and as the men shouted and the dog barked and the rain fell, still, he did not move.

Afterwards, an intrepid bobby climbed up to the top of St Paul's Cathedral to survey the damage. Between all the shattered wood and twisted metal of the scaffold, past the half-melted golden cross, with the gold pooled in thick blobs below it, revealing the cheaper metal underneath, he found a pair of empty, smoking black shoes, and a very large scorch mark.

And later, much later, searching the crypt of St Paul's Cathedral, they found Lady Lacebark lying against one of the tombs. She had just time to hiss, '*Feng xiansheng, ni shi . . .*' before she died. Dead, she seemed almost skeletal, her face fixed in a scowl even after all strength had left it, her hands too long, her arms so thin you could wrap your fingers round the elbow joint easily, her neck so long and white it could hardly have supported the weight of her head. They buried her outside a small country church in Scotland, in a very, very deep grave.

Later still, as the bells struck in the city and shutters were pushed back on to streets smelling of dead leaves in decaying forests, the rich smell you get after a cold storm in a warm morning, a soldier, picking through the stones of a staircase where a small chemical explosion had shattered half the steps, saw a hand in a dirty white glove lying underneath a pile of rubble. A few seconds later, the voice echoed through the high halls, bouncing off the sad faces of the saints, off the giggling cherubs, off the martyrs and the flickering candles lit to the dead, 'This one's still alive, sir!'

CHAPTER 26

City

It is night in the city of London, a cool empty night, full of stars ahead and a thin moon rising over the river, twinkling in the still water, bouncing off a thousand panes of glass and back again, so that the city almost glows.

In the grandeur of Drury Lane, Hamlet puts his hand to his forehead, takes up the stance that audiences across Europe recognize as 'tortured pain', and announces in a rich voice that carries to the back of the black auditorium, 'To be, or not to . . .' In the audience, someone sneezes. It is an ordinary night.

The hansom cabs flock around the Strand, and the shouts carry above the clattering of horses' hooves on the cobbles. 'Move over, move over!'

'You've got a bucket for things like that, mister!'

'You want to tell that to the horse?'

'What've you been feedin' him?'

'None of your business!'

On the battlements of the Tower, the ravens croak at each other, eyeing up the large ship sailing past Traitor's Gate, laden with meat, as they concoct their schemes for a feast. Below them, a lock turns in a particularly heavy iron door, a foot pads on a particularly cold stone floor, and a voice says from the darkness, 'You haven't won, you know?'

Iron chains clink in the darkness. Lord Lincoln lights a long wooden pipe, and puffs.

'We will still win. You can't stop us, you don't know how. We will come and we will finish what was started. This world cannot hold us back for ever, don't you see?'

Lincoln smiles. 'My lord,' he says politely, removing the pipe from his lips, '*I know.*'

Down by the river, the colliers drag sacks of dusty coal up on to the banks, backs bent, faces filthy, some wearing loose yellow cloths across their nose and mouth to keep out the dust, some coughing until black spittle clings to their teeth, while from the ships the sailors pour, searching for food, drink and company away from the sea. The houses stand on poles sticking out of the tidal mud, creaking in the wind that blows up from the estuary. Geese fly overhead in a V, heading home.

Milly Lyle rocks backwards and forwards in her armchair, staring up thoughtfully at the picture of old Harry Lyle hanging over the fire. Then, after a while, she stands up, takes the picture down, turns it over, gently pulls away the paper across its back, and from inside takes out a small gold box that sits neatly in the palm of her hand. It is engraved *ML*. She opens it. The needle of the compass swings towards North. She smiles, closes the compass and drops it into her apron pocket. When she goes back to the armchair, she puts her head on one side, and sleeps.

A door closes in a house near Hyde Park. There are footsteps on the stairs. A lock clicking. Another door opening. A door closing. Footsteps on empty, neglected planks.

A voice in the darkness. '*Xiansheng*.'

A cat miaows somewhere outside. A horse neighs down in the mews below, stamping its foot.

'*Xiansheng*.'

'It is finished, *xiansheng*?'

'It is.'

'And Lyle?' Silence. 'The Emperor will be pleased. You can go home, if you wish. The Empire may have need of you in other places. There are always needs.' Silence. 'What will you do now? You can have any place, any country. For the glory of the Empire, and our cause. Here is finished. Here is the past. There will be other battles. *Xiansheng*?'

Silence. Then, very thoughtfully, 'I think . . . I think I'll see if Mrs Oak has any more of her fine ginger biscuits left, *xiansheng*.'

A door opens. A door closes.

In the dark slums of Bethnal Green, the Missus of a house of some repute looks out at a room full of smoke, and breathes deeply the mist of forgetfulness. In the offices of the East India Company, a man with a portly belly closes a book, looks up into the candlelight and says, 'Does that mean the import of lychees is *unviable*? Goddammit, at this rate we'll have to switch to bananas!'

In the Palace, a small, dumpy woman with a tight-lipped expression and pasty face looks round the room. A chamberlain clears his throat. 'Her Most Royal Majesty Queen Victoria, by the grace of God Regina Britannicae, Defender of the Faith . . .'

In a corner, another woman sobs happily into her handkerchief. Next to her, a man with too many sidewhiskers mutters, 'Madam! You are embarrassing yourself,' and then leans towards the tall boy with the determined expression. 'And you, young man, if you think that the praise of the Queen is excusing you from your Latin verbs, you are *greatly* mistaken.'

Thomas just smiles. Inside his jacket pocket, a thick sheet of paper rustles ever so slightly. On it, he has drawn, in immense detail, a bird. Made entirely of bamboo struts and cloth.

He thinks about it, and his smile grows wider.

The thieves eye up purses as they hulk together around one of the factories of Stepney. One whispers, '*Him*.'

Another whispers, 'Tess could do 'im in a second.'

'Where is Tess?'

'Ain't seen 'er for days.'

'I 'eard something 'bout a fight. Said a man got 'urt.'

'Who?'

'A bobby.'

'Christ. She'll 'ang if she 'urt a bobby.'

'I dunno if *she* 'urt 'im . . .'

'Then where is she?'

'Dunno. Perhaps she made big?'

'Nah. Not our Tess. That's like sayin', "Perhaps there's elves" an' all!'

Later the moon shines down on a stone building of domes and corridors, nooks and crannies, ghosts and ghouls, and in a hall buzzing with low, expectant noise, like a congregation waiting on a priest, someone says, 'So, this Faraday: he's all right, is he?'

'Faraday? He's a genius, he's the father of modern science, he's . . .'

'All right, all right, bigwig, keep your hair on. Give Tate another biscuit.'

'I think he's had enough . . .'

'Tate's never had enough, have you, Tatey-watey. No you haven't, no you haven't, have you?' The voice descends into incomprehensible baby talk. A dog whines in appreciation. There is the sound of healthy teeth closing over a biscuit. There is a long crunching sound.

'I'm *bored*.'

'He hasn't got here yet.'

'This place is full of bigwigs.'

'They're scientists.'

'*He's* not!'

'Well, no, he's not, he's just an enthusiast.'

'Like you?'

'I'm . . . I *want* to be a scientist. Father's given me an

allowance now, and Lord Lincoln said that he'd be willing to allow me access to the Greenwich Observatory and if I can just . . .'

'But you're a bigwig. You don't have to do nothin'!'

'But I want to be something *more*.'

And a door opens, and someone comes in. The audience starts to clap.

'You all right?'

'It's . . . it's Faraday.'

'Father of modern science? You said.'

A little later a voice whispers hoarsely, 'What's he doin'?'

'I think he's demonstrating the interaction between electric and magnetic forces.'

'What's that?'

'It's a static generating thing. It uses a lot of static to generate . . . *things*.'

And a quiet voice says, 'It's a static discharge generator, Thomas.'

'Erm . . . quite. A static discharge generator, Teresa.'

'Oh. Is it complicated?'

'Well, obviously there's a lot going on.'

'I made one out of a kettle once,' says the quiet voice.

'Really? How?'

'I'll tell you when the lecture's over.'

In the darkness, an electric crackle, and an '*ooooh*' from the audience. Tess hisses, 'How'd he do that?'

'Well,' begins Thomas's edgy voice, 'there's a lot of charge things on the dome, because of static and . . .'

'Do you mean there's a build-up of negative charge rubbin' off from the belt thing what's carryin' the positive charge from the metal comb inside the insulatin' tower?'

'Yes. *How do you know?*'

'I read it,' Tess says simply. 'In a book.'

Next to her, Horatio Lyle starts to smile.

And the moon rises and sets over the streets of London, looking down on a million lives bumping into a million other lives, a million shoulders brushing against a million others in the street, transferring static charge from one jacket to another as they go, until the whole city buzzes with it, until every street hums with life and noise and the cries of the street sellers rise up: *'Bunch'a turnips, not sixpence, not threepence, but 'cos I see my lucky stars, today just tuppence!' 'Come 'ear the ballad of the Dutch sailor, lost at sea . . .' 'Hot cross buns! One a'penny, two a'penny . . .' 'You wan' it, I've got it . . .!' 'Birds' nests, magpies and sparrows . . .' 'Penny cures, penny cures for all ills, you ma'am . . .' 'Snakes, shillin' a snake . . .'*

. . . And the cries rise, spread out across the slanting rooftops and the crumbling chimney stacks, wake the pigeons and scare the cats, set the dogs barking and bounce off the still brass bells of St James's and St Anne's and St Mary's and St Giles's and St Paul's, and echo away, to leave just a few voices, climbing through the air.

'Mister Lyle?'

'Yes, Teresa?'

''Bout breakfast . . .'

'You can't be hungry again!'

'No, no! It's just 'cos Thomas has been tellin' me 'bout this thing called *chocolate* . . .'

'*Thomas.*'

'Sorry, Mister Lyle.'

'. . . an' I was thinkin', seein' as how I help look after Tate an' 'ave been so good with all the books an' how I ain't picked your pocket *once* . . .'

'Teresa, that is not a recommendation towards moral enlightenment . . .'

And the voices fade away, into the slowly spreading dawn.

In the east, the sun is rising.